Anna's Decision

The Harcourts, Book One

PENNY FAIRBANKS

ALSO BY PENNY FAIRBANKS

Resolved in Love Series:

Behind The Baron's Mask

Healing The Captain's Heart

Finding The Artisan's Future

Embracing The Earl's Dream

The Harcourts Series:

Anna's Decision

Dalton's Challenge

Caroline's Discovery

Patrick's Arrangement

Harriet's Proposal

The Harcourts: Another Generation Series:

A Convenient Escape

The Hidden Heiress

An Unexpected Bloom

The Necessary Lesson

An Impossible Fate

For my husband, forever and always.

CHAPTER 1

*C*hatter and laughter filled Anna's ears as she tried to read, making it difficult for her to concentrate on the book of poetry in her hands. She smiled at the page before her, the sounds of family all around her both comforting her and filling her with a strange melancholy.

Without removing her eyes from her book, Anna knew that Mama and Papa would be seated on the sofa in the middle of the room, giving them a better vantage point to watch over their children. Mama would be embroidering while Papa read the newspaper.

"Dalton, darling, you are going to wrinkle your clothes if you keep standing like that," Mama gently scolded her second eldest child after Anna. Anna knew Dalton must be leaning against the wall, peering out the window at the vast lands that would one day be his, probably deciding what adventure he wanted to go on next.

"My apologies, dearest Mama. You are right, my poor valet will have a heart attack later when he sees the sad state of my coat," Dalton chuckled, surely standing up straight and clasping his hands behind his back like a very proper gentleman.

Caroline, the third Harcourt child, played a lovely melody on the pianoforte in the far corner of the room, always sharpening her many talents.

"Are you sure you've ever played this piece before, Caroline?" Patrick, the fourth eldest, teased his older sister when she missed a note.

"Patrick, please! I'm trying to concentrate and I cannot do that when you are being so horrible!" Caroline retorted as her fingers angrily clashed against the keys of the instrument. Anna could perfectly imagine her younger sister whirling around on the bench, her chest heaving up and down with her irritation.

"How am I being horrible? I'm just sitting here innocently reading a play." Patrick's voice floated across the room from his favorite desk in another corner. He would also be making notes on whatever he read, Anna knew. He'd already decided that he would one day become an examiner of plays.

"Please, children, be kind to one another—if not for each other's sake then for mine and Mama's," Papa sighed, turning the page of his newspaper. "You do not have a headache do you, Bridget?"

"I'm sure I will in a moment if your children do not stop bickering, Martin," Mama chuckled.

A blur of movement raced past Anna and she instinctively tucked her feet beneath her chair. Harriet, the youngest member of the family, could never sit still for long. She skipped around the room, flying past Anna, and chose her next target. The girl drummed her fingers on Patrick's desk, trying to capture her older brother's attention.

"Not now," Patrick sighed, a hint of amusement in his voice.

"Patrick, you are so boring!" Harriet cried as her older brother tried to shoo her away.

As for Anna, she simply sat in her favorite chair by the fireplace, enjoying the activity that buzzed all around her. She loved this home full of children and laughter and conversation and energy.

It also stung. Anna knew she would never have a home of her own like this, no matter how hard she prayed.

"Alright, alright," Patrick groaned, finally giving in to Harriet's badgering. Anna looked up as her youngest brother picked up little Harriet—who, Anna realized with a slight jolt, was not quite so little anymore as a quickly growing twelve-year-old—and twirled her around with a little extra effort. At fifteen, Patrick's increasing strength still allowed him to easily carry Harriet around on his back or in his arms, all of which she found to be highly amusing.

"Mama, Papa, can Patrick and I take the tilbury out and drive around the fields?" Harriet asked between peals of laughter as Patrick switched the direction of their spinning game.

"Patrick, please put your sister down," Mama commanded gently from the sofa. "She is a young lady, after all. But yes, you may take the tilbury out if Dalton accompanies you."

"Of course!" Dalton grinned, nearly hopping away from the window in his excitement to get out and about. Anna smiled softly, happy to still see the cheerful little boy in her now twenty-year-old brother. He did not let the fact that he would one day become Baron Welsted affect his kind and carefree nature. Her smile quickly slipped away as she thought of the fact that the only children she would watch grow up were her own siblings and their children.

Dalton glanced over to Anna, mouth half open as if to say something, but he stopped himself short as concern clouded his expression. Anna put her smile back on, but it was too late. Dalton had already seen her melancholy mood. Or rather, Dalton had become exceedingly practiced at reading her face over the years. Anna had always been closest with Dalton despite their vastly different temperaments.

"Will you join us, Anna?" Her brother tilted his head slightly as he asked, lifting an eyebrow.

Before she could answer, the music from the pianoforte clattered to a stop. "If everyone else is going, then I must go, too." Caroline jumped up from the bench, holding her head high in her stubborn way. She did not like to be left out or feel that others were having more fun than she was.

Papa folded his newspaper, chuckling as he looked around the room at his five children. The sound always brought comfort and a sense of warmth to Anna even on days such as today when she felt hopeless. "That's settled then. The Harcourt children will have an outing while Mama and I dance about the room enjoying our time without all you troublemakers under our feet."

Resting his elbow on Harriet's shoulder, Patrick scoffed. "Surely we will find you here in the sitting room when we return, fast asleep in your seats." Harriet giggled at Patrick's joke, quickly covering her mouth with her hands when she saw Mama's scolding look. The youngest Harcourt daughter would not be as easy to mold into a proper, polite lady as her older sisters had been.

"Yes, I will join you all," Anna finally agreed with what she hoped was a content smile. It would not be long before her siblings went off on their own, starting their own lives and families. They would become too busy to spare much time for Anna. She needed to take advantage of whatever time they had left as the Harcourts.

~

THE WARM SUN gently caressed Anna's face beneath her bonnet as a cool breeze swept by, bringing a touch of lingering winter chill with it. The barouche rattled beneath her as the pair of horses pulled them along behind Patrick's and Harriet's tilbury. Looking over her shoulder, Anna took in the beautiful sight of Attwood Manor, the home they'd grown up in, rising high into the bright blue sky. Ahead of her stretched out a section of flat land with hills in the distance, evidence of spring appearing everywhere she looked.

Anna loved the Harcourts' estate. If any good came from her situation, it was that she would be able to enjoy these breathtaking lands for the rest of her life and keep her parents company as they aged.

Dalton tugged at the reins and brought their horses to a standstill. They'd reached the large, flat empty field that Papa had designated for the children to bring the carriages out unsupervised. He leapt down first, his light brown hair flying up for a moment, holding his hand out first to Anna and then to Caroline. Patrick and Harriet continued forward in the tilbury, Patrick tapping the horse into a trot.

"Don't go too fast, Patrick!" Dalton called out after them, his voice already lost beneath the sound of hooves and Harriet urging Patrick to increase their speed.

Anna put her hand on Dalton's arm. "Do not worry. We'll keep a careful eye on them from here," she reassured him, her voice soft and gentle as always.

"I'm shocked you do not plan on running right back to Mama and Papa and telling on those two," Caroline scoffed lightly, her lips pulling up at the corner in a teasing smirk.

Anna gritted her teeth, trying to let Caroline's jab pass through her. Just as Dalton opened his mouth to scold Caroline, Anna found herself overcome by her irritation at her younger sister. "Truly, how did you and I come from the same family?" she huffed, eyes narrowed at Caroline. Caroline simply tossed her head, her lovely black curls catching in the breeze.

Dalton sighed and shook his head. He knew what was coming. Only Caroline could antagonize the patient, understanding, sweet-tempered Anna into an argument. He also knew that the best thing to do when the two came into conflict was stay out of the way and let it run its course.

"I assure you that we will be out of each other's hair as soon as we marry, so you'd better hurry up with it or else I won't be able to debut in London next year. You know Mama and Papa don't want both of us out at the same time." Caroline glowered, crossing her arms over her chest. Anna grimaced at her sister's harsh reminder of her trajectory toward spinsterhood.

No one knew how much it bothered Anna to be twenty-two with not a single interested suitor to show for her multiple Seasons in London. Anna's stomach churned with regret and disappointment under Caroline's steely gaze, her truthful but painful words still ringing in Anna's ears. Suddenly the breeze around them felt too cold, raising tiny bumps all over Anna's exposed arms. She wished desperately to retreat to the warmth and safety of Attwood Manor where she could hide away from that ugly reality.

She always pretended that it did not matter to her if she never married, that she was content with wherever her path led her. But those were lies she told others in the hopes that they would one day become true for herself.

"Caroline..." Dalton hissed, his hazel eyes carefully watching Anna.

Taking a deep breath, Anna forced a smile back on her face that was plainer than Caroline's and probably plainer than Harriet's, once she grew into her features. "Don't fret over me, Dalton," she insisted quietly.

Anna had long since concluded that only one theory could explain her situation: something must be wrong with her. Not a single gentleman had taken an interest in her beyond a few dances or a carriage ride. In her three years since making her debut in London, Anna had seen so many beautiful young ladies who knew how to flirt while still remaining proper, who could keep a man's attention with a dazzling smile.

Being on the reserved, quiet side, Anna could never hope to compete with those ladies and she knew her beauty was certainly nothing remarkable. Why would any gentlemen pay her any mind when almost every other young lady in the room was clearly a better choice than Anna?

Soon, none of that would matter. Anna lifted her chin with fake confidence, steeling herself to finally make her grand announcement. "Fear not, Caroline. I shall no longer stand in the way of your opportunities. I will be staying home from London this year and quite probably next. I've found that it is hardly worth the hassle of travel. I would rather enjoy a peaceful, quiet spring here at home. I know by now that my path won't lead me to marriage and I've accepted it."

Anna finished her speech with a pained smile. She rarely spoke that much all at once, almost in one breath, but Anna knew that she needed to get it out as quickly as possible, before her courage failed her. She could at least thank Caroline for annoying her into the boldness she needed to share her decision. She could tell from the glances exchanged between Dalton and Caroline that she had not quite managed to explain it with as much grace and acceptance as she'd hoped. Her eyes went wide when she saw that even Caroline looked genuinely concerned about her.

"Please, Anna, don't do anything rash. I was just teasing, I swear," Caroline pleaded. The sun shone down on the younger woman's face, her lovely, unique, light brown eyes seeming to glow from within as they locked onto Anna. "I don't mind waiting to be presented in London, truly." Caroline bit her lip, her usually haughty voice now soft and kind.

"It's quite alright," Anna insisted. "I've given it much thought and I feel it is the right choice for me. I look forward to my role as the maiden aunt who will dote on her nieces and nephews." She delivered the last part with a chuckle, trying to sound perfectly content. One glance at Dalton's expression told her she hadn't gotten it quite right.

"Caroline, hurry after Patrick and Harriet since they've gotten a bit too far ahead," he instructed, his normally cheerful voice now carrying the weight of a young man trained all his life to shoulder responsibilities.

Caroline looked down at the ground, grasping Anna's hand in a silent apology before rushing off after their younger siblings, shouting for Harriet to stay seated lest she fall out of the tilbury.

Anna took in a deep breath full of cool, fresh air, hoping that it would invigorate her a little for the coming conversation. She knew Dalton wanted to discuss her announcement though she wished he would leave it alone. It was heartbreaking enough to finally say it aloud; she certainly did not want to explain it in excruciating detail, even to him.

"Is that really what you want, Anna?" Dalton asked, his brows furrowed. Just as Anna had suspected, Dalton went right to the heart of the matter. He rarely danced around anything, allowing his thoughts and emotions to come to the surface while still maintaining enough awareness to mind his manners. Unfortunately, Anna hadn't inherited any of that. She mostly took after Papa's quiet, thoughtful nature while Dalton had been blessed with Mama's quick wit and uncanny ability to speak the truth so kindly that it did not offend.

Anna smiled weakly as she forced her common brown eyes to meet Dalton's. "Of course it is."

Dalton frowned at Anna's answer, gently pinching her cheek. "I know you are lying, dear sister. Please, tell me what is on your mind."

Her younger brother had trapped her. Anna sighed wearily. Even just thinking about this topic exhausted her both physically and emotionally. Talking about it only compounded those effects. But she knew Dalton would not let her out of this.

"If you must know the truth," she started quietly, willing her voice to stop trembling, "I want to get married to a wonderful man and have a home full of children. Of course I do. But after my past Seasons in London, no one has shown any interest in me. I know it is because I am not charming and lively enough."

Dalton nodded silently as they slowly followed after Caroline, his gaze never leaving Anna's face. She was surprised to see that he looked so mature—different than the brother she'd known her whole life, always so full of laughter. Another pang of regret squeezed Anna's chest. She supposed that everyone else had been growing up around her while she had been so preoccupied with her future that would never be.

"The sooner I accept my impending spinsterhood, the better. Being twenty-two years old is just another mark against me. I don't have much hope that another Season will do me any good," Anna finished, her shoulders drooping slightly under the heavy weight of her confession.

Lifting her eyes, she saw her younger siblings spread out before her. Caroline stood several yards ahead, one hand holding her bonnet to her head as the wind threatened to carry it away while the other hand waved frantically for Patrick to be careful, her almost shrill voice shouting for him to be gentler with his turns. Patrick's face, usually buried in a book, shone under the sunlight, his mouth wide open in a joyous grin while Harriet cried out in excitement, the wind fanning out her blonde hair behind her like a majestic cape.

Would it really be so bad to watch this scene unfold again but with her siblings' children? Surely Anna could get used to that idea. She must. She had no choice.

Anna nearly jumped when she felt Dalton's arm wrap around her shoulders. She'd been so lost in thought that she'd forgotten he was right beside her. She leaned into his side, allowing her head to rest on his shoulder. She'd once relished the fact that she was taller than Dalton, but now his significant height advantage came in handy. Her body felt almost too heavy for her to support on her own. She may have very well sunk right into the ground if Dalton wasn't there to offer his strength.

With Dalton being only two years younger than Anna, they had grown up side by side. She could not remember her life before him. They'd stayed just as close even after all their other siblings had come along. She was immensely thankful to have such a wonderful brother like Dalton at times like this—even when his sometimes wayward behavior caused her some anxiety.

"I am fine with my choice, Dalton. Perhaps someday I shall even be happy with it," Anna insisted once more, her voice wavering slightly.

Dalton stopped so suddenly that Anna found herself jerked backward by her brother's arm, still secure around her shoulders. He turned Anna to face him, looking as serious as Anna had ever seen.

"That is not fine, Anna. You deserve to have the life you want and I know you will find it."

Anna frowned, waving a hand over the vast fields surrounding them and the hills rising in the distance. "If I couldn't find it in London, where thousands of people gather every Season, I certainly will not find it anywhere else."

Dalton took a step back and crossed his arms. Anna could see the baron he would be one day in his stance. "You should go back to London and not leave until you've found what you are looking for." His voice carried a finality in it, as if it were his decision to make. Still, Anna couldn't help laughing.

"I am sick of London—sick of seeing all the pretty, dazzling women who snatch up all the men right before my eyes before I even have a chance to say hello."

Anna's brows raised in surprise as Dalton took her hands in his. He peered down at her with such earnestness that Anna felt her resolve wavering. "Anna, you have your own beauty and wonderful qualities. It will not do to constantly compare yourself to others. The right man is somewhere out there waiting for you. I'm sure of it. Please have one more Season in London. Give yourself one more chance. I do not wish to see my favorite older sister live a life of loneliness and disappointment when I know she deserves so much more."

Dalton's words somehow stirred a tiny spark of hope in Anna's chest. She'd thought she had decided once and for all that she would quit London forever. Yet Dalton always seemed able to reach her. He lifted an eyebrow, awaiting her response.

Turning away from Dalton, Anna looked over to her younger siblings—Patrick and Harriet turning the tilbury in wide circles while Caroline watched with her hands on her hips, looking quite like Mama. Anna had always wanted to be a positive example for her siblings, but especially her sisters. She knew Caroline was desperate to make her debut next Season but she would not be allowed to do that unless Anna had married or completely given up on her dream of marriage.

Despite their many differences and their frequent clashes, Anna could not bear the thought of disappointing her younger sister. Beneath Caroline's slightly arrogant attitude existed a sweet, loving girl who deserved her own happily ever after.

With a heavy sigh, Anna turned back to Dalton, staring up at him with all the fierceness she could muster. She gave a firm nod, a tendril of dark brown hair sweeping over her forehead. "I will give myself one more chance."

Dalton's face split into a wide grin, a much more familiar expression for him, and he wrapped his arms around Anna, lifting her off the ground in the process.

"Dalton!" Anna cried out through her laughter. "Put me down immediately!" She slapped him several times on the shoulder until he finally complied.

With solid earth back under her feet, Anna took in a few deep breaths to bring herself back to reality, back to the mission she'd just agreed to. Dalton tugged at one of Anna's loose curls with a hearty laugh before running up to Caroline, taking advantage of her preoccupied state to grasp her around the waist and tickle her.

As Caroline's shrieks of laughter—followed quickly by loud scoldings—mingled in the open air with Patrick's and Harriet's shouts of exhilaration, Anna couldn't help being infected by Dalton's positivity and her siblings' happiness.

"I must be a good example for them," Anna whispered to herself, a hesitant smile slowly spreading over her face.

CHAPTER 2

*T*he atmosphere in the dining room struck Noah as quite odd. He ate dinner with his parents every evening, conversation and laughter freely flowing. That was not the case tonight. Mother and Father sat on opposite ends of the table, uncharacteristically quiet. Noah sensed the uncomfortable glances they sent to each other through the entire meal.

Despite his growing curiosity, Noah did not ask for an explanation. He quietly ate his own dinner, watching subtly. He knew his parents did not think he noticed but of course he did. Noah always took pride in his observant nature, in his ability to see truths hidden in plain sight. He used this skill to his advantage primarily when it came to determining what gifts his sisters would like on holidays or how his mother struggled more often with her knitting needles.

Still, Noah's desire to understand this strange situation before him slowly ate away at him during dinner. He silently prayed that one of them would speak up soon and give him some relief. Perhaps they would reveal news of another niece or nephew from one of his sisters.

Those occasions were typically accompanied with joy, Mother and Father buzzing with their barely contained excitement before finally giving Noah the news. Their behavior now seemed quite the opposite. Carefully lifting his eyes from his plate, Noah saw the way Father clenched and unclenched his jaw. When his eyes met Mother's for a fraction of a second, she bit her lip and quickly returned her gaze to the food dangling off her fork.

Noah cleared his throat, the sound echoing strangely in the otherwise silent dining room. Mother and Father both jumped at the sound, Father nearly dropping his fork but catching it just before it clanged against his plate.

"Is there something I should be made aware of?" Noah asked quietly, keeping his deep voice low and inviting. He could no longer wait for his parents to broach whatever subject bothered them so.

Mother dabbed at the corners of her mouth with her napkin, avoiding Noah's curious gaze. Father sighed heavily, setting his utensils down. He caught the eye of the nearest footman lingering against the wall and lifted his chin toward the door, a silent command for the servants to leave the room.

Anxiety rippled through Noah's chest, his brows furrowing as his concern increased tenfold. Whatever this news was, it certainly could not be good if Father did not want the staff to hear it. Noah's eyes locked onto his father's face, desperately trying to read his expression. All he could distinguish so far were regret, shame, and fear.

Father straightened up in his chair, returning Noah's gaze, trying to adopt a braver expression without success. Noah could see how difficult it was for Father to look him in the eyes, how desperately he wished to turn away. But he managed it long enough to deliver the blow.

"I am terribly sorry, Noah, but our estate is in trouble.

We've lost quite a bit of our money." His voice trembled slightly as he spoke those dreadful words that sent a cold shiver down Noah's spine. "Emma and Angelica will be fine since they married well but...I worry now for you, my son, and for your future family who will rely on our estate and the remaining Waynford wealth."

Forgetting his manners for a moment, Noah's mouth fell open in utter disbelief. Surely this situation warranted a little leniency when it came to proper etiquette. He wondered silently for a moment if his heart had stopped beating. He seemed unable to feel it. He'd gone numb as his father's words slowly sank in, sitting on his chest like some cruel, heavy beast.

Finally, Father tore his eyes away from his son, his face contorted in a deep shame that Noah had never expected to see on his normally jovial father. That expression shocked him back into the present moment. Time started again.

"Father, how could this happen? What could have put our estate at such risk?" Noah mumbled.

Even with his mind overwhelmed by this terrible surprise, Noah still noticed the way Mother clutched her napkin in her hands in a silent display of anger. He noticed the way Father pursed his lips, nervously glancing at the food on the table, the beautiful dishes that had been passed down through the Waynford family, the walls that surrounded them, adorned with lovingly chosen pieces of art. Noah could see the fear in his father's eyes. Losing all this was a real, perhaps even unavoidable, threat.

"Father, I need answers," Noah demanded harshly, anger masking his fear. He had no time for games of avoidance and denial. He needed the truth.

The old man flinched at the steely sound in his son's voice, a few wisps of gray hair trembling slightly. He squeezed his eyes shut as Noah's words slammed against him. Guilt erupted in Noah's stomach, almost making him feel sick. Whatever had happened clearly came with an immense amount of shame. Noah could see how painful this was for his father, his beloved father who had always loved him and guided him and done his best for their family. What could have gone so terribly wrong?

Noah forced his guilt away. He needed to hold firm and find out what happened so he could find some way to fix the situation. He would one day inherit and manage this estate, after all. He needed to understand the challenges he faced.

"Well…" Father started shakily, taking a few deep breaths before continuing. "I know you do not spend much time at White's, but I've grown rather fond of the infamous betting book in my many years there. You see, I incurred a large debt when I lost a bet about two years ago. I'd been so certain of my chances that I offered a much more generous amount than usual. You have to understand, Noah, that I was completely shocked when the other gentleman won. I felt so terribly awful and foolish, but he promised that he would collect the money I owed some other time."

"And now that time has come," Noah finished, his voice laced with bitter disappointment. Hot anger surged up through his body, only tempered by his love for Father and his immense fear of his suddenly uncertain future.

Father's head drooped down, chin resting on his chest. "Yes, the time has come. The gentleman is leaving on an expedition for India and he wants to fund his travels with the money I owe him. I just somehow thought I would have more time to gather up the funds."

A pitiful sob tore from Mother's lips, her frail body shaking with the force of her tears, a few gray curls coming loose from her simple bun. Her distress broke Noah's heart, only making him angrier that their innocent family had been put in such an awful position.

"There, there, Dorcas. Everything will be fine," Father whispered gently, putting his arms around his wife's shoulder.

"Frankland, you fool," Mother spat, her anger just as palpable as her pain. A fresh wave of shock washed over Noah. He'd never heard either of his parents utter such harsh words to the other. He could only imagine how betrayed and devastated his poor mother must feel, knowing the peril her family faced.

Seeing Mother's anguish finally released Noah's body from the paralysis of shock. He pushed his chair back, the legs scraping against the wood floor, and rushed to her end of the table. "Mother, why don't you go lay down and try to rest? Father and I will figure this out." He grasped his mother's small, arthritic hands in his, gently rubbing his thumbs over her slightly swollen knuckles, speaking as calmly as possible in the hopes of soothing her.

"Let me take her upstairs and get her settled in bed," Father offered quickly, standing from his chair. One sharp look from Noah made it clear that he would not get out of this situation that easily. If Noah must be trapped in it, then so must Father. He was the source of this problem, after all.

"I shall call for Nelson to escort her to her room," Noah announced quietly, eyes still narrowed at Father.

He peered out the door, catching a footman's attention. Noah noticed the curiosity in the footman's eye, but the man went to bring his mother's maid to the dining room all the same. No doubt the staff would whisper amongst themselves, trying to figure out the grand mystery. As Nelson hurried into the room, a worried expression on her face, Noah prayed that they would find some solution before their trusted servants caught wind of the dire situation. They all did their jobs well and did not deserve to be thrown back into the world to find new positions because of their

17

master's mistake. Especially not poor old Nelson, who had been Mother's maid and confidante since before he was born.

Nelson carefully led Mother from the room, offering gentle words of comfort all the way. Noah closed the door behind them, shutting away the sound of Mother's sniffles. Noah pulled his shoulders back and lifted his chin. He must find a way to fix this, not just for himself but for the people who depended on his family—and for his own future wife and children.

He turned to face the long dining room table again, usually a place of cheer. Now, with only Father seated at the table, it looked so dreary and foreboding. Noah went around to the other side of the table and took a seat next to Father.

He stared at the man for a silent moment, realizing how much older he looked with his face so distorted by his shame and regret. The wrinkles around his mouth, at the corners of his eyes, and between his brows had become much deeper in just these past few minutes.

Somehow, Noah's anger subsided just a bit. Father was clearly mortified and terribly upset. Noah let out a heavy sigh, dropping his chin to his chest in an almost perfect mirror of his father's posture. Everyone made mistakes—but usually not ones that would cost him his future.

Noah allowed his thoughts to swirl inside his head for a few more moments as he and Father sat in silence, each wondering what could be done. How could something like this have happened? Noah knew Father liked to play cards, gamble, and place the odd bet here and there, but never in such a dangerous way. He'd always looked up to his father as a model of responsible leadership. Father had inherited their home, Shambrook Lodge, and the money that came with it from his own father, who had inherited it from his. Being the eldest son always came with certain expectations to grow or, at the very least, protect the family wealth. Noah would have never guessed that his father would get caught up in this situation.

After what felt like hours, Noah finally had enough strength to lift his head again and look directly at Father. He had not expected to see tears gently rolling down the man's face.

"My dear boy, I am so terribly sorry for this mess I have caused." He choked out his apology, voice thick with emotion. Father squeezed his eyes shut as if he'd found himself in a nightmare and needed to wake himself up.

Gritting his teeth, Noah forced his anger aside and allowed his compassion to come forward. He got up from his seat once again and sat on the edge of the table next to his father. Father did not look up until Noah put a gentle hand on his shoulder.

As the man peered up into his son's face, eyes wide and desperate for forgiveness, Noah finally felt his anger truly subside. "I cannot lie and tell you I am not hurt and upset, Father. But I know you did not expect this to happen. You did not mean to cause us harm." The weariness in his own voice surprised Noah. These past few minutes had felt like they had taken years off his life. Hopefully, he would soon find a way to restore them.

Father gave a thin, trembling smile as he put his own hand over Noah's, shaking with a quiet sob. "I would not be surprised if you hated me for the rest of your life. How can my family ever trust me again?"

The agony in his father's voice nearly crushed Noah's heart. Even if they found some miraculous way to recover their money, he knew Father would never truly forgive himself for this. Hating Father would not recover their money either.

"I can see the truth in your heart. I can see that you love

your family and you always mean well," Noah quietly assured him, feeling his own emotion start to overwhelm him. "You made a costly mistake, there can be no denying that. But we can find a way to fix it together. I promise."

Father nodded sadly, his guilt still evident on his face. "Thank you, son. I've always admired the clarity with which you see the world around you. You are a much better man than I." He squeezed Noah's hand, still on his shoulder, as if trying to borrow some of his son's strength.

"I think that remains to be seen." Noah smiled, trying to bring some light back to their grave conversation. Father's slight smile brought a small measure of comfort to Noah's heart.

After a few moments of strained silence, Noah knew they could not put off the important question any longer. He sat up straighter, clapped his hands together, and put on what he hoped was a brave smile. "Now, we will pay the man whatever you owe and figure out a way to make the money back. Do you have any ideas?"

Father swallowed nervously, once again avoiding Noah's gaze. He looked almost as anxious as he had earlier, before he'd come clean about his bet. "I know you are not going to want to hear this," he mumbled.

"I am sure there is not anything much worse that I could hear right now, Father," Noah chuckled wryly.

"Well, in truth, the easiest way to recover the money would be for you to find a wealthy lady to marry," Father said slowly, sheepishly looking up at Noah as if he were a child waiting to be scolded.

Much to Noah's surprise, that shocked him almost more than Father's confession. He certainly did not like that idea at all.

$\approx$

NOAH BOWED his head to the young lady before him at the end of their dance set. When he stood back up to his full height, he saw that she had already hurried away to her next partner. Noah slipped between the new couples gathering on the dance floor, eager to rest for a moment and enjoy a refreshing drink. He made his way to a footman along the wall, taking a glass of punch off his gleaming silver tray. As he sipped the cool liquid gratefully, he looked back out to the dance floor at his last partner. His heart sank slightly. Though he'd only had a brief conversation with her before they took to the floor as well as a few snatches of words during the dance itself, Noah already knew that she was not the one for him. She had not seemed too interested in carrying on a thoughtful conversation.

He shifted his attention to the lively crowd surrounding him, couples old and new dancing, chatting, sometimes barely tolerating each other. Noah smiled as he brought the glass to his lips again. Such grand events like this ball always brought a wide variety of people for him to observe. When not dancing or conversing with friends, Noah enjoyed stealing away to a quiet corner to make up his own stories about what he saw.

An older couple a few yards to his left looked to be in the barely tolerating stage. Based on their age, he guessed they were only here to support a son or daughter they hoped to find a match for. The cold formality between them indicated to Noah that perhaps their own match had not been one made through love.

Another couple just beyond them, however, showed Noah what he'd always hoped to one day find. Though they looked as though they could be grandparents to the younger set dominating the dance floor, the pair looked just as happy and smitten with each other as any courting couple Noah had ever seen. The old gentleman constantly smiled down at his wife as if he could not believe he'd had the good fortune to marry her, while the kindly looking lady gazed up at her husband with stars in her eyes.

Noah sighed with a strange mixture of happiness and melancholy. He always appreciated seeing such happily married couples, especially when many of the men in his circles seemed to find their unions burdensome. But Noah knew it was possible. He had living proof of it right before his eyes at this very moment. That was what Noah had been waiting for. That was why Noah still remained a bachelor at twenty-seven years old.

Unlike quite a few men he knew, Noah looked forward to marriage. He prayed for it. Unfortunately, after several Seasons in London and courting his fair share of ladies, he still had not met anyone he'd felt a genuine connection with.

Noah wanted to fall in love. As silly as that may have sounded to some, Noah had promised himself long ago that he would not marry until he found a woman he loved with his whole heart and who gave her whole heart in return.

A young couple to Noah's right took glasses from the nearest footman. He watched from the corner of his eye as they swooned over each other. They looked ready to get married right here in the middle of this ballroom. At one point Noah would have felt a twinge of envy, wondering when such a moment would happen for him. Tonight, with Father's confession still fresh in his mind two weeks later, Noah's stomach twisted with the anxiety of his newfound reality.

He had undertaken a very serious mission—to save his family's fortune and future. He no longer had the luxury of waiting for the stars to align, for prayers to be answered, for the right woman to appear miraculously before him.

After draining the last few sips from his glass, Noah decided he needed a distraction from these unpleasant thoughts. He wove through the crowd, looking for familiar faces. Finally, his eyes landed on his good friend Phineas Tilson, sitting near one of the long tables of delicious food, his blond hair looking a little disheveled from dancing many sets. Noah considered himself lucky to catch Phineas on a break.

Like Noah, Phineas had started to receive pressure from his family to marry and produce an heir before he inherited his father's baronetcy. They also had another important trait in common—they both wanted to marry for love. They had met several years ago on a night quite like this one. They'd been in the same dance set and come away with the same pained expressions on their faces after dancing with ladies they had not cared for, quickly bonding over the experience and their similar goals. They often joked with each other that they must be the only two men in all of England who longed to marry for companionship rather than appearance, social standing, or money.

Noah quickly and quietly made his way through the guests on the edge of the dance floor, hoping to chat with his friend before Phineas inevitably jumped back into another set, always on the lookout for his future wife. Perhaps Phineas had had more luck in that department tonight than Noah.

Just as Noah finally got close enough to call out to his friend, he found himself twirling rather ungracefully back in the direction he'd just come.

"This way, Noah! Quickly!" Father whispered loudly in Noah's ear as he dragged him off, gripping his son's elbow tightly.

"Father, what on Earth is going on?" Noah demanded, trying not to stumble over his own feet.

"A baron from my club is here with his daughter and he's agreed to introduce you to her." Father grinned with what

Noah could only describe as glee. He acted as if Noah was on the verge of meeting his bride-to-be. "I believe she will be an excellent match for you. Lord Welsted says she is a very kind, thoughtful girl."

Noah's head spun as he struggled to keep up with Father, the man's excitement granting him a surprising speed. They wove through the gathering of guests toward a family standing by another table laden with pastries, cheeses, and fruits. Noah's eyes immediately landed on the young lady Father wanted to throw him at.

He watched her as they came closer, noting the way she smiled sweetly at the young man beside her whom Noah guessed was a brother or cousin based on their similar features. The smile was genuine—not like the coy, flirtatious smiles he saw many other ladies employ when they hoped to gain a man's affection.

Something about the warmth in her expression made the woman even prettier. Her dark hair glittered under the chandelier above but her large brown eyes possessed a shine all their own. Perhaps Father was right after all. A ripple of excitement washed over Noah from head to foot. He certainly would not mind getting to know this lady better.

After politely making their way through a small group that had gathered in their path, they finally arrived before Lord Welsted and his family. "My lord, allow me to introduce my son, Mr. Noah Waynford," Father blurted immediately, his eagerness getting the better of him.

Noah felt heat rise up the back of his neck at his father's lack of tact, but a quick glance to Lord Welsted's daughter eased his embarrassment. The corner of her mouth had lifted up in an understanding smile. Her father was just as good-natured, it seemed. He chuckled under his breath before turning his attention to Noah, wearing a warm smile that reminded Noah quite a bit of the young lady by the baron's side.

"It is a pleasure to make your acquaintance, my lord," Noah said with a bow.

"The pleasure is all mine," Lord Welsted returned. "This is my wife, Lady Welsted, and my two eldest children, Miss Anna Harcourt and Mr. Dalton Harcourt." The baron made his introductions, putting his hands on each of his family members' shoulders as he did so. Noah appreciated the pride with which he spoke of his wife and children. He knew instantly that Lord Welsted truly loved his family.

Noah bowed to each of them in turn, noticing Miss Harcourt's shy smile, the way her eyes darted from his face to her gloved hands clasped before her. The expression somehow conveyed a sense of mystery. Noah found himself longing to learn more, to understand her, to uncover the truth in her.

A sharp nudge in his ribs from Father reminded Noah what they'd come there to do. "Miss Harcourt, may I ask for the next dance?"

Noah fought to keep his expression as neutral as possible as he watched a strange change overcome the young lady before him. Gone was the quiet anticipation in her face that he had seen earlier when they were introduced.

"I would absolutely love to dance with you, Mr. Waynford," she said almost breathlessly with a sparkling smile that looked unnatural against her soft features. Miss Harcourt gave a slight pout before speaking again. "I'm terribly afraid that my next dance is spoken for, but please do put your name down on my card for the following one."

She reached into her reticule and flourished her dance card before Noah, holding it gingerly, as if he might snatch it from her fingers. Noah took the card and the offered pencil as gently as he could, scrawling his name on the next available line.

What on Earth could that strange flip in personality mean? Noah did his best to give a kind, inviting smile as he handed the card and pencil back to Miss Harcourt, his confusion giving way to an even stronger desire to understand this woman. He hoped to find out during their dance.

The music came to a gentle stop and another gentleman appeared at Noah's side. The man bowed before Miss Harcourt with an outstretched hand, ready to claim his dance. Miss Harcourt delicately wrapped her fingers around his, smiling with strained cheer. Noah watched as the other gentleman led her to the dance floor.

Just before they took their places in the line, Miss Harcourt glanced over her shoulder, her eyes meeting Noah's for the briefest moment.

He saw what he'd seen earlier—genuine, lovely tenderness.

CHAPTER 3

*A*nna whipped her head around to face forward again, her heart shooting up into her throat. She had hoped to get another subtle look at Mr. Waynford, but he'd certainly seen her. Somehow, her eyes had immediately found his through the crowd. He watched her with an intensity and curiosity that felt foreign to her—as if he truly wanted to see her.

Her body carried her along of its own accord as her mind brought her back to her past Seasons and the men she'd talked with and danced with and walked about with. None of them had looked at her like that.

"Miss Harcourt?" A different gentleman's voice shocked Anna back to the present moment, her surroundings rushing up to her once more, replacing those lovely deep blue eyes.

Anna's stomach squeezed with a mixture of nerves and guilt. She should not be thinking about another man while she was about to dance with Mr. Cornelius Milburn, the charming son of Viscount Milburn. She'd been so lost in thought that they arrived at the dance floor before she knew it. Mr. Milburn held his hand out toward her spot in the line that she should have already occupied.

A fierce blush bloomed over Anna's cheeks. "I-I'm terribly sorry!" she sputtered quickly as she hurried toward her spot. At the same moment, she heard her friend Esther's words ringing in her ears.

Remember, dear Anna, men like ladies who know how to flirt discreetly. You have charm. Don't be afraid to use it!

Anna flashed what she hoped was a dazzling smile at Mr. Milburn, trying to snuff out the anxiety that made her blush and stutter. "I must have gotten caught up in daydreams of dancing with you," Anna sighed, feeling horribly fake.

The older gentleman, in his early thirties, from what Papa had told her, was handsome in an almost intimidating way— quite different from the bold yet kind good looks of Mr. Waynford. Mr. Milburn's light brown hair gleamed from the candlelight surrounding them, not a single strand out of place, his nose perfectly straight with a high arch, his chin and jawline strong and sharp. The other man's features were slightly softer and smoother, but certainly no less charming.

Mr. Milburn smiled understandingly, his green eyes regarding Anna with interest. Her heart seemed to fly about her ribcage. Men rarely looked at her with any kind of interest yet somehow, two different men had given her such expressions on the very same night.

Could Anna's scheme of pretending to be those ladies she so admired and envied—the ladies who won men's hearts, fell in love, and got married—truly be working?

"I assure you there is nothing wrong, Miss Harcourt. I am just as thrilled to be sharing a dance with you." Mr. Milburn's tone carried amusement and a carefree attitude that brought Anna a sliver of comfort. She hadn't given herself away or offended Mr. Milburn with her frightful attempts at flirting.

After a few moments of dancing down the line, Anna

finally found herself in Mr. Milburn's arms. His touch on her waist was light but still enough to guide her through the steps while the hand that held hers grasped it with surprising tenderness for a man of his height and muscular stature. Anna willed herself to relax, to ease into her new persona.

To her dismay, the nerves floating about her stomach refused to leave her be as the dance went on. No matter how warmly Mr. Milburn smiled at her, no matter what he said in his light, friendly voice, Anna could not overcome the fact that she was lying. Some women could attract men with their charm and polite conversation. Anna was not one of them. The simplest conversations with even the kindest strangers felt like a battle to Anna. She never knew quite what to say or how to react.

Anna knew that she could not continue this way. She was not like those women, but she wanted to be. Her dear friend, formerly Esther Doyle and now Mrs. Parkins for the past two years, had given Anna some excellent advice during tea last week. Esther had suggested that Anna adopt the behaviors of the ladies she wished to be like, promising that it would eventually become natural to her.

Mr. Milburn gracefully passed Anna to another gentleman in the line, giving her a chance to take several deep breaths in an effort to calm herself. She prayed desperately that it would start to feel natural soon. She had only been at this ball for a few hours and she already felt utterly exhausted. Anna had underestimated how much effort and concentration it would take to uphold this facade, to constantly remind herself of how she should act and what she should say.

Anna's brief respite with another partner did not work the wonders she'd hoped it would. Once back in Mr. Milburn's arms, Anna felt the anxious butterflies storm through her stomach again, her heart hammering in her chest.

"Are you well, Miss Harcourt?" Mr. Milburn asked gently after a few moments of silence. Anna cursed herself for getting lost in her thoughts again, allowing the conversation to lapse. According to Esther, men wanted wives who could hold pleasant, interesting conversations.

Forcing herself to stay in the present moment, Anna looked up into Mr. Milburn's face. He still watched her with the same interest he'd shown before. A chill rushed down Anna's spine, but she could not tell if the sensation came from nerves or excitement.

The gentleman tilted his head to the side, a lock of hair falling across his forehead in a most charming way. Anna forced another cheery smile, hopefully not so cheery that she looked unhinged.

"I am perfectly fine, Mr. Milburn. Thank you for your concern," Anna assured him, using that lilting voice she often heard other ladies use when talking to a potential suitor. Esther's words jumped to the front of Anna's mind again.

Next, you should remember that gentlemen love having a chance to talk about their interests and hobbies. They marry ladies who ask about those things and listen attentively!

"Tell me, Mr. Milburn, what do you enjoy doing when in London?" Anna summoned all her strength and batted her eyelashes up at the gentleman in what she hoped was an eagerly interested expression.

A spark of confidence rushed through Anna as he smiled appreciatively. She had redeemed herself and seemed well on her way to making a good impression at long last.

"I primarily like to drive my carriage around Hyde Park, visit the shops, attend my friends' dinner parties, and try to squeeze in a play or two in between." As Mr. Milburn happily rattled off his favorite pastimes, Anna listened with a smile that never left her face.

Much to Anna's surprise, she latched onto his last words. "How lovely that you enjoy the theater! My youngest brother, Patrick, loves drama. He's just fifteen but he's already studying to become an examiner of plays one day."

Anna nearly beamed at her dance partner while she spoke. Surely this must be what victory felt like! She'd managed to identify an opportunity in the conversation and she'd seized it, offering her own contribution. When Mr. Milburn lifted his eyebrow just slightly, Anna's triumphant smile quickly pulled itself back into a less exuberant expression. She'd made a mistake. Perhaps it was too soon in their acquaintanceship to go on and on about her family.

Biting her lip, Anna cast around in her mind for other safe conversation topics that Esther had coached her on. "And what have you been doing to keep yourself entertained since you've been in London this Season?" Her voice wavered just slightly as her nerves rushed back in full force.

Mr. Milburn grinned and launched into a detailed explanation of his activities thus far, occasionally asking Anna a question, which she could only answer briefly before he continued describing his latest dinner party or who he'd seen at the park last week.

Anna kept her smile on her face at all times, laughing at all the right moments and occasionally offering what she hoped was a witty remark. Mr. Milburn seemed to appreciate these light interjections more than Anna's earlier discussion of Patrick's interest in the theater. To Anna's relief, she found that she preferred the conversation this way. She did not have to try so hard to come up with a constant stream of interesting things to say. As long as she kept her expression cheerful and attentive, Mr. Milburn seemed not to mind either.

As their dance neared its end, Anna allowed herself a few moments to slip back into her mind, her safe space where she did not have to impress anyone. Her mind had its own opinions on what they should do during this brief period of respite from Mr. Milburn's constant chatter.

Anna peered over her partner's shoulder, her eyes scanning her surroundings for the spot her family had chosen as their little space away from the bigger crowds. Her heart burst into flutters when she saw Mr. Waynford and his father still there, chatting with the other Harcourts.

She stole a swift glance up at Mr. Milburn, who chatted animatedly about a dinner party he'd attended last Season where something quite unexpected and amusing had happened. His sparkling green eyes stared contentedly over Anna's head as if transported back into his memories.

This suited Anna just fine. It offered her an opportunity to gaze at the younger Mr. Waynford as her current partner passed her to another gentleman in the line. Her eyes easily found Mr. Waynford again, taking in his handsome profile with its long nose, slightly rounded chin, and firm jaw—and of course those intriguing blue eyes that seemed to notice everything, perfectly framed by shining locks of dark brown hair. Nothing about him seemed ordinary.

Soon Anna found herself once again paired with Mr. Milburn. As the final turn approached, Mr. Waynford looked over at the dance floor, his eyes immediately finding hers. A strange sensation swept through Anna's entire body—both chilling and warmly comforting all at once. Had Mr. Waynford somehow seen straight into Anna's soul in that split second?

A hot wave of embarrassment quickly followed that exhilarating feeling. Anna hadn't expected to be caught staring at him. As she felt a fierce blush spread from the base of her neck all the way to her face, Anna squeezed her eyes closed, trying to shut out the swirling room that suddenly overwhelmed her, to shut out that penetrating gaze that had caught her in a foolish moment.

"Drat!" Mr. Milburn cried out as Anna's foot came crashing down on his.

They stumbled together for a moment before Anna clumsily lurched to the side, her face suddenly much closer to the polished wood floor than she knew it should be, her hands slapping down on the gleaming surface as a sharp cracking sound echoed in her ears. Then the pain came, blinding her for a moment. Tears rushed up and poured out as she heard the clatter of feet. The other dancers cleared away from her, leaving Anna feeling suddenly exposed as she partially lay on the ground, the wood cool beneath her hands in a stark contrast to the hot ache throbbing through her right foot.

Time seemed to stretch on as Anna's mind, muddled with pain, struggled to decide what to do next. Just as Anna thought she should try to get herself up off the floor, two strong hands gripped her above her elbows, hoisting her up as if she weighed no more than a feather. She felt as light as a feather as her head spun. Instinctively, Anna tried to stand on her own, the pain in her ankle immediately overwhelming her.

She cried out, somehow still aware that such a sound was extremely unladylike, but unable to control herself. Anna stumbled again, falling forward into a broad chest, masculine arms wrapping around her tenderly.

"Do you think you can walk, Miss Harcourt?" a distant but familiar voice, deep and warm, made its way to Anna through the fog in her mind. The pain rang in her ears now after her foolish attempt to put weight on her injured foot.

Anna took a few deep breaths, the pain subsiding enough for her to gather a somewhat coherent thought. "I think I've sprained my ankle," she mumbled weakly, barely able to see

33

anything around her as the tears continued to cloud her vision.

"Well, that simply will not do," the gentleman said gently. "Hold on tightly to my arm and keep your injured foot raised."

With a slight nod, Anna did as she was told, grasping onto the gentleman's coat sleeve while still trying to be mindful of her manners and not become too much of a burden. After a shaky hop, Anna jerked to a stop as a surprising realization dawned on her.

The voice beside her was not Mr. Milburn's, the man she'd expected to be at her side first to offer assistance. A quiet gasp escaped Anna's lips as she finally looked up, blinking back the remainder of her tears to clear her vision. It was Mr. Waynford's arm she clung to, not Mr. Milburn's.

"Shall we try again?" Mr. Waynford asked patiently. Anna's blush returned with even greater force than before. She nodded and forced herself to hop again, finding herself gripping her hero's arm even tighter for added stability.

In truth, Anna would have been extremely embarrassed to hang off Mr. Milburn's arm like this. They barely knew each other, but she knew Mr. Waynford even less. At least she and Mr. Milburn had had one dance together before finding themselves in this unusually intimate scenario.

As Anna made another attempt to wobble forward with Mr. Waynford's assistance, more of her senses returned to her. She heard the crowd murmuring as she paused to breathe, noticing a few more aches in her body besides her ankle. Her embarrassment temporarily overcame her pain and Anna forced herself to take another unsteady and ungraceful hop, Mr. Waynford carefully matching her pace.

They only made it a couple more steps before Mr. Milburn sprang into action, rushing to Anna's other side. "Goodness gracious, Miss Harcourt! You gave me such a fright! Do allow me to assist you," he cried loudly enough to draw even more attention to them.

Between the two men, Anna slowly hobbled off the dance floor, wishing she could melt right through it the whole way.

Mama, Papa, and Dalton rushed to meet her, their voices clashing as they all asked if she was well. "Thank you, gentlemen." Papa raised his voice slightly over the commotion in that way only he could manage—loud enough to be heard but still calm and kind. "Allow my son and I to handle the rest."

"That is quite alright, my lord. I am more than happy to help," Mr. Waynford insisted, his voice comforting and genuine, as Papa and Dalton reached forward to collect Anna.

"As am I." Mr. Milburn quickly echoed the sentiment.

"That is much appreciated, Mr. Milburn, Mr. Waynford. I promise we were just on our way to fetch you, Anna, but Mr. Waynford here moved so quickly it almost looked like he appeared at your side like an angel," Papa chuckled, giving both men a warm smile. Anna gazed up at Mr. Waynford, amazed that he would jump to her aid so readily.

"Darling, why don't these gentlemen and I take Anna to a sitting room where she can rest? You can continue your conversation here," Mama instructed without looking at her husband. Her eyes never left Anna, roaming up and down for any other obvious injuries. She put a soft, warm hand on her daughter's cheek. "You'll be just fine, my lovely girl."

"Very well then." Papa added in a conspiratorial whisper, "You know your mother has more of a stomach for these things, but do fetch me if you need anything." Anna welcomed his humorous comment in this otherwise dreadful situation.

"It's hardly a case for a surgeon, you know." Mama smiled as she motioned for Anna and her escort to follow.

"I'll come with you," Dalton insisted, trying to join their ranks.

Anna shook her head as firmly as she could without sending herself into a dizzy spell. "Thank you, but there's no need, Dalton. I'm well taken care of. I know you've promised the next dance to someone and I would hate for you to miss out."

Anna felt Mr. Waynford shake slightly next to her in a suppressed chuckle. She glanced up to see his small smile and a good-natured humor in his eyes. Her blush deepened once more, her heart sinking as she realized that she would not be able to dance with him tonight.

Mama led the way to a nearby sitting room, only pausing long enough to ask a footman for directions. Mr. Milburn and Mr. Waynford assisted her with the utmost care, never going faster than Anna could manage though it must have seemed painfully slow to them. As they made their way down the empty hall, Anna marveled at the situation she'd found herself in. Not the horrible embarrassment of spraining her ankle in the middle of a dance, but the fact that two men showed so much interest in her already. She prayed with everything in her heart that she would be able to impress at least one of them with her newfound personality—enough to want to marry her.

Because the journey was so slow, Anna had time to observe both gentlemen. When she looked at Mr. Waynford and he smiled at her with that noble honesty in his eyes, Anna felt a sting of guilt pierce her stomach. She was being false even if her intentions weren't nefarious.

Both gentlemen only knew Anna as the woman she'd been pretending to be. The realization tugged at the corners of her mouth, producing an involuntary frown. They would never know the real her—or rather, the old version of her before she eventually became this new woman.

"Is everything alright, Miss Harcourt? Should we stop and rest against the wall perhaps?" Mr. Waynford asked, peering down into Anna's face.

"I am perfectly fine," Anna chirped, putting on the brightest smile she could manage, ignoring the pain.

CHAPTER 4

"There we are," Noah whispered, carefully guiding Miss Harcourt down onto the large sofa with Mr. Milburn's help, Lady Welsted quietly fretting in the background all the while.

The young lady groaned as she sank into the plush cushions before quickly masking her pain with that same strange smile from earlier. Noah's brows furrowed as he tried to figure out why she kept adopting this veneer. At least, he suspected it to be a veneer.

Miss Harcourt noticed his expression and fluttered her eyelids. "I'm so very sorry we won't be able to dance together, Mr. Waynford, but I'll promise my very next dance to you once my ankle heals."

Noah managed a dry chuckle, sensing the effort it took her to behave so coyly. "I am sure we can arrange those details some other time. What matters most is that you rest and allow yourself to heal."

"You are so very kind." She smiled again, Noah noting the strain in her voice. What on Earth could be going on with this woman? Who was she, really?

"I do hope you will promise the following dance to me."
Mr. Milburn dropped to one knee before Miss Harcourt,
taking her hands in his. Noah couldn't help frowning at this
overly dramatic display.

Miss Harcourt's cheeks turned a very pretty shade of
pink as she pulled her gaze away from both men. She
suddenly looked quite shy with so much attention on her.
But in the next moment, her bright smile appeared again. "I
would very much enjoy that, Mr. Milburn," she blurted
eagerly.

Feeling perplexed by Miss Harcourt's unusual switches in
behavior, Noah turned his attention elsewhere. If he didn't,
he feared he would never take his eyes off her again. He
watched as Lady Welsted leaned over her daughter, propped
up against the arm of the sofa with her legs stretched out
before her, one lifted up on the softest pillow in the room.
The older woman brushed her daughter's hair back from her
forehead, which gleamed with the slightest sheen of
perspiration.

"My lady, do have a seat here." Noah's manners flooded
back to him. He pulled a nearby chair toward the baroness.

"Thank you, kind sir." Lady Welsted gratefully accepted
the chair, allowing Noah to help her adjust it so she could
still be as close as possible to Miss Harcourt.

Noah felt eyes following him. When he glanced past
Lady Welsted, he saw Miss Harcourt watching him with a
soft, sweet appreciation that seemed to suit her much more
than that excessively vibrant attitude she'd adopted earlier.
He could see the kindness in her eyes, demure yet
abundant.

Mr. Milburn pulled himself up off the floor and situated
himself on the edge of the sofa next to Miss Harcourt, taking
care not to jostle her too much as he took one of her hands in
his. Clearly, he had not taken enough care, for Noah noticed

that Miss Harcourt winced. He fought to keep his expression friendly as annoyance flared in him.

Noah opened his mouth to suggest that the other man leave the injured lady alone, but no words made it out. It hung open in quiet surprise as Mr. Milburn leaned forward, holding Miss Harcourt's gloved hand to his chest.

"I swear I will not leave your side until you are well enough to return home," he whispered gravely, nearly glaring at the poor young woman with the intensity of his earnest expression. Lady Welsted cleared her throat and Mr. Milburn quickly sat back up, suddenly seeming to remember that Miss Harcourt's mother could see and hear all his attempts to flatter her daughter.

"Please, Mr. Milburn, that won't be necessary," Miss Harcourt quickly insisted, sounding almost horrified at the thought that he would inconvenience himself even further on her behalf. She tried to push herself up into a sitting position before letting out a sharp yelp and falling back against the arm of the sofa.

"Anna! You mustn't move!" Lady Welsted scolded in that comforting way only mothers could manage. This time it was Noah's turn to fall to one knee before Miss Harcourt, his eyes darting over her face, searching for any indication of a worsening injury. He only saw her pain, which she quickly smoothed away beneath a reassuring smile accompanied by a hint of worry.

"I'm sorry, Mama. I am fine, I promise," she insisted once more. She truly seemed more distressed about causing trouble for everyone else rather than her own discomfort. "Mr. Milburn, you need not stay with me. I know you have promised dances to other ladies tonight and I do not wish to ruin your night," Miss Harcourt continued, genuine concern in her lovely deep brown eyes.

"Miss Harcourt is right, Mr. Milburn. I have no other

obligations tonight so I am happy to keep the ladies company for the remainder of their evening," Noah quickly added. It seemed to him that Mr. Milburn had started to cause the injured young woman more anxiety than she needed.

"Indeed," Lady Welsted agreed. "You've done more than enough tonight, Mr. Milburn. We are so very grateful. Do go and enjoy the rest of the ball." She caught Noah's eye for the briefest moment. He guessed that the baroness had come to the same conclusion as Noah.

"Very well then." Mr. Milburn coughed lightly with a tight smile. "I shall take my leave. I do hope you recover quickly, Miss Harcourt." He gave a low bow before leaving the room, frowning ever so slightly.

"Have you caught your breath, my dear?" Lady Welsted wasted no time returning her attention to her daughter. She continued gently stroking Miss Harcourt's hair, now slightly disheveled from laying on the sofa. It looked quite soft to Noah.

"I have, Mama. I am feeling much better already." Miss Harcourt reached up behind her to take her mother's hand, pulling it toward her cheek. She smiled against the exquisite, deep purple glove Lady Welsted wore. Noah felt himself smiling, too, at Miss Harcourt's seemingly constant desire to comfort others even though she was the one who needed comforting.

"I am sure you are," said Lady Welsted. "Nothing can get your spirits down for too long. But I will keep a close eye on you to make sure you don't overexert yourself. I know how you hate to be a bother, but you must allow me to make a fuss over you until you heal." The baroness gazed down at Miss Harcourt fondly. Noah knew his ability to observe his surroundings and read other people were sharper than most, but anyone could see how much love existed in the Harcourt family.

Lady Welsted called a footman to fetch a woman named Mrs. Parkins. Only a few moments passed before a young woman barreled into the room, nearly collapsing before the sofa, questions immediately spilling out of her mouth until Lady Welsted stemmed the flow.

"Mrs. Parkins, would you wait here with Anna while I fetch my husband and my son? Now that Anna's had some rest, I think we should return home." Lady Welsted put an understanding hand on the other woman's shoulder before leaving them behind.

"Oh, you poor dear!" Mrs. Parkins cried, taking Miss Harcourt's face in both her hands. Noah stifled a laugh as he watched the deep concern on the woman's face, assisted by a healthy dose of dramatic flair.

"Esther, I'm fine! It's just a twisted ankle. This sofa is not my deathbed." Miss Harcourt giggled quietly behind her hand. "You know I hate being fussed over."

Noah thought back to Lady Welsted's words just a few minutes ago. Indeed, the real Miss Harcourt seemed to prefer a quieter existence, though she did a fair amount of her own fussing over others. Warm air slowly filled Noah's chest as he pondered that charming trait.

Mrs. Parkins pouted playfully, tossing her head up, a few black curls bouncing along. "I cannot help fretting over you, Anna. You make it so easy!"

The two ladies laughed together for a moment while Noah thankfully remained part of the background. He did not mind being ignored for now. It allowed him to observe Miss Harcourt more closely, to see a better approximation of her true self. Noah would have been content to let the ladies continue their conversation, but Miss Harcourt's eyes suddenly darted to him and she gasped despite his understanding smile.

"I'm so terribly sorry I haven't introduced you yet!" She

covered her mouth, mortified at her social misstep though Noah quickly assured her that he'd taken no offense at all. "Mr. Noah Waynford, this is my dear friend, Mrs. Adam Parkins."

Noah bowed to Mrs. Parkins who gave a deeper curtsy than a simple son of a landed gentleman required. She looked as if she were being introduced to a marquess. "Thank you, Mr. Waynford, for helping my dear friend." Despite her obvious penchant for theatrics, Noah could hear the sincerity in Mrs. Parkins' words.

"It truly was no trouble at all," Noah insisted with a kind smile, hoping to ease some of Miss Harcourt's worries. "I shall return to the ball now that Miss Harcourt is in your capable hands, Mrs. Parkins." He stood from his chair and returned it to its proper place by the end table.

"Thank you, Mr. Waynford. You really are like an angel just as my papa said." Miss Harcourt looked at him with such genuine appreciation and care that Noah suddenly did not want to leave. He wanted to remain by Miss Harcourt's side and learn more about her.

Before Noah could take a step, Mrs. Parkins gently shook her friend's hand, a mysterious glance passing between the two women. Clearly Mrs. Parkins had something else in mind.

Like magic, that other version of Miss Harcourt suddenly appeared as she said with a simpering smile, "Do stay, Mr. Waynford. I cannot bear for you to leave just yet. We must make up for our lost dance."

Fighting a frown, Noah brought his chair back to its temporary spot by the sofa as Mrs. Parkins raised her eyebrows at Miss Harcourt in another silent but meaningful exchange. Miss Harcourt gave the slightest nod, her delicate lips pulling up in a tight smile. It couldn't hurt to stay a while longer and talk with her. Perhaps he could uncover more about her—the real her. Besides, he'd promised Father that he would try to get to know new ladies this Season.

Mrs. Parkins gazed about the room as if noticing it for the first time before announcing that she must examine a tapestry hanging on the opposite wall, mumbling something about the lack of art in her own home as she effectively left Noah and Miss Harcourt alone.

Miss Harcourt's earlier poise seemed to disappear now that it was just the two of them. She smiled nervously, barely meeting Noah's eyes. A silent moment passed between them, Noah waiting for the young woman to speak when she felt comfortable enough.

A flash of realization passed over Miss Harcourt's face, as if she'd just remembered something very important, and she sat up straighter, beaming up at Noah. "Have you been enjoying your night so far?" she asked cheerfully.

The question was polite enough but Noah, quite accustomed to the behaviors of the *ton*, could hear the flirtatious tone in her voice. He could feel his mouth pulling into a frown, then redirected it into what he hoped passed as an appreciative smile. He'd talked with his fair share of women like this, women who hoped to charm their way to the altar. The worst part was that Noah would not have minded it so much if he'd felt he could connect with any of them on a deeper level, beneath the typical pleasantries so they could truly come to understand each other. None of the ladies he'd met so far seemed to be interested in taking that journey with him.

At first, Miss Harcourt had intrigued him with those glimpses of a softness that could only be genuine, born of a truly kind heart. Yet she always returned to this typical Society lady act. He wished that she felt comfortable enough to show her real self since he felt confident by now that this dazzling facade was not it.

Still, Noah obliged the lady. "My night has been quite lovely. Even this part of it," he said with a gentle smile.

Miss Harcourt's eyes grew wide with worry. "I'm so very sorry for causing you so much trouble. You've had to miss out on so much of the night because of me," she stammered, the words spilling out of her in one breath. Before Noah could apologize for his thoughtless jest, Miss Harcourt shook her head slightly before forcing out an uncomfortable giggle. "I cannot believe you had to witness my horribly unladylike clumsiness."

So far this had been the most obvious transformation and it did not sit well with Noah. "It is not unladylike to suffer an accident. It can happen to anyone at any time," he retorted, immediately regretting the sharpness in his voice. Looking quite chastened, Miss Harcourt quietly agreed before asking Noah—with noticeably less cheer—what he'd been doing while in London.

Noah bit his lip, feeling guilty for coming across harsher than he'd meant to. "I haven't done anything too exciting," he offered quietly. "A few dinners, a ball last week, visiting friends."

Though he did not provide much in the way of conversation, Miss Harcourt still listened attentively, her pretty eyes watching him with calm interest. Noah appreciated not just the attention, but the truth he sensed in her gaze. She did not seem far away, wrapped up in her own thoughts, as so many other people did when conversing. Many had perfected the art of appearing engaged, offering only the most cursory replies on cue, while allowing their minds to stray wherever they wished.

Miss Harcourt did not fall into that group. She kept her attention on Noah for however long he spoke, a content smile on her lips, her eyes bright with focus and understanding.

"What have you done with your time in London thus far?" Noah returned, suddenly finding himself eager to see where this would lead.

Miss Harcourt's expression went blank, as if she'd only been prepared to listen rather than have a question posed to her that she must answer. With a rapid blink, she composed herself. "Oh, just the usual things us ladies like to do—walk around the park with friends, fixing up bonnets with some new ribbon, shopping for dress fabric." She gave a slight shrug and Noah felt that she wanted to say something more. Instead, she sighed wistfully. "I'm afraid it's all quite boring and certainly not worth going on about."

Noah's jaw twitched at this statement—not the words themselves necessarily, but the fact that Miss Harcourt felt the need to reduce her activities and interests to the realm of boring, womanly things. He hoped Miss Harcourt didn't see them that way, but it seemed she had come to believe at some point in her life that she was not worth talking about.

Before Noah could protest her statement, the thud of the door opening signaled the return of Miss Harcourt's family. Mrs. Parkins flew across the room, taking up her vigil by her friend's side once more. The other young woman glanced at Noah before giving Miss Harcourt an encouraging smile. Miss Harcourt managed an embarrassed one in return. She seemed unable to look Noah in the eye any longer, keeping her gaze fixed on her approaching family.

"Let's get you home for some proper rest, darling." Lord Welsted leaned over his daughter, pinching her cheek and eliciting a shy laugh in response, her eyes darting nervously to Noah for the briefest moment. The scene did not embarrass him in the least. He admired the ease with which this family doted on each other. His family was very close, but they showed their affection differently. Noah could not imagine his father pinching Emma's or Angelica's cheeks or his mother gently patting their hair past the age of ten.

Besides, Noah felt that he understood Miss Harcourt best when she had her family near. She seemed more at ease, more willing to be herself. Noah found himself hoping, much to his own surprise, that one day Miss Harcourt might feel comfortable enough to be her true self around him.

"Let me help you," Noah quickly offered as Lord Welsted and Mr. Harcourt situated themselves around the young woman. Lady Welsted and Mrs. Parkins watched with enough distance to stay out of the men's way, but still come flying to the rescue should the need arise.

Among the three of them, the gentlemen easily managed to get Miss Harcourt back on her feet—or rather, her one uninjured foot. She took a few moments to catch her breath before lifting her head to give them all a small but grateful smile that left a spark of warmth in Noah's chest.

"Mr. Waynford, we truly cannot thank you enough for all your help this evening." Lady Welsted approached, placing a kind hand on Noah's coat sleeve. Her hazel eyes, quite unlike her daughter's, seemed to search his face for a moment. Despite only knowing her for a few hours, Noah hoped that she found what she sought there.

"I would do it again in a heartbeat," Noah answered, looking over to Miss Harcourt as he spoke. Then she gave him the truest smile he had seen all night.

Lord Welsted glanced at his wife. "We simply could not forgive ourselves if we did not invite you and your family to dine with us next week." He looked so grateful that Noah nearly chuckled. The baron looked as if he would clap Noah on the shoulder if he weren't supporting his daughter.

"I'm sure we would all be honored, my lord." Noah bowed his head in appreciation and said his goodbyes as they slowly led Miss Harcourt through the sitting room, Noah bringing up the rear.

Noah bit his lip as a realization dawned on him. He'd accepted the invitation instinctively. It was only polite to do so, after all. But now as he walked behind the Harcourt family, staring at the back of Miss Harcourt's head, a strange hesitation bubbled up inside him.

The dinner might be a bit uncomfortable, for him at least, because he did not think it a good idea to pursue Miss Harcourt any further after all. Their brief acquaintanceship had been interesting in some aspects, but her strange behavior left him feeling confused rather than confident.

As the family continued toward the stairs to the foyer below, Noah prepared to reenter the ballroom. He paused outside the door, the sounds of the joyful evening on the other side feeling like a different world than the one Noah had just come from. The stairs would be difficult for Miss Harcourt to maneuver with her injured ankle. Noah took a hesitant step forward, ready to chase after the family and offer his assistance again.

Luckily, Mr. Harcourt had the good sense to lift his sister up into his arms, their mother loudly cautioning him to be careful while their father gently convinced her that they would all be fine. Miss Harcourt clung to her brother as he gingerly took the first step down the staircase. Her eyes peered over his shoulder, finding Noah watching from a distance.

She smiled, grateful and beautiful. Noah nodded in acknowledgment and a silent goodbye. Once Miss Harcourt turned her face away to watch their path, Noah's brows furrowed in confusion. As appealing as she could be in her unguarded moments, Noah doubted that he could truly fall in love with a woman so inconsistent.

Once reasonably confident that they would make the rest

of the journey down the stairs without issue, Noah signaled for a footman to open the ballroom door for him. The music and lively chatter flooded his ears, so different from the quiet calm in the sitting room.

Noah only paused long enough to scan the room for Father. When he finally saw him, Noah wasted no time in weaving through the clusters of guests to reach him. Father happily conversed with a small group of gentlemen Noah recognized from White's even though he did not frequent the club himself. As soon as Noah appeared at his side, Father offered his apologies to the other men and slipped away from their gathering, dragging Noah along with him toward a free space by the wall.

"So, what did you think of Miss Harcourt? Isn't she the loveliest creature you've ever met?" Father whispered excitedly, his gray eyes sparkling and his grin growing wider by the second.

Noah rubbed his jaw, already sensing the battle that was to come. It tore his heart to see Father's eager expectations writ large on his face, but Noah could not lie.

"I'm sorry, Father, but I do not think she is the right woman for me. I cannot court her," Noah sighed, looking down at his feet in a shameful display of cowardice. He could not bear to see the disappointment come crashing down over Father. He had clearly built up Miss Harcourt as a perfect match for Noah.

When Father remained silent for a few moments, Noah looked up. Father glanced around nervously before leaning closer to his son. "Please reconsider, Noah, I beg you." The urgency in his voice nearly caused Noah to shudder.

"May I ask why you insist that I court this particular lady?" Noah asked cautiously, eyes narrowed as he tried to read the motive in his father's eyes.

Father leaned in even closer, increasing Noah's concern.

"You see, when I was last at White's I heard that Lord Welsted is quite eager to see his eldest daughter happily settled. Since she has been out for a few Seasons, her dowry will be very generous, should she marry by the end of this Season."

The words spilled out of Father as if he might burst. A hollowness opened up in Noah's stomach as he realized Father's scheme. He looked back at the group of gentlemen Father had been speaking to earlier. "Have you heard this news directly from Lord Welsted, or from other sources?"

The corner of Father's mouth pulled down. Noah knew he would not like his father's answer and Father seemed to know it, too. "Unfortunately, I haven't been at the club at the same time as Lord Welsted so no, I did not hear it directly from him. And a ball is hardly the occasion. But I have heard several other men discussing it, quite a few of whom are planning on setting their caps at Miss Harcourt themselves or sending their sons after her."

Heat rose up through Noah's chest, frustrated and displeased. He did not like the sound of this situation, of Miss Harcourt being spoken of as a prize rather than a living, breathing woman. Of course, Noah knew that was the reality of their world at times, but he had never wanted that for himself. Just the thought repulsed him and yet Father wanted to force Noah into it.

"Is that what you were discussing with your friends when I returned?" Noah asked through clenched teeth, utilizing all his strength to keep from lashing out at Father for his absurd suggestion.

Father glanced down at his feet sheepishly. "It did come up, yes. Two of them have sons already married, but I think the other gentleman may encourage his oldest son to pursue her even though he already has a lady he's quite taken with."

Noah let out a heavy sigh, rubbing his temples as this

information soaked in. He had gotten conflicting messages from Miss Harcourt in the short time they'd spent together. On the one hand, he could see why Father would think they would be a good match for each other—money aside. Noah could not deny that he'd been drawn to her at times, that he found her interesting and warm and wonderfully kind. But then she would bat her eyes and give him a forced smile or a false laugh. Noah was not sure if he could trust this mysterious lady.

Finally, Noah made his decision. He stood to his full height, nearly a head taller than his father. "Lord Welsted invited us to have dinner with them next week and I promised I would dance with Miss Harcourt when she heals, but I do not plan on taking it further than that."

Father nervously wrung his hands, not making eye contact with Noah. "Please, my boy, at least spend some time getting to know her."

"Father—"

"Noah, Miss Harcourt could be the answer to saving our family's future," Father hissed, his voice strained with panic.

Noah took a deep breath, steeling himself to decline again. In that moment of hesitation, Noah allowed himself to truly see his father's face, to see the genuine fear there. It broke Noah's heart. He had agreed to do what he could to rectify this situation. Not even he could deny that an advantageous match offered the quickest, easiest means to do that. And this one had, quite literally, fallen into his arms.

"Fine," Noah sighed. "I will get to know her, but I am still not convinced that I will fall in love with her. And you know that I have made a promise to myself to marry a woman I love."

Father clapped his hands together, a relieved smile spreading across his face, softening the wrinkles of worry that had developed in recent weeks. "Thank you, son." He grabbed Noah's arms and squeezed, the gesture sending another wave of guilt and worry through the younger man. He did not want to fail his father, his entire family, his future. Yet this entire situation went against everything Noah stood for—truth, sincerity, and meaningful action.

Noah gave a tight smile. "Do not thank me yet. There is still a long way to go."

Yes, Noah silently agreed with himself. This story was far from over and he could not yet predict where it would take him. Perhaps, if he kept an open mind, he could come to enjoy knowing Miss Harcourt.

CHAPTER 5

*A*s quietly as possible, Anna slipped into the drawing room. She did not like drawing attention to herself, even on a night when she knew she was to be the focus. Pausing just inside the door, Anna smoothed out the front of her dress. An excited squeal from the other side of the room let Anna know her work would soon be undone.

"Anna, you look so beautiful!" Harriet cried as she threw herself at her oldest sister, wrapping her arms around Anna's waist and squeezing the breath out of her.

Anna laughed as she ruffled Harriet's bright blonde hair, squeezing her back until the girl's laughter filled the room and bounced off the walls.

"Perfectly said, Harriet," Mama agreed, her hands covering her mouth as she gazed lovingly at Anna. Papa merely nodded his agreement, so overcome with emotion that Anna thought she saw a tear in his eye.

Patrick, nestled in a nearby armchair, had taken advantage of the distraction to fold one leg under his lap. He preferred to sit that way though Mama rarely let him. Anna had no idea how he could find such a position comfortable. He looked up over his book and smiled in a silent compliment. Even Caroline, seated opposite Patrick with an embroidery hoop on her lap, looked pleasantly surprised.

"You look lovely, sister," she offered. "I do wish I could steal that dress from you, though."

Anna's cheeks reddened as their warm words and expressions flooded her. She appreciated their kindness, but Anna did not think she could completely agree. She might look lovely, as Caroline had said, but beautiful seemed a bit of a stretch.

Harriet stepped back, her eyes shining with admiration. Anna looked down at the pretty pastel green dress she wore. Mama had had it made specially for this evening. A perfect curl brushed against Anna's shoulder. She self-consciously patted her intricate hairstyle, done up in wonderful swirls with jewels nestled amongst her dark hair courtesy of her very talented maid, Ruth.

"Are you ready for the evening, my beautiful sister?" Anna turned around at the sound of that voice that was almost as familiar to her as her own. Dalton smiled at her encouragingly. He, too, looked ready for a fine night of delicious food and friendly company in his brand-new coat, his light brown hair styled in the latest fashion for young men. He watched her carefully, well aware that Anna often floundered in these situations.

A fresh bolt of nerves shot down Anna's spine. She fidgeted with her gloved fingers, the silky fabric shimmering under the light from the chandelier. Before she could think up some sort of clever answer, Dalton put a soothing hand on Anna's shoulder.

"It is going to be wonderful, I'm sure of it," he said confidently. "You have nothing to fear...though I will gladly confirm your story if you decide to play sick to get out of dinner early." He leaned in closer for the last part, careful to lower his voice so that Mama and Papa would not hear.

Anna laughed at his conspiratorial tone, appreciating the momentary relief from her anxiety—though she knew it would never go away completely. She had no idea how she would make it through dinner with one confirmed suitor and another potential suitor when she had never before dined with even one man interested in courting her.

"Caroline, Patrick, why don't you go find some other activities around the house to enjoy before bed," Mama suggested firmly, leaving little room for argument. Papa put his hands on Harriet's shoulders, ready to steer her off.

"Best of luck with your special gentlemen, Anna!" Harriet offered gleefully as Papa guided her toward the door. Anna laughed again despite her anxiety, her heart full of love for her ever optimistic and vibrant little sister.

Papa ruffled Harriet's hair as they walked past Anna. "You will do just fine, dear," he whispered comfortingly as Harriet slipped out from under his grip, floating around the room on her cloud of never-ending energy.

"Mama, please let me attend the dinner, too. I'm desperate for some real, grown up activities! Aren't I grown up enough by now?" Caroline begged even as she slowly made her way toward the door, her frustrated pout somehow making her pretty features even more charming. Anna and Mama shared a bemused glance. They could always trust Caroline to find the smallest bit of room to argue.

"I'm sorry, darling, but this night is about Anna and thanking the gentlemen who rushed to her rescue." Mama held her ground, a skill she'd perfected over the years of raising her five children, most of whom were often too willful for their own good. "Besides," the older woman continued as her third eldest opened her mouth to argue again, "you are not quite grown up just yet. You've still got a year of childhood left so you should try to enjoy it."

Caroline sighed sharply as she crossed her arms. She knew when she'd been defeated. "I would never have sprained my ankle at a dance," she grumbled as she stormed toward the door.

Anna suppressed a giggle. Caroline had always been a stubborn, often frustrating girl. Caroline paused next to Anna, giving a small smile. "Good luck, Anna," she said quietly. Her words, though simple and quickly delivered, warmed Anna. She could hear Caroline's sincerity despite her annoyance at being kept from participating.

"I'll do my best to snag one of them so I can get out of your way," Anna joked.

"You know that's not what I meant," Caroline grumbled again.

Anna caught Caroline's hand and squeezed it. "Thank you, sister." Caroline squeezed back before exiting the room in a dramatic huff.

Patrick soon followed, his eyes still glued to his book. "Have a good night, you two." He finally looked up from his book long enough to smile encouragingly at his older siblings. "I'll go bore Caroline into a stupor by reciting some lines from this play."

"Harriet, you'd best get going now," Mama called out to her youngest child who still buzzed about the room. Harriet ran after Patrick who, without looking up from his book, reached his hand out for the girl to grab. Hand in hand, the two youngest Harcourts left the drawing room.

With the children out of the way, Mama began her frantic dash through the room, tidying up herself rather than calling a maid or footman to help. She preferred to have some physical outlet for her nerves, which always appeared most strongly just before their guests arrived.

"Please try not to worry so much, Anna." Papa stood at Anna's side, his presence bringing a small measure of comfort to her. "There truly is no pressure for you to win anyone over. This is just a dinner to thank Mr. Milburn and Mr. Waynford for their help." Anna smiled appreciatively until Papa cleared his throat, suddenly looking a bit awkward. "If something more is meant to come of it, then it will. Do not force it," he finished. Of course, Papa knew of Anna's desire to marry a man she loved. Though Anna had not told him of her earlier decision to give up, Papa seemed to have sensed her hesitation to continue on what could still prove to be a fruitless path.

Still, Papa's words did soothe her slightly. He quickly patted Anna on the cheek before making his way toward Mama, imploring her to stop fluffing the pillows that had already been perfectly fluffed.

Dalton chuckled from Anna's other side as he watched their parents engage in their typical routine of one trying to talk the other out of fretting while being ignored. He caught Anna's eye and gave an amused shrug before tilting his head toward two nearby chairs.

Once they settled down into their seats, Dalton's expression grew more serious. "How are things going with Mr. Milburn?" he asked.

Anna bit her lip as she thought back on her encounters with the future viscount. "I must admit I am hopeful. He's called on me three times while my ankle healed and you were on the carriage ride with us last week. I thought he enjoyed it. What do you think?"

Dalton nodded with a smile. "Mr. Milburn does seem to be a nice enough fellow."

"But?" Anna asked, raising an eyebrow.

"Take your time and really get to know him," Dalton cautioned.

Anna frowned as she considered her brother's advice. "Do you have suspicions about him?"

"No, of course not. I just feel we haven't had an opportunity to see past Mr. Milburn's wall yet—his very chatty wall."

Anna nodded thoughtfully. She agreed with Dalton's assessment. Mr. Milburn was a perfect gentleman, always very polite during their meetings. But Anna also noticed that he never strayed from the niceties typical of the *ton*—though that was not necessarily a bad thing, she reminded herself. It simply proved that Mr. Milburn had been raised with excellent manners. Of course, Anna hoped to get to know him a little deeper before deciding if she could see a happy marriage in their future.

"Why do you look sad?" Dalton asked, his voice full of gentle concern.

Anna quickly pulled her smile on, surprised that she'd let it slip. The melancholy that had overtaken her only grew stronger the more she tried to hide it. She sighed, knowing it would be better to express her worries to her trusted brother.

"Perhaps Mr. Milburn will be my best option after all. I am not exactly in a position to be overly cautious in choosing a husband. He is very nice…even if I haven't felt that stirring of love in my heart yet," she admitted, her voice growing quieter the longer she spoke. She looked down at her hands, still fidgeting.

Dalton hummed as he allowed Anna's words to sink in. "Please do not give up so easily, Anna. If that's how you feel about Mr. Milburn, then where do your thoughts lie in regards to Mr. Waynford?"

Anna could only give a small shrug. "Honestly, there is not much to think about just yet. He's only visited me once since the dance and, even then, he did not stay long. I felt as though he was trying to figure me out the whole time. It felt strange."

It had felt very strange indeed. Anna remembered the sensation on that one and only visit with Mr. Waynford since her injury. They'd only chatted for a few minutes in the sitting room of the Harcourts' townhome, Anna's foot propped up as gracefully as possible on a stack of pillows. She would have been extremely embarrassed to have anyone else see her in such a state, but, of course, Mr. Waynford had already witnessed her at her worst on the night of the ball. They had not talked much beyond the gentleman's concerns for Anna's wellbeing before he had excused himself to leave, as he had a very busy day.

It had felt strange to be so seen, to feel that Mr. Waynford really was trying to understand her even in that short meeting.

"Is that such a terrible thing?" Dalton asked, his head tilted slightly to the side, looking at Anna curiously.

Anna sighed. "You know he would not like the real me, or, rather, the old version of me."

Anna looked up in shock when she heard the disgruntled sound Dalton made. He shook his head, clearly upset. "I still cannot understand why you are following Mrs. Parkins' advice. Wouldn't you rather catch someone's attention for who you are instead of trying to be someone else?"

A twinge of anger coursed through Anna and she could feel herself bristling defensively. "Esther is just trying to help, Dalton. After all, she's the one who's married now. She must have some idea of how this all works." Dalton shook his head again, not accepting Anna's words.

"Besides," she pressed on, "I am not being someone else. I am simply becoming a better version of myself. Soon it will be second nature." She sat up even straighter, lifting her chin in defiance as she'd seen Caroline do countless times. It always made the younger woman look so confident. Anna hoped she could convey the same feeling, even if her fingers still twisted themselves into knots.

"Sister, you do not need a second nature. You are perfectly fine as you are right now. The right man, your future husband, will see that," Dalton argued, his voice rising slightly in his passion.

Anna shot a worried glance over to Mama and Papa, but they remained occupied with making last minute adjustments to the already perfect drawing room. Papa had lost this round, joining Mama in her mission to tidy.

Since she lacked a solid rebuttal for Dalton's statement, Anna decided to brush it off and move past it. "If one of them is truly interested in me, it seems to be Mr. Milburn, since he's visited me several times while Mr. Waynford has only visited once."

Dalton's eyes narrowed curiously as he lapsed into silent thought. "I know you are my older and much wiser sister," he finally started, "but, if I may, I would caution you once again to wait and see where the situation takes you with both gentlemen."

Anna gave a wry smile. "I shall consider your sage advice, dear brother."

The drawing room door opened, admitting their guests. Anna jumped up from her seat, curtsying with as much grace as she could manage given the hammering of her heart and the twisting of her stomach.

When she straightened, Anna met Mr. Waynford's eyes first. As he observed her again, a delicious shiver ran up and down her back, combating the heat gathering in her face. Despite her anxiety, Anna found herself smiling shyly at the gentleman from across the room. The corner of Mr. Waynford's mouth pulled up in an exceedingly charming expression, causing Anna's heart to burst into flutters.

Anna forced herself to turn her attention to Mr. Milburn and his father, Viscount Milburn. Somehow, her anxiety had transformed into exhilaration for that brief moment when she'd seen Mr. Waynford. Perhaps it was better to have more guests after all. Anna thought she might become completely overwhelmed by the intensity of Mr. Waynford's gaze if she did not have something else to distract her.

Viscount Milburn and his heir both looked around the grand drawing room, clearly impressed. The room spoke of beauty, from the wonderful artwork to the exquisite furniture, all chosen carefully by Mama and Papa. Still, Anna knew the two gentlemen probably only found the room impressive for a baron's family. Coming from a family of viscounts, Anna was sure that they were accustomed to even finer rooms.

Mr. Milburn's eyes soon led him to where Anna and Dalton lingered a short distance away while their parents welcomed their guests. As soon as he noticed her, he gave his greetings to Mama and Papa and rushed forward with a glowing smile.

Before Anna could even take a breath to say hello, Mr. Milburn launched into a rapid speech. "How delightful to see you again, Miss Harcourt! You as well, Mr. Harcourt. I have been so looking forward to this dinner and I am immensely grateful that you have finally healed. I do hope we can dance together again very soon."

Anna caught Dalton's eye. They shared a rueful smile as Mr. Milburn continued, lavishing praises on their beautiful home. Dalton's brow jolted up for a fraction of a second. Anna knew exactly what he thought. A chatterbox like Mr. Milburn might prove to be overwhelming for Anna's reserved nature.

At least he even wanted to speak with her, Anna assured herself. She listened attentively as Mr. Milburn updated her on everything he'd been doing since they saw each other a week ago. Anna, though shocked that he could fit so many activities into one week, remembered Esther's suggestions to nod frequently while making occasional exclamations. Encouraged, Mr. Milburn began a detailed explanation of his plans for the following week, leaving Anna without any real opportunities to join in. Again, Anna did not mind. It saved her from constantly trying to formulate clever responses and interesting anecdotes.

Just like at the ball, Anna realized that she could take a quick look around the room while Mr. Milburn happily went on about his life without him noticing. With just her eyes, Anna slowly searched the drawing room and soon found what she'd been unconsciously looking for. Mr. Waynford stood by the window, talking with Dalton, while Mama and Papa did the same with Mr. Waynford's parents and Viscount Milburn.

Another jolt hit Anna squarely in the chest as she realized that Mr. Waynford still watched her with that same intensity as before. Whenever her gaze fell upon him, she found him looking back at her.

She bit her lip before smiling nervously, suddenly feeling exposed. Anna knew she should spend time with their other guests, yet she felt a longing somewhere deep inside to continue meeting Mr. Waynford's eyes. Unfortunately, Mr. Milburn had not yet provided her an opportunity to tactfully turn her focus elsewhere or invite the other gentleman into their conversation.

Mr. Waynford quietly chuckled at Anna's expression, dipping his head in an understanding nod, a lock of brown hair tumbling out of place. Relief flooded through Anna. At least he did not find her rude for unintentionally ignoring him. He seemed to understand her concerns without her having to say anything out loud. While Mr. Waynford may not have been terribly interested in Anna, he at least seemed to have a good sense of humor about the situation.

Dalton had noticed the silent conversation that passed between Anna and Mr. Waynford. He gave Anna a sly smile, an expression Anna knew meant he had something up his sleeve. Anna quickly returned her focus to Mr. Milburn, not sure she wanted to know what scheme Dalton had hatched. It only took her a few moments to find out. As soon as Mr. Milburn mentioned something about the museum he'd visited yesterday, Dalton seized his chance.

"Are you a lover of art, Mr. Milburn?" he asked cheerily from his spot by the window. "Then you must allow me to show you this painting just over here. It's been in the Harcourt family for many years and I am well versed in its history." He gestured to the opposite wall, an almost comical grin on his face.

"Ah, yes, indeed. Pardon me, Miss Harcourt. I will return soon so we can resume our conversation," he mumbled through a disappointed smile.

Though she'd been hoping for a reprieve from Mr. Milburn just moments ago, Anna felt a lightness in her chest. No man had ever sounded so disappointed about not being able to spend more time with her.

As Mr. Milburn drew up next to Dalton, the younger man drew his attention to a painting on another wall. "Do look over there, Mr. Milburn. That is another excellent piece. Perhaps we can discuss that one later tonight." Mr. Milburn turned to look in the direction Dalton pointed, which gave Dalton the perfect opportunity to catch Anna's attention and nod his head toward Mr. Waynford, who had turned to examine an intricately painted vase on a nearby end table.

When Mr. Waynford looked back up toward the other

two men, Dalton quickly spun around and guided Mr. Milburn to the promised painting. As soon as he'd turned, Anna scrunched her nose at the back of her brother's head. She knew he just wanted to help, but she did not want him to be so terribly obvious about it. She would have been mortified if Mr. Waynford had seen Dalton's less than subtle encouragement to Anna.

Mr. Waynford chuckled as he closed the distance between them. Anna smiled as she turned to Mr. Waynford, finally standing before him where they could see each other clearly. She much preferred to be able to hear his laugh rather than just see it from afar. It was light and warm, carrying the feeling of a shared secret.

"I must admit I quite enjoy seeing displays of teasing between siblings. It reminds me of the days before my sisters married. We constantly annoyed one another—in the best ways, of course."

Though Mr. Waynford's eyes remained gentle and understanding, Anna felt herself blushing with almost as much force as she'd done when she'd sprained her ankle. She'd hoped to avoid mortification, but instead she walked right into it. Mr. Waynford must have witnessed the unladylike expression she'd directed toward Dalton.

She swallowed, fighting back her sudden urge to fly from the room, feigning illness as her brother had suggested earlier. "You see, Dalton knows me better than anyone so he has perfected the art of getting under my skin," she explained with a nervous smile, praying that a touch of humor would mask her embarrassment.

Mr. Waynford nodded knowingly, but before he could reply, Anna remembered Esther's lessons, remembered who she was supposed to be.

Clearing her throat, Anna put on the most charming smile

she could manage, narrowing her eyes in that sweet way that she'd seen those elegant ladies employ. "I must wonder what you mean about annoying each other in the best way. I do wish my siblings could be a little more understanding of my poor nerves," she sighed with a touch of drama. She remembered Esther doing that quite often when they'd both been unmarried young women. She always managed to gain the attention and sympathy of whichever man she spoke to.

Mr. Waynford narrowed his eyes as if he didn't quite believe Anna. Her nerves swirled around her stomach once more as she fought to keep her expression pleasant. Had he seen through her act? Or perhaps he was trying to unmask her?

After a moment of uncomfortable silence, Mr. Waynford gave a small smile. "I think you will feel differently once you and your siblings have moved on in life. I thought I would be relieved when my older sister and younger sister both married and moved out of our family home to start their new lives."

The softness in his voice somehow made Anna feel better. He did not seem angry with her, at least, and he clearly cared deeply about his family, which led her to believe that he would certainly shower his future family with love and warmth. The thought sent a wave of hopeful excitement through Anna from head to foot.

"I miss them both, even though they go right back to badgering me whenever we find ourselves in the same room again," he confessed, his eyes far away with an endearing nostalgia. Anna did not want to interrupt his thoughts by speaking so she remained silent, patiently waiting for him to continue. "I wish I had appreciated them more when they still lived in our family home. Even though we always teased each other and argued, it showed in a strange way that we cared. In the end, I always know that we'll be there for each other."

Mr. Waynford looked at Anna pointedly, his gaze piercing through her. Anna's eyes grew round with surprise that this almost complete stranger would feel comfortable sharing such profound thoughts and intimate details of his life with her.

Her heartbeat picked up speed as something inside her responded with genuine interest—not just the interest she thought others wanted to see from her. She longed to hear more of what this man had to say because she truly wanted to hear it rather than just trying to prove that she would be an attentive wife. His words resonated with her.

Anna smiled. This time, it was her real smile. "I think I understand what you mean. In truth, I will miss my siblings when we part. I love them all dearly both for the traits we share and the traits that make us all so very different from one another." Caroline's face flashed through Anna's mind as she spoke. She shook her head, amused at the memories of her younger sister pouting and whining.

Mr. Waynford eyed Anna curiously. "Who was it you thought of just now? Mr. Harcourt, perhaps?"

They both glanced over to the opposite wall where Dalton still conversed with Mr. Milburn, hardly letting a moment pass without making some comment on the painting before them. Dalton seemed not to notice the way Mr. Milburn constantly peered over his shoulder at Anna and Mr. Waynford. His expression pleasantly surprised Anna. He clearly seemed eager to return to her or at least keep the other gentleman away.

"Dalton does give me his fair share of grief," Anna chuckled fondly. "I actually thought of my younger sister, Caroline. We are opposites in many ways, which often causes us to clash, but I love her all the same. In fact, Caroline's views and attitudes have certainly caused me to reconsider my own at times. I sometimes find myself wishing that I could be more like my younger sister even though it should be the younger admiring the elder."

Mr. Waynford nodded thoughtfully, his eyes never leaving Anna's face, always reading her. Yet another surge of embarrassment rumbled through Anna's stomach. She'd spoken so frankly. Perhaps she had offended her guest with these personal thoughts. They were still quite new in their acquaintance, after all.

"I do not think that learning from others has an age limit or hierarchy. Knowledge is invaluable, wherever it comes from."

Anna smiled appreciatively, relieved that she hadn't made a complete fool of herself. This conversation with Mr. Waynford had felt so much more natural than the several she'd had with Mr. Milburn so far—even with those embarrassing moments. She did not feel as much of a need to maintain her interesting Society lady act. Talking to Mr. Waynford had actually been easy, perhaps even comfortable.

Much to her disappointment, Anna did not have much time to enjoy the feeling as the butler announced that dinner was ready.

~

ANNA'S PULSE quickened with anxiety once more as they made their way through the first course. She knew the soup must be delicious, yet she could barely taste it thanks to her nerves, which had grown even more powerful than in the drawing room.

A dinner like this always felt so formal, especially when both her suitors sat on either side of her. Mr. Waynford's parents sat across from them and Viscount Milburn sat at the head of the table next to Mama, who would no doubt try her best to keep the older man awake through the meal.

Mama had tactfully suggested that the two younger gentlemen sit with Anna since they were responsible for helping her and no doubt had much to talk about. The elder Mr. Waynford looked downright delighted while Viscount Milburn, aged and already looking quite weary from the evening's activities, seemed to have little energy to care one way or another as long as he was appropriately seated.

Mr. Waynford had accepted the suggestion gratefully while Mr. Milburn praised Mama for coming up with such a brilliant plan.

Anna also noticed that Mama and Dalton exchanged amused glances while Papa sent Anna a rueful smile from his spot at the other end of the table. Being on the reserved side himself, Papa knew that having to converse with both men would be challenging for her. But if Mama deemed it so, then it would be so. Anna returned the bravest smile she could, hoping to ease her father's concerns. This would indeed be a difficult evening for her still developing new persona.

Mama, Papa, Dalton, the older Waynfords, and Viscount Milburn quickly settled into a pleasant conversation while Anna remained trapped between her two suitors—if she could even consider Mr. Waynford a suitor. Even if he was just a guest rather than a potential match, Anna would still have to do her best to keep both men entertained.

Once again, Anna soon found that she did not have to worry about that very much. Mr. Milburn happily led the way through their conversation.

"Have you ever been to Yorkshire, Miss Harcourt?"

"Unfortunately, I have not yet had the opportunity," Anna sighed, trying Esther's tactic again.

"Such a shame!" Mr. Milburn gasped, his soup spoon stopping halfway to his mouth in shock. He certainly seemed more receptive to Anna's attempts at flirtation than Mr. Waynford. "You would love it, I assure you. My father's seat originated in Yorkshire three generations ago and our family has lived there ever since."

"I am sure it is beautiful—"

"It truly is a sight to behold. From the windows in our drawing room, you can see miles upon miles of wonderfully vast green pastures and fields. We have excellent gardens as well, of course, and a pinery. Have you ever tried pineapple before, Miss Harcourt?" The words flew from Mr. Milburn's lips so quickly that Anna wondered if he'd taken a breath.

"Only once before," Anna offered, prepared to explain the lavish dinner party she'd attended at her great aunt's home in Kent.

"Such a delightful fruit, is it not?" Mr. Milburn smiled at Anna with something like pride, as if he was glad Anna could relate to his elegant lifestyle. Of course, Anna had only tasted pineapple once. The Harcourts did not have the luxury of tending an exotic plant like a pineapple, though it did not surprise her that Mr. Milburn's family could.

The future viscount went on for several more minutes, detailing the beauty of the expansive lands he would one day inherit, that perhaps Anna would one day call home. She had no doubt the Milburns' estate was just as glorious as he described, but she found it increasingly difficult to offer so much as a simple word of wonder let alone ask a question about a detail that interested her.

For someone as shy as Anna, she supposed this was a better alternative to having to hold up her end of the conversation, though she wished she could have had a chance to ask about the type of sheep the Milburns raised on their farm since the Harcourts also kept sheep.

As Mr. Milburn took a deep breath to continue his speech, Mr. Waynford cleared his throat. Anna glanced over to him, seated at her right and thus far silent. She smiled apologetically. She did not wish to ignore him, but Mr. Milburn, once again, would not let her get a word in edgewise. To Anna's surprise and relief, Mr. Waynford seemed to find the situation more amusing than offensive as he lifted a knowing eyebrow. Anna sensed that he understood her present predicament perfectly well.

Anna returned her attention to Mr. Milburn, who did not seem to notice that her thoughts had been momentarily occupied by someone else.

"Our paddock is quite generous for our many horses. Those great beasts need so much space to roam so they do not grow restless and ornery," Mr. Milburn continued.

Anna stifled the urge to frown as she slowly came to a realization, Mr. Milburn chatting away in the background all the while. If she did marry this man, at least she would not have to worry too much about utilizing the act she'd been learning from Esther. Mr. Milburn seemed perfectly content to be his own conversation partner, allowing Anna to relax as she listened.

A surprisingly melancholy heaviness settled over Anna as this thought sank in. Somehow, the thought of finally being married did not sound as ideal as it had before. Of course, Anna would still rather marry a man she loved, who loved her in return. As she'd told Dalton earlier, perhaps that option had passed her by. She'd thought any marriage would do as long as the gentleman was pleasant.

The longer Anna listened to Mr. Milburn without really participating, she wondered if perhaps truly sharing a life with her husband would be better after all. As she watched Mr. Milburn animatedly describe the conservatory at his family's estate, his eyes transported to the country rather than remaining in the Harcourts' dining room, Anna gave herself a harsh but necessary reminder.

As she'd told Dalton earlier, Anna did not have the luxury of being picky. She was sure that she could find some measure of happiness with Mr. Milburn, if he did indeed want to marry her. Surely she could get used to a life filled with his never-ending stream of cheery thoughts. Besides, Anna did not like to talk very much herself. Couldn't this be a perfect situation?

Mr. Waynford cleared his throat again. Just as Anna turned to ask if he was well, the gentleman leaned forward slightly, giving Anna a knowing look.

"I hope you don't mind, Mr. Milburn, but I would be very grateful if you could tell us more about your horses. I'm always fascinated to hear about the different breeds since my family only has a handful at our home in Somerset," he politely interjected. Anna's mouth fell open ever so slightly, shocked at how easily Mr. Waynford maneuvered himself into their conversation, taking advantage of the exact moment Mr. Milburn took a breath.

Mr. Milburn frowned slightly. He hadn't been expecting his line of thought to be disrupted. He quickly gathered his composure and gave Mr. Waynford a welcoming smile, his green eyes narrowing for a fraction of a second.

"Of course I would be delighted. Since I enjoy the sport of racing myself, I have two very handsome Thoroughbreds that I also take fox hunting in the winter. We naturally have several Yorkshire Trotters for our carriages and a beautiful pair of Cleveland Bays." Mr. Milburn did not miss a beat as he quickly settled into this new conversation. Before he could continue, Mr. Waynford turned his attention back to Anna.

"Miss Harcourt, do you enjoy riding?" he asked with such pleasant manners that Mr. Milburn could not claim that any sort of rudeness had occurred. Again, Anna found herself admiring the skill with which Mr. Waynford handled the situation. He, too, seemed to be a quieter type of man—but only when he chose to be, Anna guessed. He certainly did not flounder through conversations like she did when her anxiety and desire to impress got the better of her.

Normally, Anna would have felt quite nervous about suddenly being brought into focus, but this time the nerves did not bother her quite as much. She felt glad to have a chance to share her opinion, limited though it may have been.

"As a matter of fact, I find horses to be a bit intimidating." She glanced from one man to the other, trying to gauge their reactions. "I hardly ride sidesaddle, but when I do, I never go above a walk. I enjoy carriage rides, though, as long as someone else is driving." Mr. Waynford nodded apprecia- tively, a gently encouraging gleam in his eyes. Anna chuckled as she thought of someone else she knew who could not get enough of those majestic animals. "My youngest sister, Harriet, on the other hand, is quite obsessed with horses. I'm sure she will be an expert rider when she grows older. She already loves taking the reins in the family tilbury."

Mr. Waynford listened attentively and a bubble of hope floated up through Anna's chest. She somehow enjoyed the feeling of being asked her thoughts, of being heard.

Mr. Waynford spent the rest of the evening artfully drawing Mr. Milburn's endless stream of conversation into a more open direction, allowing himself and Anna chances to speak for themselves.

Anna's admiration for the gentleman grew as they sat through several more courses. Not only did he always have something insightful to offer, but he also paid equal attention to everyone, making sure each person had a chance to get to know someone else at the table. It made the dinner feel less formal to Anna, as if they were all good friends gathering together after a long time apart.

As they neared the end of the dessert course, Anna watched Dalton and Mr. Waynford playfully debate the best types of hats, both smiling and laughing as they went back and forth between the merits of toppers versus beaver hats. As she watched their easy banter, Anna realized the sad truth. Mr. Waynford was simply a very good man. He was kind and respectful to everyone. Any special attention she thought she'd noticed when he turned the tide of the conversation—or even on the night of the dance when he'd rushed to her aid before anyone else—came not from some fledgling interest in her, but rather from the very nature of his being. He was a good man while Anna remained nothing special.

Before Anna's spirits could sink too deeply, Mr. Milburn drew her attention back to him. Anna peered up into his handsome face full of sharp features, a tiny flicker of hope igniting in her heart once more.

"Miss Harcourt, would you join me for a ride about Richmond Park next week?" he asked loudly. "It reminds me a bit of my beloved Yorkshire." He lowered his voice slightly and leaned closer to Anna, a mischievous smile bringing a hint of playfulness to his expression. "I assure you, you will not be asked to drive."

Anna's poor spirits lifted just as quickly as they'd withered. Mr. Milburn must truly be serious about courting her if he already wanted to see her again.

"Of course, Mr. Milburn! I would enjoy that very much," Anna quickly agreed, hoping she conveyed an air of sweet, ladylike surprise and excitement rather than the eager hope of a woman nearly at her wit's end.

To her right, Mr. Waynford gave an awkward chuckle that sounded more like a pained cough. Anna turned her attention to him. For the first time since Anna had known him, Mr. Waynford looked a tad flustered. Anna found it to be quite endearing.

"I was also just about to ask if you would like to accompany me to Somerset House next week," he mumbled quietly, his eyes darting across the table to his parents. Anna was too stunned to look herself, but she was sure everyone in the room had stopped to stare at her and the two gentlemen.

She could only look back and forth between Mr. Milburn and Mr. Waynford, well aware that she looked quite foolish and uncivilized, but unable to pull herself out of her overwhelming shock. Both men had just invited her on outings. Dalton finally broke Anna's reverie by catching her eye from across the table. He wore one of the most excited grins Anna had ever seen on him, and that was quite the statement, considering Dalton's default facial expression was a smile.

Somewhere beneath her initial shock, Anna knew that she was living through something she hadn't imagined even in her wildest dreams. She'd always known that she would be lucky to be courted by even one man, yet two had just expressed their desire to spend more time with her. Perhaps one of these gentlemen would one day be her husband.

"Of course, I understand if you are busy," Mr. Waynford quickly added, a hint of panic in his usually calm and confident voice.

Anna realized that she'd been lost in her thoughts for too long. She turned to face Mr. Waynford so quickly that she nearly knocked her drink over. "Absolutely, Mr. Waynford. I'm looking forward to it." Anna beamed, now unable to keep her eagerness to a manageable level.

She almost felt as though she would burst with happiness from this amazing turn of events. Two men courting her! Could this really be happening to Anna of all people? Were her prayers finally being answered after a lifetime of worrying and wondering when her happy ending would come?

Anna's smile faltered when she noticed the look passed

between Mr. Waynford and his parents, especially his father. His mother, a kind and quiet older woman, looked tentatively hopeful, but his father looked almost more eager than Anna herself.

Something about that silent conversation between them brought Anna crashing back to reality. Surely Mr. Waynford's family must have some hopes for a match made between their son and Anna. She glanced back up at Mr. Waynford from the corner of her eye, suddenly terrified to look him in the face. His brows furrowed and a muscle in his jaw twitched. Perhaps Mr. Waynford was not as interested in Anna as she'd thought just seconds ago.

Anna bit her lip, sadly letting go of the elation she'd only been able to experience for a moment. She knew she should not be surprised. Her personality and appearance had never won her any attention until recently, but her family's wealth might attract a man.

It seemed that Mr. Milburn was the only man truly interested in Anna. As she cleared her plate of fruits and sweetmeats, she began to wonder if Mr. Milburn even cared for her. At least, it was impossible to tell this early on.

If Anna guessed correctly about the glances shared between the Waynford family and the younger Mr. Waynford's discomfort after inviting Anna on an outing, then Mr. Waynford sought a wife with social status. On the other hand, Mr. Milburn seemed to want a wife who would happily absorb all his words and ideas.

The rest of the conversation passed by Anna without leaving much of an impression. Mr. Milburn returned to his soliloquy while Mr. Waynford continued his efforts to talk with Anna and the other people at the table. Anna could hear herself responding when needed, but she could not bring herself to really put the proper amount of effort in. She'd let her hopes get too high. Now she needed to be more realistic.

She would still spend time with them both and pray that one would propose, but Anna knew she needed to constantly remind herself that she had most likely already lost her chance at true love. Anna would have to settle for any marriage now, hoping it would be a tolerable one.

CHAPTER 6

*B*right sunlight glinted off the water of the Serpentine River while chatting voices and clacking hooves flooded Noah's ears. If he had to choose, he would prefer life in the country with its quieter, calmer pace. Still, he had to admit that he certainly enjoyed some aspects of life in London, especially places like Hyde Park that offered a little country within the city.

Noah looked around to see dozens of people out and about, enjoying the pleasantly warm afternoon. It was not the promenade hour yet so not as many people had ventured out, most of them walking leisurely rather than riding about in extravagant carriages. Noah did enjoy being out during the promenade hour, though, as it allowed him to observe a wide variety of people.

He had intentionally arrived early to have some time to himself for this exact purpose. Noah turned his back to the river, his gaze traveling over the people surrounding him. He tried to read their expressions and even their lips, hoping to catch a glimpse into them for these few seconds of observation.

Indeed, Noah saw what he believed to be genuine happiness, love, and friendship. He also saw quite a few interactions with a specific goal in mind—whether it be marriage or forging a powerful connection or something else entirely—rather than having a meaningful conversation simply for the sake of it.

"Good afternoon, my friend!" Phineas called out behind Noah. He turned to see an elated grin on the other man's face.

"It certainly seems to be a good afternoon for you," Noah laughed as they began their slow walk by the river. Phineas remained lost in thought for several moments, the joy never leaving his face as he gazed ahead with a soft smile.

Finally, Noah could take it no longer. "Do you care to share what occupies your mind?" he prodded gently.

Phineas jumped as if he'd forgotten Noah walked by his side. After the surprise wore off, Phineas grinned once more. "I think I have met the perfect woman, Noah," he sighed happily, trailing off as his mind carried him away to the woman in question.

Noah beamed as well, happiness swelling through his chest. He loved to see his good friend so exhilarated and hopeful. "Could you elaborate about this perfect woman?"

Of course, Noah wanted to hear more about her, whoever she was, but he also wanted to bring Phineas back to the present moment. He looked so blissfully unaware of everything but his thoughts of this woman that Noah half feared he might walk right into the river if no one prevented it.

"Her name is Miss Cora Bishop," he started, his words coming out faster the longer he spoke. "We met about two weeks ago at a dinner hosted by a friend of mine from my club. Miss Bishop is his younger sister, who has just made her debut in Society this Season. I'd heard my friend speak of her before, but not in great detail, so I never gave it any thought…that is, until I saw her at the dinner. I swear, Noah, I cannot describe the feeling I got when I laid eyes on her. She is the perfect embodiment of charm, grace, and beauty."

Noah nodded thoughtfully as his friend spoke. He idly wondered if he knew the feeling Phineas spoke of, the feeling of being immediately taken with someone. Miss Harcourt flashed through his mind for a moment, but he pushed her away. Surely those circumstances could not be compared to Phineas's experience, unless Miss Bishop also played some mysterious game of dual personalities.

"Of course, I did not think she would be interested in me, but she agreed to several outings with me," Phineas continued, nearly breathless now in his excitement to share his romantic tale. "I must say we have gotten along very well thus far. She seems to be just as fond of me as I am of her in this short period. Noah, I do believe my dream of making a love match will soon be fulfilled!" he cheered, drawing a few curious glances their way.

"I'm so very happy to hear that, my good man." Noah clapped Phineas on the shoulder. He swore he could feel his friend buzzing with excitement.

"Mama and Papa were thrilled when I told them about Miss Bishop. They are desperate to meet her, but I want to wait a while longer for that. I want to be more certain of her feelings first—and I do not want my parents' enthusiasm to scare her off." Phineas laughed, the sound so refreshing and infectious.

Noah laughed, too, knowing Phineas's parents nearly rivaled his own in their eagerness to see their sons married. He could feel the joy radiating from his friend and it seeped into Noah. Phineas had been searching for his future wife for so long, resisting his family's pressure to marry.

As Noah watched Phineas's face, he could see that his friend really was falling in love with this lady. He prayed that

Miss Bishop would truly be the one for Phineas. If anyone deserved a happy ending, it would be him. Knowing his own situation and the distasteful scheme he'd agreed to, Noah was not sure he could say the same for himself.

"I'm terribly sorry for rambling on about this without even asking how your endeavors have been going." Phineas cut himself off, eying Noah curiously. Noah must have let his misgivings show on his face.

He knew exactly what his friend hinted at. Of course, he had told Phineas about Father's less than subtle request that he pursue Miss Harcourt. He sighed, not entirely sure how it was going himself. It had been two days since the dinner at the Harcourts' home and he still felt uneasy when he thought about it.

"That does not sound good…" Phineas offered cautiously.

"No, no, that's not it," Noah quickly corrected him. "I must confess I am not sure what to make of the situation."

Phineas shrugged as if Noah's problem was no more complex than choosing which coat to wear. "Perhaps we can make sense of it together."

Noah smiled ruefully. Phineas had always been the more naturally optimistic of the pair, despite their similar struggles in the marriage mart.

"I only agreed to court Miss Harcourt to humor Father and Father did say he thought she would be a good match for me. The strangest thing is that I do see it at times, yet other times her personality becomes so different. I cannot latch on to who she really is or why she's doing this," Noah explained. The heaviness in his voice surprised him.

Phineas grew thoughtful, a line appearing between his brows. "I would very much like to meet this Miss Harcourt one day. She certainly sounds interesting."

"She is, Phineas," Noah sighed. "That is what frustrates me so much about her. I am truly interested in the sweet, loving side of her that I see, not this faux charm that some-times appears. It does not seem natural for her, but she keeps reverting to it for some reason. The real charm I see—at least, I believe it to be her real charm—is so much more endearing to me. It's as if she thinks I want to see a different side or a different person entirely."

"Perhaps she just needs some time to get more comfort-able with you before she lets all her walls down," Phineas suggested before giving a quiet cough. "Have you heard anything more about Miss Harcourt's fortune?"

Noah did not hide his frown. He did not like discussing that topic. It was true that he had initially agreed to get to know Miss Harcourt because his family needed money, and, much to Noah's vexation, he'd heard even more people sharing the rumors of the lady's very handsome marriage portion.

Worse still, Noah knew that talking about Miss Harcourt's wealth made him sound the same as so many others in Society—people who only cared about increasing their material goods. Noah was not that person. At least, he wasn't when he'd thought he could afford it.

"I have heard more rumors, yes. More gentlemen have learned of Miss Harcourt's…situation. It certainly seems that I am not the only one who is interested in that detail. Of course, you know I would not be doing this if I had any other choice," he quickly added. His words had not quite conveyed what he'd meant. He was not interested in Miss Harcourt's money in the way the other men surely were. He had no choice but to be interested in it.

"I know, my friend, I know." Phineas put a comforting hand on Noah's shoulder though it did not seem to do much.

"I detest the way all this sounds." Noah shuddered, Phineas's hand falling away. "But it is the truth of the matter right now. I must do this for my family."

Phineas frowned. "Perhaps some good will come of this situation somehow," he offered, though with less cheer than before.

Noah shrugged, suddenly too hot under the afternoon sun, his coat now restrictive though it had been comfortable a few minutes ago. "There is another man who appears quite serious about courting her—Mr. Milburn. He's the son of a viscount."

Phineas's brows shot up in surprise. "Ahh, Mr. Milburn. I have heard of him, and I'm not sure I like what I've heard."

Noah stopped in his tracks so suddenly that Phineas continued on for a few more steps before realizing he'd left Noah behind. "What do you mean? Tell me immediately. I do not wish for Miss Harcourt to come into harm's way," he demanded, his heart racing.

"No, no, it is nothing sinister," Phineas quickly clarified, raising his hands up, palms out as if trying to calm a wild animal who may attack at any moment.

"Then what do you not like about him?" Noah asked more calmly, only slightly relieved that Mr. Milburn was not the violent or cruel criminal he'd feared just a moment ago.

"I've just heard that he's vain and arrogant. At first when you mentioned him, I was surprised that he would feel the need to pursue a woman simply because of some rumored dowry. Though his father is only a viscount, they have quite enough wealth of their own. Given what I know of him, though, it does make sense. Supposedly, Mr. Milburn is never satisfied with what he has, always seeking to grow his reputation, his connections, his closet, his lands, his fortune. It seems that he views Miss Harcourt as a means to that end. Besides, I am sure he would love to brag that he won the woman every man in London chased after all Season."

Noah's lip curled in a snarl, earning him a startled look from a nearby couple who had the misfortune of being in his line of sight at that moment. He quickly regained his manners and smiled at them apologetically. The anger and disgust did not leave so easily, though. He hated the sound of Mr. Milburn's plan even though he knew that their goals were really not so different. At least Noah could sleep a little easier tonight knowing that his motives were slightly better than Mr. Milburn's. He needed to save his family from ruin, while Mr. Milburn only coveted more of what he already had.

"I have an important question for you," Phineas continued, a hint of curiosity as well as mischief in his eyes as he watched for Noah's reaction.

"Go ahead." An alarm of suspicion sounded in Noah's mind as he searched his friend's face, trying to guess what he would ask.

"Do you think you could marry this lady, even if there is no love between you at the start? Sometimes love does come after the marriage, so I've heard, so do not forget that as a possibility."

An important question indeed. Noah slipped into deep thought as he pondered his friend's words. As much as he wanted to save his family, Noah could not deny that he was extremely uncomfortable with the position he'd been put in by no fault of his own. Despite Miss Harcourt's double personality, Noah knew that she still deserved a happy future and a husband she truly loved.

If he married her solely for financial reasons, Noah would be robbing them both of that chance. Yet if he did not, or if he did not find another wealthy woman to marry instead, his family would fall into destitution. He would never be able to properly provide for future generations of Waynfords.

Noah's mind took him back to the few interactions he'd had with Miss Harcourt thus far. He'd felt some stirring of something, though he could not yet be sure if it could or should develop further. If he married Miss Harcourt, which version of her would he really be committing the rest of his life to?

"I hate to admit that you bring up an excellent point," Noah jested.

"Believe it or not, wise old Mr. Waynford, I possess at least half a brain." Phineas laughed as he slapped Noah on the shoulder. "But do tell me more about how right I am."

"Well, it remains to be seen if you will be right in the end," Noah carefully reminded him. "But your suggestion does merit some consideration. I still have more time to get to know Miss Harcourt before I decide if I could at least be content with that kind of marriage. When I think about her, I find that I am drawn to her and I long to learn more—or at least solve the mystery of who she really is. I can sense a kindness of spirit in her all the same.

"Perhaps I could at least enjoy a companionable marriage with her...even if love never grows between us. That would not be so terrible, would it?"

"Mr. Waynford, good afternoon." An unexpected voice called Noah's name, snapping him back to his current surroundings.

He looked around, somewhat surprised to find himself back in Hyde Park. When he got so deep in thought like this, he often became blind to anything else but the possibilities he envisioned.

His surprise increased tenfold, his heart shooting up into his throat as he realized Miss Harcourt now approached from the opposite direction, accompanied by her friend from the dance, Mrs. Parkins, and a gentleman Noah assumed to be Mr. Parkins.

She looked quite happy to see him, her smile soft and warm. Yes, Noah thought to himself, perhaps he could appreciate a life with Miss Harcourt. Any man would be happy to receive such a lovely expression.

Noah shot a meaningful look to Phineas who immediately nodded his understanding. "Good afternoon, Miss Harcourt," Noah called back.

As they quickly closed the distance between their two groups, Noah carefully observed Miss Harcourt. Today, she looked so gentle and unassuming—not to mention so very pretty in the soft glow of the afternoon sunlight, her pale purple walking dress flowing gracefully with each step.

"How lovely it is to run into you so unexpectedly, Mr. Waynford," the young woman said as they finally stood before one another. Her voice was pleasant, but her eyes, and the way they crinkled slightly at the corners as she smiled, told Noah that she meant every word she said. "This is my friend, Mrs. Parkins, whom you met at the ball a few weeks ago, and her husband Mr. Adam Parkins." Noah bowed to the couple and in turn introduced Phineas.

"Why don't we all walk together along the river?" Phineas suggested brightly. "A fine day is always made more enjoyable with pleasant company."

Miss Harcourt nodded her agreement before Mrs. Parkins subtly elbowed the young woman in the side. It did not escape Noah's notice, however, and he paid even more attention to the silent communications between Miss Harcourt and her friend. Miss Harcourt gave Mrs. Parkins a confused look for a moment before seeming to realize something.

Noah watched the transformation happen once more. Miss Harcourt switched, an almost unnatural smile stretching across her face, tugging at her soft features. "What an excellent idea, Mr. Tilson!" she cried, her voice slightly shrill.

Disappointment and confusion flooded Noah. He could

not figure out why Miss Harcourt would act like this when it clearly did not suit her. Even she looked uncomfortable as she tried to keep the smile on her face. Of course, Noah enjoyed her smile—but only the real one. This one looked so forced and difficult for her to maintain. From Noah's brief interactions with these ladies, this vibrant and animated behavior seemed to be more natural for Mrs. Parkins.

"Mr. Tilson, why don't you join my husband and I? I recognize your last name and I must figure out if you come from the same family of Tilsons I know." Mrs. Parkins gestured for Phineas to come closer, her expression triumphant as she sent a meaningful glance to her friend.

Noah forced a bemused smile at Miss Harcourt. He got the impression that Mrs. Parkins thought she'd slyly orchestrated a situation in which Noah and Miss Harcourt could have some privacy. Based on Phineas's knowing expression, Mr. Parkins' rueful smile, and Miss Harcourt's wide eyes, everyone in their party knew exactly what Mrs. Parkins was up to.

"That would be lovely, madam." Phineas graciously accepted Mrs. Parkins' invitation. As soon as he stepped up next to the couple, Mrs. Parkins immediately took off back in the direction they'd just come.

"Tell me about your family, Mr. Tilson. Do you perhaps have a cousin named Maria who lives in Surrey?" She wasted no time in throwing questions to Phineas as her quick pace carried them further away from Noah and Miss Harcout, her husband trailing behind.

There was nothing left for Noah to do but offer his arm to Miss Harcourt. She blinked rapidly at him as she accepted, very carefully placing her hand on his arm with the utmost elegance. They started their walk behind the trio, who had already gained quite a distance, keeping a more leisurely pace.

"How have you and your family been since I last saw you all?" Noah asked.

"We are all doing very well indeed," Miss Harcourt assured him cheerfully. "I am so very excited for our outing to Somerset House. If only the next few days would pass quickly! Isn't it quite miraculous for us to meet so unexpectedly like this?"

Noah silently agreed. London was a large city and, though Hyde Park and the Serpentine were popular spots on a lovely day like this, he would never have guessed that he would come across Miss Harcourt in the same place at the same time. He did not usually think too much of signs, but Noah could not help wondering what this chance meeting could mean.

Perhaps it really was just a coincidence, but he would take advantage of it regardless. He could still use this as an opportunity to decipher Miss Harcourt's switches in behavior, and if such a dual personality could lead to a tolerable match.

"Mr. Waynford? Are you well?" Miss Harcourt asked with that same lovely, genuine care Noah had started to recognize. He must have been quiet for too long.

Noah looked down into her face and saw that her eyes were just as gentle and concerned, her expression conveying a sincere desire to understand whatever bothered him, and perhaps even see if she could help. He could read all that right there in her expression, so different than it had been a few moments ago.

He smiled, feeling himself soften. "I assure you I am well. I've just been enjoying the beauty of the day and this pleasant surprise."

Miss Harcourt smiled back, full of warmth and contentment. A thrill of happiness shot through Noah. He was glad he could make Miss Harcourt smile like that. If only he could see more of this side of her. Noah knew deep in his bones that this was her true self—not the flirtatious, animated veneer she wore. Noah knew without knowing how he knew that what he saw in Miss Harcourt now was not something that could be fabricated.

"How have you and your family been recently?" she asked, tilting her head back far enough so she could look him in the eyes without her bonnet getting in the way.

"They've been doing very well. They are all enjoying the Season and catching up with all their London friends. I must admit we've all been quite busy. I find it a little over-whelming at times even if I do enjoy seeing my friends and exploring."

Miss Harcourt hummed thoughtfully, her serious expression charming. "Yes, I do agree that London comes with many benefits. Still, when I am here I can't help missing the simplicity of country life. Yet when I am home in Somerset I find myself missing days like this in the city. Isn't that strange?"

"I am sure you would never come to London if you had a charming companion like me in Somerset," Noah said in a playfully haughty tone. Normally he would not say some-thing so forward and arrogant, even as a joke, but somehow he wanted to test Miss Harcourt, to see which side of her would come forth next.

Miss Harcourt laughed, her shoulders trembling and her nose scrunching as the sound spilled from her, carried off by the breeze. Noah found the sound to be both genuine and enjoyable.

"Ah, yes, my lifelong home does have many charms, but none that can compare to a certain gentleman I know," she smiled slyly, her warm brown eyes sparkling with merriment.

Noah's mouth almost fell open in surprise. He'd antici-pated a bashful response with a light scolding for being so brazen. He hadn't expected her to tease him back so readily. Miss Harcourt clearly possessed an endearing and witty sense of humor, all while maintaining the heart of her sweet nature.

"Of course, my younger sister Caroline would be terribly angry with me if I stayed in the country while she herself is so excited to finally be out and enjoy all that London has to offer," she continued with a bemused sigh. "And once Caroline is angry, there is not much that can soothe her besides a trip to Gunter's or our ice shop at home."

"I know all too well the anger of sisters." Noah gave Miss Harcourt a commiserating look, suddenly feeling relieved. He enjoyed hearing these personal stories and seeing that Miss Harcourt adored her family.

Miss Harcourt nodded sagely. "I am glad I never had to know the anger of an older sister like you did. I'm sure it is an experience all its own."

Noah found himself laughing more loudly than he'd intended, once again drawing curious stares from passersby. "Too right you are, Miss Harcourt." An exhilarating lightness spread through Noah's chest as he looked down at his companion and he saw her surprised delight at his reaction.

"I'm afraid I must ask you to lower your voice, Mr. Waynford." She tried to sound serious, but she could not fight the smile that tugged at her lips. "Everyone in the park will think I am some sort of comedic master, and I am not quite ready for all that attention."

Brilliant! Noah found himself thinking over and over again as they walked on for several more minutes, asking each other polite questions and giving thoughtful, sometimes humorous answers. It seemed that when Miss Harcourt was not so concerned with behaving in a certain way, she became an excellent conversation partner. She always had thoughts to share and smart observations to make.

"Anna! Mr. Waynford! You must hurry!" Mrs. Parkins called from further up the path, startling Noah and Miss Harcourt out of their pleasant banter. She beckoned frantically for them to come closer, pointing to the river.

Miss Harcourt sighed with a fond smile. "Once Esther has her sights set on something, it is usually best to go along with her," she advised.

Noah admired her insight about the people around her. Perhaps she would even like to join Noah in his hobby of observing people and trying to decipher them. She would certainly have interesting opinions to add. Before Noah could get too caught up in those thoughts, they arrived at the riverside where the rest of their group waited.

"Oh, how sweet!" Miss Harcourt cooed as they saw the object of Mrs. Parkins' excitement. A family of ducks lingered by the bank, idly swimming in circles, the tiny yellow chicks diligently following behind their mother.

Phineas came up next to Noah and caught his eye, lifting a curious eyebrow. Surely he expected a detailed report from Noah later. Noah found that he looked forward to sharing his new knowledge of Miss Harcourt—and the welcome warmth that enveloped him—with his friend.

"I rarely see them this close to the bank. Aren't they so precious?" Mrs. Parkins gripped her husband's arm, her bottom lip nearly trembling with that sensation that only babies of any species could produce.

"Indeed they are, my love," Mr. Parkins agreed, patting his wife's hand.

Miss Harcourt's gasp caused them all to jump, four heads whipping around to stare at her. "Look there! One of the ducklings is stuck in the mud."

She brought a gloved hand to her cheek, her fingers pulling against her skin, her eyes darting around the riverbank searching for something that might help. It took Noah a moment, but he soon found the poor little duckling, a barely visible ball of feathers with two desperately flapping wings, more black than yellow.

"Thank goodness we have the perfect man for the job," Phineas announced smartly, grabbing Noah by the shoulder and pushing him forward slightly. Noah sent his friend an unamused glance, which only earned him a lighthearted shrug in response. Of course, Noah knew that Phineas had given him a chance to play the hero and impress Miss Harcourt.

Noah carefully stepped closer to the bank. He would have volunteered even if Phineas had not done it for him. He crouched down without hesitation, well aware that most well-mannered gentlemen would never be caught kneeling on the ground in danger of falling in mud just to help a trapped duckling. Even a simple creature like this duckling deserved a chance at life, so Noah did not mind getting a little dirty.

He leaned forward, stretching his arm as far as it would go in his fitted coat. At first he feared he would not be able to reach the duckling, but with a grimace and a grunt of effort, Noah finally caught the little bird. His fingers sank into the cool, wet mud as he scooped the duckling out. As soon as it was free of the mud, it leapt out of Noah's hand and landed in the river, eagerly rejoining its family.

As cheers sounded behind Noah, he triumphantly tried to stand again. He'd moved too quickly, his foot slipping on a patch of mud. Noah felt himself losing his balance, his arms flailing as he desperately tried to prevent the inevitable. He slipped further down the bank, his walking boots filling with mud, certain that he would soon look just like the duckling he'd rescued.

A pair of hands grasped Noah by the wrist as he felt himself tipping backwards. Instinctively, he grasped back.

When he looked up, Noah nearly lost his balance again. Miss Harcourt held him up, both hands now wrapped around Noah's wrist, her chest heaving with the effort of keeping Noah upright. Their eyes met for a silent, breathless moment.

"Goodness gracious, Anna!" Mrs. Parkins moaned. "Surely you've ruined your slippers and the hem of your dress."

Noah tore his gaze away from Miss Harcourt's, looking down to see that she stood in the mud with him. When he looked back up, she still did not seem to care in the least despite her friend's admonition.

"Are you hurt?" Miss Harcourt asked.

She did not seem to realize that she'd done something quite brave and selfless. One's true nature showed through most in times of distress or when quick action was needed. This, Noah now knew without a doubt, was Miss Harcourt's true nature.

"No, and I have you to thank for that," Noah mumbled, still in awe. He came back to his senses enough to at least fight his way out of the mud, pulling Miss Harcourt along behind him, their hands still wrapped around each other's wrists. Phineas and Mr. Parkins jumped up to assist them, Phineas taking Noah's free arm while Mr. Parkins offered his hand to Miss Harcourt.

"I'm so terribly sorry about this mess I've caused." Noah took a moment to take in the state of Miss Harcourt's shoes and dress now that they had made it to solid ground, guilt turning his stomach upside down. He knew enough about ladies' clothes from Emma and Angelica to know that they did not come cheap, yet Miss Harcourt had ruined them for his sake.

Miss Harcourt tucked a strand of dark brown hair back under her bonnet. She laughed, her eyes squeezing shut as she tried to get a hold of herself. The rest of their group joined in, hesitant at first but soon growing bolder, no doubt irritating the other park goers.

When the laughter subsided, Miss Harcourt's expression had returned to that beautiful serenity. "Please do not apologize, Mr. Waynford. I would much rather make sure you are well than fret over my dress and slippers."

Noah's heartbeat picked up speed. The young woman narrowed her eyes at him and Noah panicked, wondering if his staring had made her uncomfortable.

"Just a moment, Mr. Waynford." Even Miss Harcourt's commands were gentle. Noah gave himself over to her mercy. She pulled a white handkerchief out of her reticule and held it up. "You have a spot of mud on your cheek. Shall I wipe it away for you?"

"Please do," Noah whispered, unable to encourage his voice to a normal, confident volume. As Miss Harcourt took a step closer, nearly toe to toe with him, Noah's chest tightened in anticipation. Time seemed to slow as he watched Miss Harcourt, felt her fingers brush against his cheek through the thin fabric of the handkerchief.

"You know, we seem to have fallen into the habit of rescuing each other," Noah mumbled, suddenly second guessing everything he said or did. Would Miss Harcourt appreciate it, find it amusing or insightful?

Miss Harcourt pulled her hand away and Noah immediately missed it. "We do seem to fall in each other's presence quite a bit, don't we?" She giggled at her own jest, her eyes falling away from his shyly. Noah felt nearly lightheaded at the perfection of her response and the way she'd seen an opportunity in his words that even he himself hadn't realized.

"Yes," Noah coughed, trying desperately to rein in his swirling thoughts and emotions.

"Fear not, Mr. Waynford." Miss Harcourt smiled understandingly. "Everyone needs rescuing from time to time."

Noah could only nod at this astute observation, his mind too overwhelmed to form an equally intelligent response. For the first time in their brief acquaintance, Noah sensed a subtle but meaningful stirring in his heart.

Perhaps Miss Harcourt could rescue him in more ways than he thought.

"We really should take you back with us, Anna," Mrs. Parkins interrupted, pulling Noah away from his strange thoughts that contained both excitement and anxiety. "I should get you cleaned up before you go home or else Lady Welsted will never allow you to see me again."

Mrs. Parkins had covered her mouth with one hand, her brows furrowed. She looked as though the possibility of being denied Miss Harcourt's presence was the worst thing that could happen to her. Noah almost chuckled quietly to himself. He suddenly felt that he could truly sympathize with her on that account.

Miss Harcourt turned away from Noah to take her friend's hand in hers, the hand that had just touched Noah's cheek. "Mama would do no such thing. I'll make sure of it."

Mrs. Parkins fussed over her friend once more, just as she'd done at the dance, leading her away from the riverbank while Mr. Parkins followed behind. For all her theatrics and influence over Miss Harcourt, at least Mrs. Parkins genuinely did her best to care for the other woman.

"You've shown remarkable bravery today, my friend," Phineas said loudly as he rejoined Noah, a few people glancing their way to catch a glimpse of the hero. "Of course, I wish Miss Bishop could have been here. I would have jumped into that mud myself to rescue the duckling." He shook his head, disappointed at his lost opportunity to impress his lady.

Noah let his head fall back as a loud laugh escaped him. Soon he heard another light giggle join in. Miss Harcourt looked over her shoulder at them. "I'm sure we can all make a pact that you can tell this Miss Bishop of your good deed and we will not contradict you, Mr. Tilson. But only if you do not mind giving away the credit, Mr. Waynford."

Noah laughed again, feeling lighter than he had in a long while—since his father had given him the terrible news. He realized that he hadn't thought about that since he and Miss Harcourt had started their walk together. He'd been too captivated by her to think of anything else.

CHAPTER 7

*E*yes lingered on Anna, just for a moment, but long enough for her to notice. Did she really seem so out of place beside a man like Mr. Milburn? He had the type of handsome looks that women fell for and men envied.

She did her best to shove her self-conscious thoughts away, to stay focused on what should have been a pleasant trip with Mr. Milburn. What did those people matter? If Mr. Milburn wanted to spend his time with her, that was his choice. He must see something in her even if no one else did.

Anna turned to look up at the gentleman who had been blocked from view by her bonnet. He noticed her gaze, giving her a shining smile. "Lovely day, don't you think?"

"Absolutely," Anna agreed, trying to channel her anxiety into excitement. "I'm afraid I don't spend enough time at Richmond Park. I always forget how beautiful it is. And your curricle is a beauty all its own."

She knew she rambled a bit, but for once in Anna's life, she needed the distraction of conversation. She could still feel eyes finding her, watching, judging.

"I quite agree," Mr. Milburn chirped happily, staring

ahead with his chin lifted proudly. "As I said at dinner, it reminds me a little of my beloved home in Yorkshire. I do hope you have the opportunity to visit someday. This carriage is very handsome, isn't it? We've brought other carriages as well. I find it always good to have a variety for different activities. A coach or gig would not suit such a fine day as this."

Mr. Milburn rambled as well, picking up the thread Anna had managed to pull from herself and unspooling it with his own thoughts. They soon settled into a companionable conversation, primarily supplied by Mr. Milburn. Unlike before, Anna made sure to absorb every word he said. She would not allow her mind to wander for fear that it might drift back to the other park goers and why they seemed so curious about her today. Besides, Mr. Milburn deserved to be listened to just the same as anyone else, even if he had an awful lot to say.

"Miss Harcourt, would you like to take the reins?" he offered after finishing an interesting tale about his cousin Robert who once fell into the river on the Milburns' estate and had to be fished out by a chain of men.

Anna's eyes bulged not at the thrilling conclusion of his story, but at his suggestion. "Pardon? I-I mean to say that I am terribly sorr—"

Mr. Milburn's laugh interrupted her rapid, stumbling apology. "No, Miss Harcourt, it is I who should be sorry. I only meant to tease you a bit. I remember perfectly well that you do not like driving. Please forgive me for frightening you."

Despite his apology, he seemed rather amused. Anna slowly relaxed, letting out a strained giggle. "How cruel of you, Mr. Milburn!" she cried in playful vexation, gently tapping his arm with her gloved hand.

She'd seen Esther do that many times during their

Seasons together. Men always found it charming. Esther still did it with her husband on occasion. Though Anna got the impression that Mr. Parkins found it less charming now, he still went along with it to amuse his wife.

"I hope you know I would never do anything to make you uncomfortable." Mr. Milburn's eyes burned into Anna's, his green irises even brighter in the late afternoon sunshine.

Her heart flipped and her pulse raced as she realized how close they sat in this curricle. Before she could say anything, one of Mr. Milburn's hands abandoned the reins. He squeezed Anna's hand, his thumb tracing a few gentle circles against her glove before returning to the reins.

Anna simply stared at Mr. Milburn as he guided the horses along the path, confident and experienced. Dumbfounded was the only word she could think of to describe how she felt.

He remembered what she had said at dinner and had tried to use it as their own private joke. Of course, Anna had completely mistook him as being serious. He had seemed quite serious with his last words, with his shockingly passionate gaze.

Perhaps, after getting used to his humor and his long-winded conversation, Anna could truly fall for Mr. Milburn. She'd had her misgivings about their compatibility at first, but the more she got to know him, the more Anna could see herself not simply settling but actually enjoying their relationship.

Her eyes roamed his face, so self-assured and beautiful—everything Anna was not. Would he grow to love her? His earlier words seemed to indicate that he might. Could Anna grow to love him? For the first time in their courtship, Anna thought love could be possible with this man. Anna pulled her gaze away from Mr. Milburn, shaking her head. It was still far too soon for that, Anna reminded herself as an image of Mr. Waynford swam unbidden through her mind.

Despite the silent scolding she gave herself for thinking of her other suitor, Anna could not help wondering what this day would have been like with Mr. Waynford.

"Do you see that gentleman over there, walking with the handsome black cane?" Mr. Milburn's voice quickly shoved all thoughts of Mr. Waynford away.

"Certainly," Anna replied, as cheery and vibrant as she could manage.

"That's Lord Neve, an old friend of mine. Quite a charming chap once you get past his gruff attitude."

Mr. Milburn waved to the man in question, whose face immediately went from a seemingly permanent frown to a surprisingly warm smile. He slowed the curricle down to chat with Lord Neve for a moment, introducing him to Anna. When he heard her name, Lord Neve's eyes narrowed slightly as he examined her face, causing Anna to instinctively lean into Mr. Milburn's side.

"I am sorry about that," he chuckled nervously as he urged the horses to continue. "See, gruff attitude."

The same happened a few more times as Mr. Milburn pointed out a friend or acquaintance, stopping to make introductions when possible. Not all of them looked at Anna as curiously as Lord Neve had. In fact, most of them greeted her with perfect politeness. Unfortunately, Anna did not miss the fact that several of her new acquaintances seemed perplexed by her.

"Are you well, Miss Harcourt?"

Anna's head jerked back up. She hadn't realized she'd let it fall, that she'd been staring at her hands clasped around her reticule for some unknown amount of time. She gave Mr. Milburn a sweet, gracious smile.

"Do not worry about them," Mr. Milburn continued with

a nonchalant shrug of his shoulders and the handsomest smile Anna had ever seen. "They are either jealous or surprised that I am out with such a beautiful young lady today. No doubt they are wondering why an angel like you is wasting her time on a clod like me."

Anna's heart flipped again. She knew he either must be blind or so enamored with her new persona that she seemed more attractive than she really was. Still, his words planted a seed of hope in her, already blooming ever so slightly.

As they continued, Mr. Milburn pointed out more people he knew, made introductions, and occasionally shared an amusing or interesting story about the person in question. Anna marveled at his ability to make and keep so many acquaintances. Outside of her family, Anna's only real friend was Esther, whom she only saw in London. She'd also been friends with the two young ladies who lived on the estate closest to Attwood Manor, but they'd lost touch after the ladies married and moved away.

Perhaps, after spending more time with Mr. Milburn, Anna could learn from his social skills, further improving her new personality. Anna knew she could use all the help she could get in that department if she wanted to have any hope of making a suitable wife for Mr. Milburn—or landing any match at all.

Anna just could not fully relax on the trip. She thought it a terrible shame that she should spend her time on this lovely day with a charming gentleman wrapped up in paranoia.

No matter what she did, Anna could not forget all those eyes.

ANNA STEPPED DOWN from the carriage, her slippers barely making a sound against the road beneath her. She doubted she would have heard it anyway if there had been a sound. The pounding of her heart was the only noise she could hear.

She gazed up at Somerset House, the grand building that shared a name with her beloved home in the country. Anna had been to the Royal Academy's annual exhibition several years in a row—since her very first Season—and she always had a wonderful time.

The crowds overwhelmed her on occasion, as dozens upon dozens of people crowded into the building to view the exhibits. Anna would not allow that to deter her. The beautiful art was well worth it.

Today, Anna found herself unable to truly look forward to the experience. Her anxiety rendered every other feeling insignificant. She would be spending an afternoon with just herself and Mr. Waynford, along with one of the Harcourt footmen, for the first time. There would be no friends or family who could offer her encouragement or come to her aid if her nerves got the better of her—and it certainly seemed like they would put up a decent fight today.

In an effort to distract herself, Anna made her way to the stone railing that looked over the River Thames, her footman giving her enough space to think quietly. She gingerly set her hands on the smooth railing, the heat from the stone seeping through her gloves as the sun showered her in its light. Though the day was not terribly hot, Anna felt tiny beads of perspiration popping up on the nape of her neck.

The fact that her mind constantly replayed that chance meeting by the Serpentine did nothing to help. Anna had enjoyed it so very much. Mr. Waynford had seemed so curious about her and willing to listen. Though they must have only walked and talked for perhaps half an hour, Anna felt sure that they would not have run out of topics to discuss. Better yet, Anna had only noticed later that day that she'd allowed her mask to fall away. Mr. Waynford hadn't seemed to mind. She'd enjoyed his sense of humor and had been thrilled to see that he seemed to appreciate hers as well.

So why did she feel so nervous today? Anna looked out over the sparkling water of the Thames, the current slow and peaceful under the light breeze. Of course, Anna could not think about that day without thinking of the duckling incident. Her face reddened at the memory of Mr. Waynford's bravery and her own shocking boldness.

No matter how hard she'd tried, Anna could not banish the image of Mr. Waynford valiantly marching into the mud and how handsome he looked as he put all his energy and focus into freeing the duckling. Much to her embarrassment, Anna could not help swooning a little every time she thought of it. Though the damsel in distress had only been a baby bird, Mr. Waynford had been a hero in her eyes all the same.

Then there was the matter of Anna's behavior. She still could not believe that she'd taken hold of him when he had almost fallen in. That alone was quite brazen for Anna, but she justified it to herself by claiming that instinct must have inspired her. Though that still did not explain why she would do something so truly shameless as to wipe his face with her handkerchief. Anna shuddered at the thought, all the embarrassment she should have felt at that moment overwhelming her now.

Anna had never done something like that in her life. How often had she seen a gentleman at a dinner or dance with a bit of food clinging to the corner of his mouth and she had never said a word for fear of offending them? Yet it had been so natural to reach up and brush Mr. Waynford's cheek. Anna remembered exactly how that moment had felt. Even through the handkerchief and her gloves, Anna had felt the heat coming from Mr. Waynford's skin, the warmth of his breath on her face.

He'd been so kind and inviting that day, putting her at

ease in a way she'd never felt around any other man. Anna wished that she could feel that relaxed right now. Instead, she felt like she might faint from the force of the butterflies spinning in her stomach.

"Such a beautiful day, isn't it?"

Anna jumped with an embarrassingly inappropriate yelp as someone beside her spoke.

"Goodness, I did not mean to startle you," Mr. Waynford apologized with a chuckle, the corners of his eyes wrinkled with mirth.

With a hand over her chest, still recovering from the surprise, Anna muttered, "You do not seem very sorry at all, sir."

The gentleman lifted an eyebrow. "What could possibly give you that impression?"

Anna blushed once more. She wondered if perhaps her blush would soon become a permanent feature of her face with how often she'd been doing it of late. The only way she could recover now would be to disappear. How could she have been so rude? Something about this man brought out a different side to Anna.

"My apologies, Mr. Waynford! You just shocked me into letting my manners slip." She adopted the sweetest voice she could manage.

Mr. Waynford's cheer dimmed slightly even as he offered Anna his arm. "Do not fret over it. The fault is all mine," he insisted quietly. The playful tone in his voice had all but vanished.

Anna sheepishly put her hand on the crook of his elbow and they walked toward Somerset House. She glanced up at Mr. Waynford from under her bonnet. His eyes deftly traveled over their surroundings, from the well-kept grass to the beautiful building before them to the other people arriving to view the exhibit.

Perhaps he had seen through her attempts at flirting. Perhaps they had enjoyed a nice meeting at Hyde Park, but Anna still feared the possibility that being her true self would not keep him intrigued.

They walked through the doors of Somerset House and up the stairs toward the Great Room in silence, Anna's heart growing heavier with each step. Trying to figure out some way to repair the damage she'd done within the first five minutes of their day, Anna's anxiety took her on a whirlwind of second guessing all her past actions and words.

The air around Anna suddenly felt different, full of buzzing excitement and awe. She knew they'd arrived at the magnificent exhibition room. She looked up, craning her neck to see all the way to the ceiling as the walls had been filled from top to bottom with paintings. All Anna's worries left her alone for a moment as she sighed with wonder, over-whelmed by the beauty surrounding her.

"Is this your first time at the Royal Academy exhibits?" Mr. Waynford asked, his voice softer and his smile kinder.

"I have visited before, but it still takes my breath away to see this glorious architecture and artwork and all these people sharing this experience together."

Mr. Waynford nodded thoughtfully, looking almost impressed. Anna's heart skipped a beat at the expression, her hope slowly reigniting.

"I feel the same. I know many people come here just because it is the fashionable thing to do, but I think the majority end up appreciating the true purpose of the exhibits. It's hard not to when such beauty is staring them in the face." His eyes softened as he spoke, never removing them from Anna. Her heart began to thunder now. Could he be implying that he included her in that beauty?

Such a thought was so foreign to Anna that she guiltily pushed it to the back of her mind. She should not make those kinds of assumptions yet lest she get her hopes up only to have them crushed later. She knew Mr. Waynford was a perfect gentleman, kind and considerate to everyone, even silly little ducklings who got stuck in mud.

They walked together in silent awe for a few moments, drinking in the artwork that stretched all the way up to the ceiling. The ceiling could be considered art in its own right with its delicately designed moulding. They each retreated to their own thoughts, the atmosphere between them pleasant though they exchanged no words.

"There must be even more paintings than last year," Anna whispered. "How can they possibly keep finding these amazing new paintings to add?"

"How many times have you been to the Royal Academy?" Mr. Waynford asked.

Anna bit the inside of her cheek as she formed her answer. "I've been several years in a row now," she admitted quietly. Though Mr. Waynford surely knew she had been unable to make a match yet, it still hurt Anna to even allude to her multiple Seasons in London. She glanced nervously to Mr. Waynford, waiting for him to realize that he courted a woman on the verge of spinsterhood.

"How lovely that you've been able to experience the exhibit so many times," he said with a kind smile.

Anna nodded gratefully, her anxiety slowly retreating. If he'd heard about Anna's desperate situation, he kept it to himself.

"I've also visited quite a few times. I wonder if we've been in this same room at the same time in the past and we just did not know it." He looked at Anna thoughtfully, his eyes reading her face as if he might remember it amongst crowds of the past. "If you don't mind my saying, I think we are very fortunate to be here together now."

An exhilarated smile took over Anna's features before she

could stop herself. Mr. Waynford's words sent a thrill of bliss through her. Not just his words, she quickly realized, but the sincerity with which he said them.

"I think you are quite right, Mr. Waynford." They exchanged contented smiles. Anna would have been happy to keep standing there staring at Mr. Waynford had an old gentleman not grumbled about them blocking the view as he walked past.

Anna felt mortified until she saw Mr. Waynford suppressing a laugh. "Do not mind him," he muttered, still trying to keep himself together. "He must not realize that we are the view."

It was Anna's turn to force her laughter back, her hand flying up to her mouth. Feeling encouraged, Anna decided to carry the conversation forward and keep them moving through the room. "Which subjects do you like best, Mr. Waynford?"

"I love landscapes," he answered immediately.

"I admire your taste." She nodded approvingly as she gestured toward a large painting nearby that would suit Mr. Waynford. Once again, Anna could see the laughter behind his smile.

They paused before the landscape Anna had pointed out, both tilting their heads back to better appreciate the massive painting. "These bright green sloping hills remind me of our home, Attwood Manor, in the hills of Somerset," she commented, her eyes roaming over the artist's exceptional skill in forming every blade of grass and the nearly translucent clouds in the perfectly blue sky.

"It must be a beautiful place," Mr. Waynford agreed. "Where would one find Attwood Manor with this painting as a reference?" He leaned forward to get a closer look, his eyes roaming the lands, stopping at the details that caught his attention.

"Hmm…" Anna leaned forward as well, transforming the painting before her with memories of her home. "Perhaps somewhere around here." She pointed to an area of flat green land toward the middle left, hills rising to the right and forest behind. "It is not an exact likeness, of course, so this is only an approximation. I'm afraid you would still get quite lost if you tried to find Attwood Manor even with this painting as a map."

"Oh, I do not think I will need the painting." Mr. Waynford gripped his chin in his strong fingers, looking rather scholarly. "I can just ask you to tell me how to get there."

"Is that so? Are you planning on making a visit?" Anna asked with amusement. Somehow, she found it so easy to joke back and forth like this with Mr. Waynford. Though her question suggested a relationship beyond this one Season in London, Anna knew that it would not offend him or come across as too forward.

"I cannot tell you that, Miss Harcourt. That would ruin the surprise." Mr. Waynford smiled mischievously, watching Anna from the corner of his eye. Anna's heart danced. He always knew exactly what to say even to her ridiculous suggestions.

The next landscape they examined showed a magnificent mountain range that left Anna breathless. "Can such a place like this really exist?" she asked, taking a step forward to see the way the shadows created a complex rocky surface.

Mr. Waynford came up next to her, his hands clasped behind his back. "I cannot say that this particular place exists, but there are certainly places like it. It reminds me of the mountains I saw when I visited the Continent. There truly is nothing quite like them on this Earth," he murmured, his voice full of admiration.

"I hope I will be able to see mountains like this someday," Anna sighed wistfully.

"I hope you will, too." Mr. Waynford gave Anna a brief smile before returning his gaze to the painting. They remained there for quite some time, Anna wondering what he saw in his memories, what he'd experienced in the time before she'd known him.

When Mr. Waynford came back to his senses, he gently scolded Anna for not dragging him away so she did not have to stand there, bored.

"It was no trouble at all," Anna insisted. "Believe it or not, I find it quite pleasant to simply stand next to you in companionable silence. We could stare at this painting for another hour and I should still be content." Though her words had started as a playful jest, Anna soon realized how serious she was, suddenly finding it difficult to breathe under Mr. Waynford's intense gaze.

"I'm very glad you think so, for I feel the same," he agreed, his voice thick with something Anna could not put a name to, though she already longed to hear it again.

"Pardon me," a young man said politely as he and the lady on his arm slipped past Anna and Mr. Waynford to get closer to the mountain landscape.

Mr. Waynford held his arm out for Anna again and they continued on their path. Anna glanced over her shoulder at the couple before the crowd engulfed them completely. She wondered if they were newlyweds or a courting couple. She wondered if they assumed the same thing about her and Mr. Waynford. The thought that others might see them that way made Anna shiver with excitement.

"Is something wrong?" Mr. Waynford asked as they stopped before another landscape, his eyes searching her face, completely ignoring the artwork.

While Anna appreciated his attentiveness, she certainly could not tell him what had caused her reaction. That would be far too forward, far too soon. She searched around the room for something to say when she realized that the answer was right in front of her.

"I just felt a bit cold suddenly, that's all." She pointed to the exquisite landscape before them, an ocean scene of green and blue waves, frozen as they broke upon a golden shore. "It makes me think of a windy day at Brighton Beach," she explained, hoping she'd successfully dodged his suspicions.

Mr. Waynford furrowed his brow, his eyes exploring the painting in silence. Anna breathed a sigh of relief. She did not have the confidence yet to move from light teasing to true confessions.

"Is it not incredible how the artist captured the many colors of the water and the soft power of the waves?" Anna said it more for herself than for anyone else's benefit, unable to contain her wonder. She lapsed into silence as she stared at the painting, feeling herself transported to that very shore. She could almost smell the salt in the air and feel the way the wind tangled her hair while the sand slipped beneath her feet.

Somehow, despite her magical reverie, Anna eventually became aware of eyes upon her. Pulling her attention away from the ocean, Anna looked to her left to see Mr. Waynford staring—not at the painting, but at her.

The intensity in his eyes made Anna wonder for a moment if perhaps she'd gone slack-jawed or done something equally embarrassing. That feeling quickly dissipated, replaced by a warm, comfortable pleasure. No, he did not look offended or disturbed by something Anna had done. He looked captivated.

"My family stayed in Brighton for a few months two years ago. I was not brave enough to try the bathing machines, but I loved walking along the shore and listening to the waves," she explained, returning her gaze to the painting.

Mr. Waynford nodded, seeming to finally notice the ocean landscape before them. "I have never been to Brighton, actually. Can you believe that? Based on the picture you painted with your words, I would very much like to go someday."

"I do hope you will be able to visit soon." Anna clasped her hands before her chest, suddenly filled with an intense desire for Mr. Waynford to experience everything he could possibly want in the world. Brighton was beautiful, an amazing experience, but Anna knew that Mr. Waynford would see things in that place that Anna would have never considered, creating the seaside town anew through his perspective.

The gentleman turned so sharply to face Anna that she took a half step back, startled by the sudden movement. "Miss Harcourt, what kind of paintings do you like best? I'm afraid we've spent too much time already on the subjects dearest to me. I should very much like to know what is dearest to you now."

His words startled Anna almost as much as his rapid spin. She hadn't expected him to ask her what she wanted to see. "I am more than happy to stay here and keep discussing these landscapes," she insisted. "There are so many we still haven't seen yet." Anna hoped Mr. Waynford could see her sincerity. She truly would be content to pass the whole day in this room, going from one painting to the next, getting lost in their beauty. Anna would never grow tired of Mr. Waynford's unique insights.

Mr. Waynford shook his head at Anna. "That will not do, I am afraid. We are spending this day together, so we should both have an opportunity to enjoy and contemplate our favorite pieces."

That same warmth she'd felt earlier spread through Anna, seeping out from the middle of her chest through every part of her. Could Mr. Waynford truly be this willing to learn about her interests, just as she was about his? The glint in his eyes and the half-raised brow told Anna that he did indeed want to know her better.

He waited patiently for Anna's response. For now, she could only gaze up at this charming, intelligent, kindhearted man while a realization dawned on her. She was finally able to articulate to herself that melancholy feeling that had haunted Anna since her first unsuccessful Season.

No matter how many times she told herself to accept any offer that came her way, she'd actually come to dread a future married to a nice man who did not truly love her or take a genuine interest in her. She dreaded the possibility of spending her days listening to someone else as he talked for hours on end or being left to her own devices while he went about his day, never asking Anna what she thought or wanted. She dreaded the thought of being a stranger in her own marriage.

Mr. Waynford did not make her feel that way. He drew her in, tried to get to know her, wanted her to participate in their conversations and activities. Anna felt as though she was a part of his world.

She could not suppress her grin, trusting that Mr. Waynford would not take offense to such an unladylike expression. He always seemed to prefer that Anna show her true self, even if it sometimes strayed from the polite manners she'd been brought up with.

"My favorite exhibit is the Hall," she confessed proudly, standing a little taller.

Mr. Waynford's eyes widened with surprise for a moment before he returned Anna's grin. "Then we must go right away," he announced, offering his arm to her. As soon as she took it, they were off, Anna giggling under her breath as she nearly trotted to keep up with Mr. Waynford's long strides, the Harcourt footman doing his best to follow.

Surely they must look quite silly, but Anna did not care. She could not remember the last time she'd had this much fun, felt this open and free.

They flew through Somerset House, the hallways passing by in a blur. Anna watched Mr. Waynford's excited expression as he led them to the Hall, unable to tear her eyes away from his handsome profile, from the smile on his lips.

Once they stepped through the doors into the grand Hall, Anna did allow her attention to leave Mr. Waynford. They fell silent as they both gazed around, frozen just inside the doors. The footmen along the walls all stood silently as well in an almost perfect imitation of the magnificent plaster casts of statues that guarded the area. The only sound came from an artist's pencil scratching away at his paper as he sat in a far corner, sketching in the peace and quiet of this less frequented exhibit.

Anna and Mr. Waynford took a slow turn around the room, still enveloped in comfortable silence. Anna could feel Mr. Waynford's awe and admiration radiating from him as his observant eyes absorbed the sculptures, almost too incredible for their simple minds to witness.

Each statue was unique, though they all seemed to come from the same material. Some depicted human men and women standing tall and proud or serene and contemplative. Others depicted regal centaurs and other creatures of myth. Busts of stoic faces with empty eyes gazed out with purpose and ancient knowledge.

They both agreed, without saying a word, to sink down onto a bench along one wall, facing the other wall where several statues and busts stood, forever captured in their various poses and expressions. Anna stared in quiet appreciation, her eyes always finding some new detail that overwhelmed her with its genius. She knew Mr. Waynford did the same and she felt no guilt or anxiety for abandoning him in favor of her own thoughts. She knew, with a comforting certainty, that he understood.

When Mr. Waynford's voice did break her concentration after a period of time that felt like seconds and hours all at once, it did not startle her. Instead, his voice by her side felt natural and welcome, as if it flowed into her mind, nestling perfectly amongst her thoughts.

"What makes the statues your favorite?" he asked quietly, his leg nearly brushing against hers. It seemed wrong, even disrespectful to bring noise into this sacred place.

Anna smiled as she thought of her answer, so at peace with everything—even herself. For the first time, being herself around anyone other than her family and dearest friends felt possible. It felt more than possible. It was right. Anna's thoughtful silences and opinions did not bore Mr. Waynford. In fact, he welcomed them.

She turned to face Mr. Waynford for a moment. He watched her patiently and curiously. Anna allowed herself to be watched as she did the same with him, realizing that it did not feel as uncomfortable as she'd thought. Being seen by the right person came with a sense of belonging that Anna had never thought she'd feel with a man.

Anna faced forward again, wondering just what it was about these statues that amazed her so. "It is hard to put into words," she admitted with a quiet laugh.

Mr. Waynford smiled understandingly. "I suppose I have asked you quite an impossible question."

"Still, I will do my best." Anna inhaled, determined to keep her promise. After a moment, the words seemed to fall right into Anna's mind effortlessly. "The statues are my favorite because I cannot fathom how stone can be made to look so soft. How could the sculptor capture the gentle curves of the human form or the way fabric flows in a breeze?"

"I see," Mr. Waynford mumbled as he gazed at the statues, pondering Anna's explanation.

"I always wished I could reach out and touch the statues to find out if they really feel like stone. Perhaps the process of carving somehow made them softer."

When Mr. Waynford did not respond, Anna glanced at him from the corner of her eye. He smiled at her with a hint of amusement but also something else. Admiration, perhaps?

Anna realized with a jolt that her hand had started to lift of its own accord, as if she really would reach out across the Hall and brush her fingers against one of the sculptures. She'd thought she'd had her fill of blushing for the day, but apparently that was not to be the case. Her face flamed as she realized that she must look utterly ridiculous. She quickly brought her hand up to her hair, adjusting a curl that did not need adjusting.

Mr. Waynford chuckled kindly before glancing around the room. No one seemed to be paying them much mind. Even Anna's footman stared around the Hall in amazement. Mr. Waynford leaned forward, his face coming so close to Anna's that she could almost feel his lips on her skin. He brought his fingers to her cheek, slowly guiding them to the strand of hair she'd just fussed with. His eyes captured hers with an earnestness that made Anna dizzy, yet grounded her at the same time. Mr. Waynford tucked the curl behind Anna's ear tenderly—lovingly.

It seemed that Mr. Waynford found Anna's rambling and absentminded gesture—things she would have once been mortified over—to be endearing.

Mr. Waynford pulled back, creating the appropriate amount of distance between them once more. Despite the erratic, overwhelming fluttering of her heart, Anna wished he would return…and stay longer.

"I've never thought that way about statues before," he admitted quietly, looking across the hall once more. "Perhaps it is the sculptor who brings softness to the statues with the gentle, loving work of his hands. He must tirelessly chisel and smooth the stone to create every minute detail. It is that human touch that transforms the stone from something cold and inanimate to this miraculous thing with a sense of life and knowledge."

The almost emotional tone in his voice brought peace to Anna's heart. She'd found herself wondering many things so far today, not the least of which was how the same man could make her feel both exhilarated and calm, sometimes within the same breath.

Anna nodded her agreement, allowing his words to sink in in the welcoming silence of the Hall. Even with all the men she'd met throughout her Season, she'd never come across someone who possessed such a genuine thoughtfulness, let alone someone who enjoyed and encouraged conversations with her—conversations they could equally contribute to and build from.

She could see through her peripheral vision that he still looked ahead so Anna took the opportunity to observe him. Hope bubbled up inside her as well as a realization—the realization that maybe she did not want to settle for being a silent, listening wife, more of an accessory to her husband than a partner.

Sitting in the Hall of statutes with Mr. Waynford, Anna finally felt for the first time in all her years of searching that she may not be too late after all, that she could still find that meaningful, loving relationship.

Mr. Waynford turned to Anna, his mouth open as if to say something. Anna gasped at having been caught shamelessly staring, but the gasp devolved into a coughing fit. She squeezed her eyes shut, thankful that she would not have to see the expression on Mr. Waynford's face.

"You there! Please, bring a refreshment as quickly as you can," Mr. Waynford commanded the nearest footman who immediately set out, the clicking of his shoes on the wood floor echoing through the room. "Miss Harcourt, are you alright?" As soon as the footman had been sent on his mission, Mr. Waynford returned his attention to Anna, his voice and eyes full of concern. He took her hands in his. Anna found herself gripping them tightly as another wave of coughs wracked her body.

Too overwhelmed by a whirlwind of emotions, Anna kept her eyes closed as she struggled to catch her breath. She'd once again managed to land herself in a disgraceful situation, yet it did not smother the hope she'd felt earlier. In fact, her hope only grew, tentatively but noticeably. She wanted to learn more about this gentleman who did not care that he'd just caught a lady brazenly staring at him, this gentleman who always rushed to her rescue.

"Y-Yes, Mr. Waynford. Thank you. I am already feeling better," Anna stuttered, the cough subsiding enough for her to speak.

"Ah, here, this will help." The footman returned in record time, bearing a silver tray with a cup of tea. Mr. Waynford passed the cup to Anna, thanking the footman for his help. He watched as Anna drank, cautioning her to go slowly. As the warm, delicious liquid traveled down her throat and spread through her body, Anna finally came back to herself.

She sighed, filling her lungs with air. "Much better."

"Are you sure you're feeling well enough to continue? Or would you prefer to return home?" Mr. Waynford demanded, his eyes still searching Anna's face for any other issues.

"I am perfectly fine now, I promise! I want to stay. There is still so much more to see," Anna insisted, though she had to admit that she appreciated his concern and attention.

In truth, Anna could only hear Mr. Waynford's words now, bouncing off the walls of the Hall, filling her ears. She hoped to escape this area so she could clear her head and not make a fool of herself again. Finally accepting Anna's assurances, Mr. Waynford helped her up from the bench and placed her hand on his arm, leading them back out to the rest of the Royal Academy exhibits.

A few hours later, after more wandering and discussing and laughing, Anna and Mr. Waynford found themselves standing outside Somerset House once more, the fresh air dancing past them and the Thames sparkling nearby.

"What did you think, Miss Harcourt?" Mr. Waynford asked, a question she almost never heard from the men she'd hoped would court her.

With a refreshing contentment filling Anna from head to toe, she said, "I had a wonderful time." How many times had she said that phrase, without really meaning it, hoping to impress a gentleman who hadn't asked?

"As did I," Mr. Waynford agreed softly. "I am so happy that you enjoyed it. It's always a pleasure for me to hear you talk about the arts. I hope to hear more of your thoughts on other subjects in the future."

Anna smiled—a real smile, not one of the coy ones Esther had taught her. Before she could say anything else, her carriage pulled up beside them.

"I will call upon you again soon," Mr. Waynford assured Anna as he helped her up. Just before he closed the door, Mr. Waynford peered his head inside the carriage. "And do think about what you would like to do next. It's your turn to decide."

He closed the door before Anna could respond, the driver

tapping the horses with the reins, carrying her away from Somerset House. She turned around in her seat, peering out of the small window behind her to see Mr. Waynford watching her go, a thoughtful smile etched on his face.

Anna lifted her hand to the window in a small wave. Even from this distance, Anna could see Mr. Waynford laugh as he waved back. She settled back into her seat, her smile never leaving her face, replaying the day in her mind during the ride home. When the carriage rolled to a stop before the Harcourts' townhouse, Anna wished that the ride could have been longer. She wanted to spend more time reveling in all those lovely details so they would remain fresh in her mind.

The driver opened the door for her and Anna reluctantly climbed out of the carriage, slowly making her way up the front steps, clinging to the last few seconds she had before the dream must inevitably melt away as she returned to her normal life.

"Oh, Anna, there you are." Caroline's expectant voice broke through Anna's musings. She looked up to see her younger sister passing through the foyer with a sketchbook in one hand and a collection of pencils in the other. "Your other gentleman is here," she said with a mischievous look on her face.

Anna frowned in confusion for a moment before Caroline's eyebrow lifted impatiently, cluing Anna into her meaning. She gasped when she realized that Mr. Milburn must be here. "Caroline, do not say it that way! It sounds rude!"

Unbothered as always by Anna's scoldings, Caroline easily shrugged this one off as well. "Papa has requested that you join them in the drawing room if you returned in time from seeing your *other* gentleman."

Anna's mouth flew open to scold Caroline again, but the younger woman threw a sickeningly sweet smile over her shoulder as she hurried away down the hall. Anna would have to let her go for now since she had a guest waiting, though she wanted nothing more than to chase after her sister, lock her in a room, and recite their old governess's many rules for ladylike etiquette until Caroline learned her lesson.

Instead, Anna summoned her composure and made her way upstairs to the drawing room, nerves assailing her once more. It had been so nice to let go of her anxiety for a few hours with Mr. Waynford. Now that she would have to entertain Mr. Milburn, they came roaring back. She thought she could start being herself around Mr. Waynford, but what about the other gentleman, as Caroline so aptly put it?

Anna paused at the drawing room door, listening to the muffled voices inside. She realized how backwards her fears felt. She'd spent more time with Mr. Milburn than Mr. Waynford, after all. If she felt this relaxed around Mr. Waynford, surely she could handle an afternoon with Mr. Milburn.

"Are you ready to enter, Miss Harcourt?" asked the footman, waiting by the door with his hand poised on the knob. Anna braced herself with a deep, slow breath, and nodded.

As soon as she appeared in the doorway, Mr. Milburn jumped up from his seat by the sofa, beaming with cheer. "Miss Harcourt! I'm so glad we didn't miss each other." He rushed to Anna's side, barely giving her any time to get into the room. He picked up Anna's hand and placed it on his arm, leading her toward the sofa where Papa sat, looking as flustered as Anna felt.

Papa knew that Anna had been out with Mr. Waynford today, so seeing another guest would probably stretch her nerves. "Anna dear, why don't you sit next to me so you can tell me about your day?" he suggested just as Mr. Milburn stopped before the chair next to his, about to help Anna down into it. "My hearing is not the best, you see, Mr. Milburn."

Anna hid her giggle behind her hand as she sat next to Papa on the sofa, knowing that he and Mr. Milburn had just been chatting at about the same distance with no issue. Besides, Papa's hearing was perfectly fine. To his credit, Mr. Milburn nodded graciously and resumed his seat, positioning himself on the edge of the chair so the baron could supposedly hear him better.

"Lord Welsted tells me you visited the Royal Academy exhibits today," Mr. Milburn started. "Truly marvelous, is it not?"

"I wholeheartedly agree." A wave of relief washed over Anna. She should have no problem carrying on an interesting conversation now that she knew she and Mr. Milburn shared a common interest in the exhibits.

"Surely you visited the Hall of statues? I swear, it amazes me every time no matter how many times I've seen it." He sighed in awe. Anna's eyes widened.

"You enjoy the sculptures as well?"

"Absolutely!" he cried, his eyes latching on to Anna, shining with excitement. Or was it pride? Anna could not quite tell, though she sensed that Mr. Milburn was happy to impress her. She felt almost giddy at the thought that a gentleman wanted to impress her when she had spent all her time trying to get men to spare even a second glance in her direction.

"That is always Anna's favorite exhibit," Papa offered, watching the exchange with a bemused expression. When Mr. Milburn wasn't looking, he gave Anna an encouraging wink. Yes, Anna agreed with Papa's silent assessment. She would be able to handle herself in this conversation after all. At least, better than she usually did.

Mr. Milburn nodded wisely. "Of course it is. I would expect nothing less from a bright lady like you, Miss Harcourt. People get too caught up in all the paintings, but I find it impossible to enjoy them as much. You cannot even see half of them as they are either almost at your feet or almost on the ceiling."

"Indeed." Anna smiled as she thought back on the beautiful Great Room, every inch of wall space taken up by a talented artist's work. "I suppose that is why they put the best and most popular ones at eye level," she offered. "But they are all treasures if one looks closely enough."

"Too right you are," Mr. Milburn readily agreed. "Do you have a favorite painter, Miss Harcourt? I find Rembrandt's subjects to be fascinating."

Anna did not have a chance to answer Mr. Milburn's question as he gave a long, detailed explanation of his favorite Rembrandt works and his merits as a painter. Anna tried her best to listen contentedly, appreciating Mr. Milburn's enthusiasm as much as she could.

Soon, Anna's thoughts drifted off. She knew the gentleman would likely not notice, as long as she nodded here and there. As much as she wanted to be proper and respectful and give her guest the attention he deserved, Anna could not help thinking of Mr. Waynford and the wonderful time they'd had. She thought of the way his blue eyes grew deeper when he became fixated on a piece of art, the way his mouth drifted up at one corner while he analyzed, the way his brown hair rose and fell like the gentle waves of a calm sea.

"Anna, how did Mr. Waynford enjoy the exhibit?" Papa asked, tearing her away from her daydreams about her other gentleman. He gazed at his daughter knowingly. Mr. Milburn may not have noticed that Anna's thoughts had carried her far away from the drawing room, but Papa certainly had.

"Ah, you went with Mr. Waynford?" Mr. Milburn asked, surprised.

"Yes, he invited me last week at dinner," Anna reminded him gently.

"Yes, yes, of course. I remember now," Mr. Milburn chuckled awkwardly. "Goodness, I must have forgotten everything else after our lovely carriage ride a few days ago."

"It was lovely indeed," she quickly agreed, hoping to soothe the man. Of course, hearing about other suitors must not be terribly comfortable.

Turning her attention back to Papa, Anna said, "Mr. Waynford enjoyed it very much. He has quite the eye for detail."

"I am sure he does," Mr. Milburn added, a surprising tightness in his voice.

"Pardon?" Anna asked, not quite sure she'd heard correctly.

"It is nothing to trouble you with, Miss Harcourt. I know Mr. Waynford to be a very intelligent man, so it does not surprise me in the least that he is a lover of the arts, as we are."

Anna nodded slowly, still curious about Mr. Milburn's strange words, but glad to see that he bore no ill will to the man who was essentially his competitor. Only a man truly secure in himself would so readily compliment a rival.

"In fact," he mumbled, "I am quite glad he got to visit Somerset House. He truly does not deserve the position he's been put in, poor man."

This certainly caught both Anna's and Papa's attention. They exchanged concerned glances. "What could you mean by that, sir?" Papa asked cautiously, never one to enjoy prying into someone else's business.

"Goodness, I must have been thinking out loud again." Mr. Milburn let out a short, nervous laugh. "As you know, once I get started on a topic, I could go on forever and ever." His eyes darted between the baron and his daughter.

Anna might have suspected her suitor of attempting to bring his rival down in her estimation, but he really seemed to have let something slip unintentionally. She had certainly learned that the talkative Mr. Milburn rattled off information as easily as breathing.

Papa's eyes narrowed as he awaited a proper explanation from Mr. Milburn.

Realizing he would not get out of this easily, Mr. Milburn swallowed and continued. "I just meant to say that Mr. Waynford's father is not doing very well at the moment."

"Goodness, he never mentioned..." Anna's hand flew to her mouth in shock. She would have had no idea that the elder Mr. Waynford suffered from some sort of injury or ailment. He'd seemed perfectly fine at the dinner last week, but Anna knew that many illnesses could be invisible. The younger Mr. Waynford had also given no indication of his father's situation.

"I'm very sorry to hear that." Papa bowed his head. "We will be praying for the whole family."

Anna would have nodded her agreement, but she remained frozen in surprise. She wondered how long Mr. Waynford had known about his father's condition, whatever it was. The information painted every interaction with him in a different light. Even today, he had never let his worries or sadness show on his face, surely to keep from upsetting Anna or ruining a happy day.

"Please do not mention my mistake," Mr. Milburn pleaded. "It is still a sensitive subject for them and I know they are trying to put on brave faces."

Anna's heart sank at Mr. Milburn's request. She wished she could jump into the carriage that very minute and race to the Waynford home—as inappropriate as it would be for an unmarried lady to appear on a man's doorstep—and comfort him, say soothing words in his ear that might help him forget his pain for a moment.

She also did not want to risk bringing him more pain by talking about the situation before he was ready. In addition to praying for Mr. Waynford's father, she would pray that her own Mr. Waynford would soon feel comfortable enough to share these melancholy thoughts with her, to allow himself to lean on her.

Mr. Milburn bit his lip before bringing the conversation back to the safe topic of art. There was not much more to be said on the matter of Mr. Waynford's father, apparently, nor should any more be said. "Miss Harcourt, which pieces stood out most to you? I have not made my visit yet, but I will keep an eye out for any you deem worthy."

With great difficulty, Anna pulled her thoughts away from Mr. Waynford long enough to tell Mr. Milburn about the several landscape paintings they'd enjoyed. Though she had to admit that she appreciated the way Mr. Milburn worried for the other man, Anna could not stop thinking about just how strong Mr. Waynford was. He'd put on such a brave face that Anna would have never seen through it.

CHAPTER 8

*N*oah glowered out the window of the carriage as it rattled along toward the Harcourts' home. He certainly looked forward to the musicale and spending more time with Miss Harcourt, but he had not anticipated being trapped in such close quarters with his sisters for the whole ride.

Emma, his older sister, and Angelica, his younger, both sat across from him while their parents and husbands rode in another carriage, his nieces and nephews at home under the care of their governesses. Noah had insisted that they should ride with their husbands while he went with Mother and Father.

Clearly, Emma and Angelica had other plans for him. They'd claimed they wanted to share the carriage with Noah because they'd only just arrived in London a couple weeks ago and hadn't had a chance to see each other yet, Emma citing the fact that they had much to catch up on.

The only thing Noah's sisters seemed interested in catching up on was his relationship with Miss Harcourt. They'd spent the ride thus far bombarding him with their overlapping questions, filling the carriage with an almost unbearable level of noise.

He sighed as he ignored yet another inquiry, completely blocking it from his mind. Nothing he'd said so far had satisfied them, so they had ended up nagging him into sullen silence. Noah wished he'd been firmer about them riding with their husbands instead of him.

"Noah!" Emma's shrill voice finally broke through her brother's efforts to remain aloof. He did feel a little guilty for behaving so immaturely—but only a little.

"What is it, Emma?" Noah responded through gritted teeth, not removing his eyes from the window.

"Are you going to propose to Miss Harcourt?" she asked so calmly that she could have been asking Noah if he planned to buy a new hat.

Noah's head snapped around to face Emma. She had always been the most outspoken of the Waynford children and she'd badgered him even more than their parents about getting married and having children. Even Noah was shocked that she would be this frank.

"It is too soon for me to know. I will not make this decision lightly, even with all that is at stake," he muttered, his agitation showing through clearly.

Even as he said it, Noah felt a stirring in his heart, something that told him that he was closer to a decision than he'd let on, even to himself.

"Please do not fight," Angelica begged her older siblings with an exasperated sigh, always the peacemaker even though she'd thrown her fair share of questions at Noah. "I apologize for our prying, brother. We just want to get to know the woman who might soon be our sister."

As he usually did when Angelica intervened, Noah softened. "I am sorry as well for being so harsh earlier. I know you have the best intentions, even if you have strange ways of showing them." He shot a playful glare to Emma who scrunched her nose at him.

Emma might be two years his senior, married for ten years to Mr. Reuben Brett, and a mother of three, but when she visited Noah, they always managed to revert to their childish teasing. Angelica, though only twenty-four, had married Josias Simonds, Baron of Simondsby, and already had two sons. She did not stoop to their old antics as often as her older siblings, kindly reminding them that a baroness should behave a little more maturely.

They watched him expectantly, their faces almost perfect mirrors of his own only with softer, more feminine features. No matter how they frustrated him, Noah would always adore them. He decided to finally end their suffering.

"Now, do not start making any wedding plans yet, but I will admit that I am growing quite attached to Miss Harcourt. As I said earlier, however, there is still more to discover before I can be sure that we will be a good lifelong match."

Emma sighed haughtily, which only served to annoy Noah again. She still seemed displeased with his answer. "You always were quite the pragmatic one," she laughed. "Take it from me, Noah. Love and marriage are not always about pragmatism, even in a situation like this. You have a heart, you know. You've spent all these years claiming you've followed it, so do not ignore it now."

Noah bit his lip in frustration. "Thank you, my wise sister. I know you are an expert on all things marriage related."

"I mean it, Noah," Emma pressed on, a sudden sincerity in her voice. "You really must be quite fond of Miss Harcourt since your letters did not talk much about any of the other ladies Father has tried to introduce you to. And goodness knows he has tried."

Noah fell silent again while Angelica chuckled. "Emma does make an excellent point," she chirped.

He looked out the window again in a huff. He recognized this row of homes. They were almost there. "Please do not make a fuss out of this at the musicale. I already have a hard enough time keeping Father in line."

Emma and Angelica exchanged sympathetic glances. "We will be on our best behavior," Emma promised solemnly, putting her hand over her heart.

Noah leaned back in his seat. He trusted his sisters to keep their word. It was Father he had doubts about.

Indeed, as the butler led the couples upstairs to the music room, Noah walking alone behind them, Father stopped and grasped his elbow. Pulling him down to whisper in his ear, Father said, "You must make a lot of progress with Miss Harcourt tonight, Noah. You are running out of time to secure her affections. I know Mr. Milburn has shown quite a bit of interest as well, and as the news continues to spread, surely more gentlemen will be after her."

Noah did not keep his sigh to himself this time. "Father, I am painfully aware of our circumstances. I assure you I am doing my best, so please allow me to handle it my way."

Father nodded with a sad frown. "I know, son. I'm sorry," he mumbled as they stepped into the Harcourts' music room. Noah looked down at his Father, the man he'd once idolized for his strength and confidence. Now he grew older and frailer by the day, especially with this new stress weighing him down.

Guilt twisted Noah's stomach into knots. "I know you are just trying to help." He put a gentle hand on his father's shoulder, suddenly acutely aware of how fragile, how human he seemed. Father gave a smile that did not convey any sense of happiness as he put his hand over Noah's.

Noah only wished that repairing the family fortune did

not have to fall so squarely on his shoulders, especially since he had not destroyed them. He quickly shook his head, banishing that thought to the farthest corner of his mind. He could not hold that over Father's head forever. The older man had apologized many times over. Noah could see in the deepening lines of his face and the difficulty with which he smiled now that he would carry this guilt for the rest of his life. Noah did not need to make it any worse. This was his reality now and he needed to accept it once and for all.

"I have everything under control, Father. I promise. You raised me to never give up, after all," he whispered warmly.

"The Waynfords are here." Noah heard a lovely voice call their name. He looked up to see Miss Harcourt curtsying before coming toward them. She smiled so kindly, excited to see him. Her eyes swept over his family and she looked just as pleased to see them all.

Noah's heart relaxed. "Everything is perfectly fine," he whispered to Father again, feeling the truth of his words in his bones.

The Waynford family bowed and curtsied to Miss Harcourt and her parents, who followed close behind. Even as he bowed, Noah did not take his eyes off her. She radiated serene beauty in her white dress, a green sash tied around her waist, her hair done in a simple but elegant style that left a few curled strands to frame her soft face.

Everyone exchanged happy greetings as Father introduced their party. All the while, Noah remained captivated by Miss Harcourt. He could not deny that he'd been thinking about their outing at Somerset House, replaying it over and over again in his mind—though not much of the artwork had made a lasting impression. Instead, he thought about Miss Harcourt's curious expression as she offered her opinions on the art, and especially when she'd spoken of the sculptures.

He'd felt a true connection in the Hall. Miss Harcourt had

a wonderful, intelligent mind. He also knew from their walk by the Serpentine that she had a kind, selfless heart that made him think he'd met an angel on Earth.

Noah silently scolded himself as he felt a rare blush threaten to spread across his cheeks. He recalled Miss Harcourt wiping the mud off his face with her handkerchief and the way he'd sat so close to her in the Hall of statues, his lips nearly touching her forehead as he'd adjusted her hair.

What was he, a silly schoolboy experiencing the first flutters of his heart? Noah hoped he could keep those memories away or else this night would turn out to be torturous.

As Miss Harcourt caught his eye, her eyebrows darting up in a silent question, Noah realized that perhaps he really was experiencing the first of something.

He gave a firm nod in response. Miss Harcourt smiled so warmly, almost amused. He wondered if she could read his thoughts on his face and suddenly felt mortified at the idea of being so obvious when even he was not ready to put a name to his feelings. Noah had always been the one who read people, not the other way around. Yet somehow, Noah felt that perhaps Miss Harcourt could match his skills when she wanted to. Still, he refused to get anyone's hopes up until he was more certain of his eventual course of action.

"Please feel free to talk amongst yourselves or take refreshments. We are still waiting on a few more guests before we start the entertainment," Lord Welsted announced in his quiet way.

Noah turned his attention to the baron, who stood apart from the group, observing the interactions as his wife effortlessly engaged their guests in conversation. Clearly Miss Harcourt had inherited her coloring from her mother, as the baron had dark blond hair and green eyes, but her gentle nature came from her father. He knew from the few times he'd seen them together that all the family members were kind, respectable people.

"Would anyone like to join me for refreshments?" Miss Harcourt asked, shyly lifting her empty glass.

"I think we should be off to claim our seats," Angelica responded, looping her arm through Emma's. "We are both so short, you see, so we always try to sit where we will be able to see."

Noah's bottom lip jutted out, impressed by Angelica's quick thinking. Emma looked like she wanted to protest, but a knowing look from Angelica told her to go quietly. Reuben and Josias followed behind their wives as they walked down the row of chairs toward the small stage.

"Lady Welsted and I were just discussing her beautiful flower arrangements," Mother said with subdued excitement. Noah was glad to see that the ladies had something in common that would keep them occupied for quite a while.

"Indeed, I was just about to ask Lord Welsted about his thoughts on that strange style the fashionable set is wearing these days." Father stepped closer to the baron, his hands clasped before him. As subtly as he could, Father wiggled his fingers at Noah, shooing him.

Noah turned to Miss Harcourt with a gentlemanly smile. "I suddenly find myself in great need of a glass of punch."

"Right this way." Miss Harcourt nodded understandingly, leading Noah to the back of the room toward a long table covered in a bright white cloth, trays upon trays of gleaming silver platters spread out with all kinds of delicious meats, fruits, cheeses, nuts, and more glasses of punch than Noah could ever need.

He hadn't expected that something as simple as a musicale could look so elegant, or perhaps he had slowly started to adjust himself to the thought of a different lifestyle—a lifestyle without expensive silverware and expensive dishes and expensive entertainment. That desperate part of his mind told him that if Miss Harcourt did come from such lavish surroundings, perhaps the whispers around London about her dowry were true after all.

Noah shook his head, forcing those thoughts away. Not now. He wanted to enjoy his evening with Miss Harcourt without those worries, just as he had at the Royal Academy. He hadn't thought about his mission once while they'd worked their way through Somerset House. All that had seemed so distant and inconsequential—until, of course, Noah found himself alone in the carriage that he'd been wondering if they should sell.

"Are you well, Mr. Waynford?" Miss Harcourt asked, an unexpected weight in the question. Noah returned his attention to her, reminding himself once more that he'd been looking forward to this night since they'd received the invitation last week—and not just because he loved musicales.

"Yes, quite well." He coughed, taking a rushed sip of his drink, hoping to wash away his concerns.

"I'm glad to hear it." She smiled, but the expression contained a sadness that only brought Noah's concerns rushing back. Had he done something wrong? Had she heard something? "I hope you know that I am always praying for the best for you and your family," she whispered, her eyes dropping to the glass in her hands.

"Thank you, Miss Harcourt. That is very kind of you. I do the same for you and your family as well," Noah responded, trying to keep the confusion out of his voice. He wondered at the strangeness in her tone and expression.

Noah could not wonder long, however, as the room slowly filled with more guests looking for seats, eating, and chatting with each other. Soon, Noah and Miss Harcourt stood shoulder to shoulder by the refreshment table as more people came to fill up their plates with food.

Every time their arms brushed against each other, Noah felt some kind of current pass between them. His heart beat a little faster with every slight, accidental touch. They slowly sipped at their glasses of punch, exchanging observations about the room and the new guests as they arrived. As they spoke, Noah noticed Miss Harcourt glance down a few times to smooth out her skirt, or her hand dart up to pat her perfectly styled hair.

It dawned on Noah that she must be nervous about her appearance. He felt like a fool for not realizing it earlier. He turned so sharply to face Miss Harcourt that he felt a small splash of punch land on his glove. Startled, she stared up at him with big, lovely, curious eyes.

"Your glove—"

"You are…" Noah interrupted, searching for some way to finish his sentence that would adequately describe what he felt at that moment.

"Anna, there you are. Mr. Waynford, so glad you could come tonight," Mr. Dalton Harcourt called out to them, approaching with the customary bounce in his step. He smiled cheerfully as he stopped before them, clearly already enjoying the evening. "How are you—" he started to ask Noah, but his eyes darted from his sister to Noah and back again.

Mr. Harcourt's expression faltered. He seemed to realize that he'd interrupted something. He looked over his shoulder from the direction he'd come. "Ah, I think I've heard someone call for me. I'll save a seat for you both in the front." The young man turned on his heel and strode away, disappearing as quickly as he'd come.

The interruption had cost Noah all his nerve. His head swirled and everything in the room seemed to be flying around him—everything except Miss Harcourt.

"What were you about to say, Mr. Waynford?" Miss Harcourt asked, a hopeful gleam in her eyes.

Noah cleared his throat. "...beautiful. This room is beautiful. That's what I was trying to say," he lied, his stomach already in knots from the guilt. He'd taken the coward's way out.

If she was disappointed at all, Miss Harcourt hid it well. She looked around the grand music room. "I agree. I really should take more time to appreciate it. It is such a lovely room, even if I see it almost every day when we're in London. I'm afraid I've become rather used to it. But you are right. It's beautiful."

Miss Harcourt brought her focus back to Noah, looking him squarely in the eye before continuing. "It would be such a terrible tragedy to take life's beauties for granted, no matter how simple or mundane they may be."

Noah smiled, his heart melting. Her words resonated deeply, even more so now that Noah faced the possibility of losing all the common beauties he'd been accustomed to. He wished he hadn't waited to appreciate them until it was almost too late. He longed to hear more of her wisdom and insights, to see the beauty of the world through her eyes.

"You are absolutely right, of course," Noah mumbled almost in awe. Miss Harcourt's small smile could not hide her pride and happiness.

Lady Welsted approached on her light, gliding steps, looking every bit the generous and warm hostess. "You'd best take your seats now," she suggested, waving them off toward the chairs. "The musicale will be starting soon." The baroness hurried off to warn the remaining guests who still milled about the room.

Noah and Miss Harcourt walked together through the rows of chairs, spotting Mr. Harcourt in the second row from the front. He turned as they approached and nodded to the empty seats next to him. Noah noticed his family seated on the opposite side of the aisle, a few rows further back. He glanced at them, uncertain if he really should be sitting apart from his family.

Emma caught his eye and glared at him, giving a sharp shake of her head while Angelica smiled encouragingly. Mother wore an expression of reserved hopefulness while Father nodded so enthusiastically that Noah feared his few remaining strands of gray hair, already stretched perilously thin across the top of his head, would fly right off.

That settled it. Noah followed Miss Harcourt to the row her brother occupied, giving a small wave to the adjacent row where her father and another young lady sat. Based on the sparkle in her eyes and the charmingly arrogant expression on her face, Noah guessed she must be the sister Miss Harcourt had spoken of before, the one she loved despite their often frustrating relationship.

Mr. Harcourt, seated at the end of the row by the aisle, stood and gestured for Noah and his sister to take the inner seats. Miss Harcourt went first, gracefully tucking her skirts around her legs to make more room for everyone. Noah slipped in next to her while Mr. Harcourt resumed his seat at the end on Noah's other side. The room suddenly felt much hotter as he realized how close they were, as close as they had been on that bench at Somerset House. Noah tugged at his cravat, hoping to get some relief from the heat that engulfed him, but he knew the attempt was futile. He could not escape the heat, not if he planned to stay near Miss Harcourt.

Another sensation soon signaled to Noah that a pair of eyes watched him from afar. He peered around the room for a moment before finally spotting the culprit. The young lady seated by Lord and Lady Welsted stared at him with her strange light brown eyes that were not quite hazel, giving her elegantly sharp features even more intensity.

Noah leaned closer to Miss Harcourt, his heart doing an impressive flip when his knuckles accidentally brushed against the back of her hand. "Is that young lady on the other side your younger sister?" he whispered, noticing the way his breath moved a dark brown tendril of hair that hung loose by Miss Harcourt's ear.

Miss Harcourt sighed knowingly, not bothering to look in the direction he'd indicated. "Yes, that would be Caroline. Is she staring at you?"

Noah chuckled at the fond exasperation in Miss Harcourt's voice. "Indeed she is. I hope I have not done something to offend her."

"No, I'm sure you haven't. She is simply a curious, friendly creature—friendly to all but me, it seems. She's been eager to catch a glimpse of you. She claims my unimaginative descriptions give her nothing to work with."

"Ah, so you speak of me often?" Noah narrowed his eyes teasingly as Miss Harcourt's widened.

"Of course I do," she said hurriedly. "I often talk about the lovely trips we go on, though Caroline finds our topics of conversation to be too dull for her taste."

Noah nodded approvingly, his chest swelling with a surprising amount of satisfaction. Surely Miss Harcourt must be quite fond of him, too, if she spoke about him to her family. "Unfortunately, not everyone is as sophisticated as we are." He lowered his voice conspiratorially, wearing a sly half-smile.

"Oh, goodness!" Miss Harcourt covered her mouth with her hand as laughter rippled through her. "Do not let Caroline hear you say that. I'm afraid it would not end well for you. In Caroline's opinion, she is the epitome of sophistication."

Noah's eyebrows shot up as he glanced over at Miss Caroline. "Could she really do that much damage?"

"Her sharp tongue can deliver quite a lashing when provoked." Miss Harcourt shuddered. "She begged Mama and Papa to allow her to attend the musicale tonight and she promised to be on her best behavior, so hopefully she will keep that promise. Though she is not usually one for causing a scene among guests—just her poor, defenseless family."

Noah chuckled as he watched the younger Harcourt daughter, now facing forward, eyes glued to the small stage. Her chin tilted up ever so slightly, her shoulders pulled back elegantly. Despite her regal air, Miss Caroline did look quite capable of causing mischief.

"And has she passed the test so far?" Noah asked.

Miss Harcourt laughed again, this time forgetting to stifle the sound with her hand. It rang in Noah's ears, so lovely and free. Miss Harcourt looked around sheepishly, hoping that no one else had heard.

"Our definitions of what constitutes best behavior can differ quite wildly," she continued in a whisper. "But I shall give credit where credit is due. Caroline has been doing quite well, aside from her brief battle with Mama about her hair."

Noah saw what Miss Harcourt meant. Though her dress complimented her older sister's, Miss Caroline had chosen a far more elaborate hairstyle, tiny jewels shining within her black tresses. In fact, a quick glance about the room told Noah that the young lady's hair far outdid every other woman's.

"She'd asked the maid to put her hair in that complex style and by the time Mama saw it and demanded Caroline simplify, Caroline argued that it was far too late to change it," Miss Harcourt continued, her exasperation evident.

"I must admit, that is quite a clever plan," Noah offered.

"Yes, if only Caroline could put her cleverness to a use

other than vexing people," said Mr. Harcourt, catching their conversation. "I told Mama and Papa not to let her come tonight. Now that she's had this little taste of freedom, it will be nearly impossible to keep her contained until she debuts next Season." He shook his head with an exaggerated frown.

"You are probably right." Miss Harcourt chuckled ruefully. "But in the end it will be worth it to see the sheer joy on Caroline's face tonight."

Noah admired the warmth in Miss Harcourt's words, her ability to see positives in seemingly any situation.

Mr. Harcourt scoffed playfully at his older sister. "I'll leave you to handle Miss Caroline's moods when Mama and Papa refuse to grant the rest of her requests."

Miss Harcourt glared at her younger brother. "I'm afraid I'm going to be quite busy with Mr. Waynford, as we have many exciting plans that I absolutely must not miss."

Mr. Harcourt let out a hearty laugh. Noah joined in, once again impressed with Miss Harcourt's wit. He hoped she was sincere in her desire to spend more time with him. Something deep inside him told Noah that they would never run out of interesting things to do or discuss. They could make anything entertaining, insightful, and meaningful.

Noah's laugh stopped abruptly. He covered his lapse with a cough, brushing aside the Harcourts' concerns. His latest revelation had nearly frozen him in his tracks. Perhaps Miss Harcourt had been the one making progress with Noah rather than the other way around.

"Good evening Mr. Harcourt, Miss Harcourt...Mr. Waynford." Another voice joined their conversation. Noah's jaw clenched instinctively with surprising force. "Miss Harcourt and I have quite a few plans ourselves, do we not?" Mr. Milburn took the seat on the other side of Miss Harcourt, watching her intently though his smile was pleasant enough.

"Yes, indeed," Miss Harcourt admitted, shooting a

nervous glance to Noah. "You see, Dalton? I shall not fall victim to your follies." She teased her brother with ease, though Noah sensed a shift in her demeanor. She seemed a little more tense, her spine a little straighter, and her smile a little tighter.

Or did Noah only see what he wanted to see? He pursed his lips as he watched Miss Harcourt shift her attention to the newcomer, asking after him as any polite person would do. Noah swore he could see something missing in her eyes as she looked at Mr. Milburn, something he saw when she looked at him—a spark of happiness.

Of course, Noah's growing infatuation could simply be telling him that there could be no way Miss Harcourt felt as comfortable with Mr. Milburn, or anyone else for that matter. He could be fooling himself into imagining signs of her preference for him.

The thought made Noah's chest squeeze with pain, making it harder for him to breathe, as if a weight crushed him from the inside out. Yet as soon as Miss Harcourt turned back to him, smiling excitedly as she informed him the music would start at any moment, the pain subsided.

Noah was shocked at how much better he felt when her eyes found his—and how bitter he felt when he thought of her forming an even more meaningful connection with another gentleman. He'd only just admitted to his sisters that he was developing feelings for Miss Harcourt. He just hadn't expected them to grow so quickly and with such force.

"I must thank you once again for inviting me. I'm so very fond of music. I've been looking forward to a good musicale all Season and I have no doubt the Harcourts will put on a wonderful event." Mr. Milburn's voice grated at Noah's ears. He felt so foolish for being so annoyed at a man who really had done nothing wrong. Noah could not even judge Mr.

Milburn's motives for pursuing Miss Harcourt since they were not too different from his own.

Noah pushed those thoughts away, determined to enjoy the evening despite this unwanted addition. He must not think about his situation. When he pondered it for too long, when he saw Miss Harcourt's innocent, trusting face, Noah felt sick. Even if he truly had become attached to her, couldn't the argument be made that he was still deceiving her?

Mr. Harcourt, having gamely engaged Mr. Milburn in conversation, managed to let the man know the music would begin soon. He turned forward, the movement distracting Noah from his distressing thoughts. He glanced over at the younger man, who gave him a tight smile. Again, Noah found comfort in the fact that he seemed to be the preferred suitor amongst the Harcourt family as well.

When the music began, Noah allowed himself to relax, enjoying the entertainment, absorbing the peaceful atmosphere radiating from Miss Harcourt. For now, all that mattered to Noah was the beautiful melodies floating to him from the stage from a variety of talented musicians including a string quartet, a harpist, and a vocal performance accompanied by pianoforte.

Of course, whenever Noah realized again how close he and Miss Harcourt sat, the heat returned to his body in full force, as if he stood outside under the brightest sun. To Noah's great relief, everyone was too focused on the performances to pay him and his anxiety any mind.

As illogical as it seemed, Miss Harcourt caused great agitation in Noah's nerves, but every sight of her sent a gentle wave of calm over him. Joy lit her face, a small smile gracing her lips. She often leaned forward slightly as if trying to get even closer to the music, to allow it to envelop her. Though Noah returned his attention to the music, he always maintained some awareness of Miss Harcourt by his side.

As the current piece came to an end, Miss Harcourt leaned close. "How are you enjoying the evening so far?" she whispered.

"I am enjoying it immensely," he assured her. He certainly did appreciate the excellent music. Miss Harcourt made it even better. Noah silently hoped that they would have a chance, perhaps during the mid-musicale break, to discuss their thoughts on the pieces and performances.

All too soon, Miss Harcourt turned away from Noah and posed the same question to Mr. Milburn. Before Noah could get too carried away with his displeasure, the music started again with a romantic, lilting pianoforte piece.

Noah allowed himself to be swept away again, partially for the enjoyment of the music and partially so he could gather his opinions for later discussion with Miss Harcourt.

To Noah's pleasant surprise, the intermission arrived in what felt like no time at all—a true testament to the skill of the musicians. When Noah shifted in his seat to ask Miss Harcourt if she would like to join him for another glass of punch, he found her already being led away by Mr. Milburn.

"Would you like to chat with the lord and lady?" Mr. Harcourt asked, a hint of consolation in his voice. "They greatly admire your intellect and I'm sure they would love to hear your thoughts on the musicale thus far. Despite how she acts, Mama has been quite anxious about its success."

Noah looked back at Miss Harcourt, chatting kindly with Mr. Milburn. "I should like that very much," he agreed, stifling his reluctance.

"Mr. Waynford, I trust the entertainment is to your taste?" Lady Welsted asked as the two men approached.

"Of course, my lady." Noah bowed to his hostess, hoping to alleviate some of her nerves. Though she carried herself with confidence and grace and managed the evening with expertise, Noah could see what Mr. Harcourt had meant now that he knew what to look for. The baroness's gloved fingers twisted around each other. Her smile was trapped somewhere between hope and dread.

Lord Welsted, on the other hand, looked more anxious about the guests slowly creeping closer, no doubt eager to make a positive impression on their host. They seemed not to realize that the best impression they could make would mean allowing the baron to seek them out at his own pace.

The more Noah watched Miss Harcourt's family, and her parents in particular, the more he could see where the lady got quite a few of her traits. Her generous heart, Noah knew, was all her own.

"Allow me to introduce you to our other daughter, Miss Caroline Harcourt." Lord Welsted latched onto Noah's presence. Noah could see the hope in his eyes that the other guests would give him space now that he'd joined a conversation with someone else.

"A pleasure to meet you, Miss Caroline." Noah bowed his head to the young lady. She offered him a curtsy that had been practiced to perfection.

"How lovely to finally meet you, Mr. Waynford." She smiled knowingly, but the expression was not devious or mean-spirited. In fact, Noah thought he saw a glimmer of hope in her eyes.

Yes, Noah remembered what Miss Harcourt had said about her sister. Despite her stubborn ways and sometimes overly prideful attitude, the young lady possessed a kind heart that truly wanted the best for others—even if she put herself on a pedestal at times. As different as they were, the sisters had at least that much in common.

Despite only knowing Miss Caroline for a few minutes, Noah somehow found himself hoping that he would not disappoint her. As the family slipped into pleasant conversation, he looked over his shoulder, searching for Miss Harcourt. She now stood by the back wall near the table of food, nodding politely as Mr. Milburn prattled on about something. As if sensing his gaze, Miss Harcourt's eyes met his. She gave an apologetic smile that eased Noah's heart ever so slightly.

"Mr. Waynford?" A polite, lilting voice forced Noah to pull his gaze from Miss Harcourt. "Have you been enjoying getting to know the Harcourts?" Miss Caroline asked with an almost imperceptible lift of an eyebrow.

Lord Welsted cleared his throat, giving his daughter a pointed look. "Caroline, I think it might be getting a bit late for you."

Miss Caroline whirled around to her mother. "Mama, I am not tired at all."

Noah chuckled, giving the young woman a helping hand. "I am enjoying it very much, Miss Caroline. Everyone has been so kind and welcoming."

She turned back to Noah with a beaming smile, perhaps thanking him for indulging her and proving to her father that she was simply being friendly.

"You two should head back to your seats now," Lord Welsted suggested to Noah and Mr. Harcourt. "The next half will be starting soon." Noah did not miss the firm glance he gave his younger daughter and the placating smile he gave his wife.

As he and Mr. Harcourt returned to their seats, Noah stole a glance at his family. He breathed a sigh of relief when he saw that they chatted with each other and the nearby guests cheerfully, enjoying themselves—and blissfully unaware of him for once.

Before resuming his seat, Noah found Miss Harcourt once more, slowly making her way back with Mr. Milburn by her side. By some miracle, the other gentleman melted away from Noah's awareness. All he could focus on was the fact that Miss Harcourt still seemed to be searching for him, too.

A DIFFERENT BUT still pleasant sound filled the music room, the sound of chairs moving, feet shuffling on the rug, content voices chatting. The musicale had come to a triumphant end. Noah still heard the last few notes ringing in his ears, washing over him. He always felt uplifted by beautiful art and good company. Even Mr. Milburn could not take that from him. Now, if only Noah could steal that long awaited moment with Miss Harcourt.

Just as he turned to her, Mr. Milburn stood from his chair, looking determined to monopolize her attention yet again. Before he could open his mouth, Mr. Harcourt stood as well.

"Mr. Milburn, I would greatly appreciate it if you could join me for a drink. I've been eager to discuss the performances with you since I know how fond you are of music." The gentleman's brow furrowed for a fraction of a second before graciously accepting Mr. Harcourt's friendly invitation.

"Miss Harcourt, may I introduce you to my sisters?" Noah quickly offered, determined not to let Mr. Milburn block him again—or to waste Mr. Harcourt's assistance.

The young woman glanced nervously from Noah to the row where his family sat to Mr. Milburn. Her eyes lingered on the viscount's son for a moment. "That would be lovely, Mr. Waynford."

Noah would have rather found a quiet corner to talk, just the two of them, but she seemed in need of rescuing so this would have to do. Besides, he would have to introduce her to his sisters eventually. Perhaps it would be better to get that out of the way sooner rather than later.

Mr. Harcourt stepped out of the way to let them pass, immediately closing the distance between himself and Mr. Milburn once Noah and his sister had made it into the aisle. "Did you have a particular favorite?" Mr. Harcourt asked the gentleman, wasting no time in leading him toward the back of the room.

Noah smiled to himself as he and Miss Harcourt made their way through the crowd of guests who lingered in the aisle. Her brother was quite an observant and thoughtful man. Hopefully, Noah would have a chance to thank him for all his help at some point in the near future.

Emma and Angelica barely waited for introductions before they began to gush about the wonderful entertainment, immediately pulling Miss Harcourt into their little group so they could praise her family for hosting such a lovely evening.

"Miss Harcourt, you must tell me where Lord and Lady Welsted found that amazing string quartet. I'm sure I will hire them if Josias and I ever host a musicale," Angelica insisted, her eyes glowing with genuine curiosity as well as a desire to make Miss Harcourt feel comfortable.

"I cannot help noticing that you, Lady Welsted, and your sister all wear such lovely gowns," Emma chimed in, grasping Miss Harcourt's hands as if they'd been friends for years. "My modiste has recently retired and I've found that I just do not like her replacement as much. Would you mind telling me where you ladies have your dresses made? This beading is exquisite."

Noah watched Miss Harcourt carefully, her eyes glancing from Angelica to Emma and back again as they fired their questions and compliments at her. He took a step forward, prepared to intervene. The poor young woman looked quite nervous to be conversing with these loquacious ladies. Much to Noah's relief, Miss Harcourt's expression soon softened into a smile. Though still overwhelmed, she appeared more relaxed by the moment. He sensed that she really was glad to be part of the conversation now that she realized her new companions were friendly, if a tad overzealous.

This was a very good sign indeed. Miss Harcourt and his family would surely get along very well, unlike some families Noah knew where the in-laws barely tolerated each other. Noah turned away from the rest of the group, keeping his expression hidden. His brows knit together in deep thought.

He still needed to be sure that they would get along well enough first before worrying about everyone else. Or, perhaps, did he already know deep down that they would make a good match despite his insistence that he needed more time to fall in love?

A tap on his shoulder startled Noah out of his thoughts, reminding him that this was not an ideal place to work out these important questions. He turned to see Josias, Angelica's husband, looking at him with a mischievous smile.

"My apologies," Noah coughed. "My thoughts must have drifted."

Josias elbowed Emma's husband, Reuben, in the side, pulling him into the conversation. "We are very familiar with that look on dear Noah's face, are we not?" the young baron whispered. Noah's brothers-in-law shared a meaningful glance that told him he would soon receive another one of their well-intentioned but not always useful lessons.

"Certainly, Josias," Reuben enthusiastically agreed, thankfully keeping his voice low enough that only the three of them could hear. He tilted his head toward Miss Harcourt.

"Yes, as I am sure you have heard from my wonderful

sisters, Father introduced me to Miss Harcourt as our possible savior," Noah sighed.

Reuben and Josias shared another look. Noah gritted his teeth, not looking forward to whatever would come next. "Your expressions all night have told us a different story," Reuben whispered conspiratorially. "It seems to us that she is not just a possible match, but the *only* match. I daresay, she is the only woman in the room as far as you're concerned."

Noah smiled tightly. "She is the only woman I am courting in this room at the moment." He failed to keep the frustration out of his voice.

"Come now, brother, we are just teasing." Josias put a hand on Noah's shoulder, smiling ruefully. After having known each other for many years, they had all discovered each other's limits when it came to playful, brotherly antagonizing. Josias seemed to realize that Noah was dangerously close to his limit.

"Do think about what we said, though," Reuben added. "Sometimes others can see it better than you can." His eyes drifted to Emma and Noah's irritation subsided slightly. His brothers-in-law did know a thing or two about falling in love.

"And please do not tell our wives we bothered you," Josias whispered quickly. "I love Angelica, but we know she is the scariest of them all when she gets angry." He chuckled fondly at his memories of crossing Angelica and—usually rightfully —earning her ire.

"This will stay between us," Noah promised. "I do not want to see you a broken man." He patted Josias on the arm, knowing full well that beneath Angelica's calm and sweet demeanor she had a truly fearsome temper when she'd reached her own limits of aggravation.

Reuben and Josias left Noah to his own devices, engaging Mother and Father in conversation while Noah lingered near the ladies. He tried to listen as Miss Harcourt talked about a piece she particularly enjoyed. The tension building up in Noah's shoulders, traveling all the way up to his temples, made it difficult for him to stay. His brothers' words rang in his head, distracting him from everything else.

He had hoped to spend more time discussing music with Miss Harcourt, getting to know her better, but it seemed that part of the evening had ended. "Please excuse me. I must step outside for some fresh air," he mumbled to the group. Miss Harcourt's brows turned up in surprise.

As Noah made his way through the Harcourts' lovely townhouse, he just felt more muddled. "Why does everyone keep pushing me in this direction?" he asked himself as he went. "If this is where I am meant to go, I must come to that conclusion for myself."

Even if he had a particular goal in mind, did he still not have a right to choose a wife who suited him? There was the matter of Mr. Milburn as well. The other man had tried to keep Miss Harcourt to himself all night, which had put a dent in Noah's ability to discover more about the woman he might marry one day. Her unusual flips in behavior had nearly stopped since their trip to Somerset House, but Noah still needed to know more.

Yet his developing feelings certainly made Noah curious to see where this would go. He'd thought that he would be able to take his time falling in love, to be sure of himself and his intended. Now, a time limit dictated his pace. How could he be sure that his feelings for Miss Harcourt came from a place of genuine love rather than a place of desperation?

Noah knew by now that he found Miss Harcourt to be quite charming, but charm would not be enough to make a successful marriage. He did not want his earnest desire to find a solution to his family's debts to influence his heart into making a decision he would spend his whole life regretting.

So, Noah wondered as his anxious energy propelled him through the front doors, would he regret Miss Harcourt?

Once outside in the cool air of the night, Noah felt less claustrophobic. The gentle breeze restored him, eased his mind. The questions did not leave so easily, however. He knew he would have no choice but to confront them directly, and that time rapidly approached.

He was so accustomed to being in command of his thoughts and emotions, of having a clear head. This confusion he'd been thrown into unsettled him—so much so that he'd run away from a little harmless teasing from his brothers-in-law.

After glancing up and down the quiet street to ensure no one was nearby, Noah leaned back against the stone banister of the Harcourts' front steps. His head fell back and he stared up at the night sky, getting lost for a few minutes in the simple but magical beauty of the stars.

"Mr. Waynford?"

Noah whirled around, standing up straight like a proper gentleman. Miss Harcourt waited at the top of the stairs, watching him with concern. Noah had gotten so lost in his easy, uncomplicated thoughts about the stars that he hadn't heard her approach.

"Miss Harcourt," Noah mumbled, trying to gather his wits. "What brings you out here?"

She gave a bemused smile. "You, of course."

Noah's heart resumed that painfully rapid pace, familiar yet still exciting. Miss Harcourt looked radiant under the pale light from the stars above, like an angel sent down from the heavens just for him.

"You mustn't worry about me," he insisted quickly, her concern filling him with a light, bubbly warmth. "I just needed some time to myself to...ponder the music."

Miss Harcourt came down the steps, her eyes lowered to

watch her footing while her hand carefully hovered over the banister. She was the epitome of gentle grace. "I was actually quite looking forward to asking you about your thoughts," she said as she took the last step, standing before Noah, her eyes drifting up to meet his.

Her words made Noah far happier than he'd expected. To know that she too valued his insights, enjoyed their conversation, sent Noah into a dizzying spin that was both foreign and comfortable all at once. They quickly settled into an entertaining, insightful discussion of the musicale, both Noah and Mis Harcourt equally sharing their delights.

"If you could choose only one favorite, which would it be?" Noah asked, feeling a little devilish.

"How could you pose such a question to me, sir?" Miss Harcourt gasped in exaggerated shock. "You know it is impossible to choose a favorite amongst so many magnificent performances," she scolded gently, trying her best to look stern despite the smile twitching at the corner of mouth.

"Such a terrible burden you bear, Miss Harcourt. But if anyone can bear it, I'm sure it is you." Noah bowed his head solemnly, also finding himself unable to completely banish his smile.

After a few moments of deep and serious thought, Miss Harcourt sighed with a wistful smile. "If I absolutely had to pick a favorite," she started, raising an eyebrow at Noah who nodded firmly, "it must be the harpist."

Noah lifted his fingers to his chin in a thoughtful pose. "Interesting, very interesting. And why might that be?"

"Goodness, not only do you force my hand in choosing my favorite performance, but now you ask me to explain why?" Miss Harcourt covered her heart with her hand, looking quite scandalized now.

"Surely that is a natural follow-up question, is it not?"

Noah asked, his skin tingling either from the cool night breeze or from this stimulating, humorous little debate with Miss Harcourt—or perhaps both.

The more he came to know her, the more Noah admired her sharpness of wit and her playful humor. He suspected that only a lucky few had allowed Miss Harcourt the time she needed to show them beyond her quiet, reserved nature. Noah's chest swelled with pride. He considered himself to be one of those very lucky few.

Miss Harcourt shook her head in faux disappointment. "If you insist…"

"I do."

The lady's smile took up nearly half her face as she stared at Noah, glowing brighter than any star he'd ever seen. "Do you truly have no compassion for my poor nerves?" she asked teasingly.

"I am afraid I do not." Noah gave a remorseful frown. "Now, stop delaying, Miss Harcourt."

"Ahh, yes, I do digress. My apologies," she said with a wry smile. Noah could see from the sparkle in her eyes that Miss Harcourt rather enjoyed this banter, the way they could jest while knowing that they both remained perfectly comfortable. Indeed, Noah could not remember the last time he'd had such a refreshing conversation that challenged his intellect and entertained him at the same time.

"I find it so difficult to describe why the harpist captured my heart so, but I shall try my best. For you." Miss Harcourt flashed a shy smile to Noah, dropping her gaze to her fingers, nervously pinching at the white fabric of her dress.

Noah did not mind the loss of eye contact. Those words were enough to make him a jittery mess, too. Would he ever become used to this strange feeling Miss Harcourt produced in him? Would he be able to convince himself that this feeling had a name?

"Do not do it just for me, Miss Harcourt. Do it for yourself as well," Noah suggested, his voice low and full of meaning, his body aching to close the distance between them.

Miss Harcourt nodded thoughtfully, her smile almost surprised. Perhaps she had not heard that often enough. Noah's heart sank with the thought.

"I know most other guests would choose the dramatic string quartet or the grand and lively trumpets as their favorites," she started, pausing to formulate her feelings into words. "While those pieces were certainly beautiful, they lacked something I only found in the harp. Simplicity." She nodded, lifting her face to look at Noah once more, feeling the conviction of her own thoughts.

"Yes, I loved the simplicity of the harp. On its own, there is nothing to distract the listener from the music. I could hear each and every note and how they melted into each other and lifted each other up. I could see their journey in my mind's eye and feel it in my heart as the harpist painted the story in the air."

Transfixed, Noah stood in complete silence as he stared at Miss Harcourt, her words painting their own story for him. He felt as though he had experienced the performance anew through her. He wanted to experience more of the world in this way.

Miss Harcourt blushed from the intensity of his gaze. "That did not make much sense, did it?" she chuckled.

"No, it made perfect sense," Noah insisted quietly. "Thank you for sharing that with me. You've given me a new way to think about that performance—perhaps even about the instrument itself. I never paid the harp much mind, yet you have opened my eyes to a new appreciation of it. And you spoke with such eloquence that it simply stunned me for a moment."

"You are far too generous, Mr. Waynford." Miss

Harcourt's blush deepened. Now, Noah wanted nothing more than for her to look at him, to see the sincerity in his eyes—in his heart.

"Miss Harcourt, Lady Welsted seeks your presence." The stiff voice of the butler caused both Noah and Miss Harcourt to jump.

"I shall be back shortly," Miss Harcourt said over her shoulder. The magic of the moment had been broken. She looked Noah in the eyes. He could see regret in them.

"Go on." Noah tilted his chin toward the door. "We can talk more when we see each other next for an activity of your choosing."

Miss Harcourt glanced over her shoulder, then back to Noah, smiling thoughtfully to herself. "I am so very glad you had a nice evening. I did, too." She took a deep breath, a spark of excitement radiating from her. "I am glad I decided to come to London after all," she whispered, seeming to forget about Noah's presence for a moment.

"Why did you not want to come to London?" Noah could not stop himself from asking, though he knew he wasn't meant to hear Miss Harcourt's last sentence. Besides, the question was a bit forward for their current relationship. Yet if Noah wanted to continue courting this woman with a serious intention to marry her, he must dig deeper.

Miss Harcourt bit her lip, her eyes wide with embarrassment. Noah immediately regretted asking that impolite question. He was pushing too far, too soon. He may just scare her away before he could understand her better—after he'd finally caught glimpses into the true heart beneath.

Noah wanted more than glimpses now. He wanted the whole picture, but he could not get that far if he offended Miss Harcourt into ending their courtship. She looked down the street before them with a sad smile. It caught Noah off guard, making him regret the question even more.

"I am not usually one for tackling such sensitive subjects with someone I've only known a relatively short time, but I'm sure there is no point in hiding it." She sighed, pulling her shoulders back to brace herself for whatever she said next. "I am sure anyone who knows my family also knows that I have been out for several Seasons now without making a match."

Noah's mouth nearly fell open in surprise. He certainly wasn't expecting their conversation to take this turn. He wasn't expecting Miss Harcourt to be so frank, yet he found her honesty refreshing, her boldness admirable. Despite her obvious discomfort with the subject, she still allowed Noah into this unpleasant part of her life.

Miss Harcourt shrugged, not a very ladylike gesture, but, then again, the topic was hardly ladylike. She looked up at Noah, smiling to mask her pain. The smile did not fool him. He could still see the pain in her eyes. His heart hurt for this young woman who did not deserve this obstacle life had thrown at her.

"I was not planning on coming to London this Season—or likely for many Seasons," she started slowly, shedding her anxiety as she spoke. "Dalton convinced me to try it again." Miss Harcourt's eyes met Noah's, her sweet, gentle heart as well as her bravery shining through. "I am glad I allowed him to convince me or else I would have never met you, Mr. Waynford."

"I am very glad he convinced you as well," Noah said quietly, the atmosphere around them transforming into something profound, almost magical. "My Season has been brighter because of you and I am so very thankful for that."

"Miss Harcourt," the butler called again.

"I wish I did not have to leave you out here on your own." She frowned at Noah before hurrying up the stairs.

Noah watched her go. Something deep inside him told

Noah that he was indeed on the right path. He had finally seen more than a glimpse.

Miss Harcourt paused at the door, looking over her shoulder at him, her profile illuminated under the silvery moonlight. She displayed a serene smile before disappearing inside.

Now that Noah had gotten a little closer to the full picture, his desire to discover more only grew deeper and stronger.

CHAPTER 9

*A*nna looked down yet again at her lovely evening dress, brushing her hands over the soft pastel blue fabric as if she could also smooth away her excited anxiety. Lovely darker blue embroidery swirled over the gown in intricate designs of vines and roses. She felt no need for anything more extravagant, though she knew most of the people at the opera tonight would be dressed in their absolute best.

Not long ago, Anna would have fretted about being too plain to be noticed. Tonight, Anna had chosen this beloved dress without any hesitation. She did not worry if she would be too plain. Somehow, Anna felt that she knew he would see beyond her unassuming simplicity.

Mama's sniffle caused Anna's head to jerk up in surprise. The older woman stood several feet away, dabbing at her eyes with a handkerchief.

"Whatever is the matter, dear Mama?" Anna asked gently, stepping closer and holding her hands out to her mother.

The baroness pushed Anna's hands aside and pulled her into a tight hug instead. Anna peered around Mama's head as

156

they wrapped their arms around each other. She noticed Papa watching further back in the foyer with a bemused smile and pride in his eyes.

Anna chuckled breathlessly as Mama squeezed her tighter, a few warm tears falling onto Anna's cheek. "Now, what's all this? I am just going to the opera. I've done it many times before." She patted Mama's back softly, trying to soothe this unusual burst of emotion.

Mama pulled back, but kept hold of Anna's arms, looking her daughter up and down. Her smile trembled as she tried to get herself back in order with only slight success.

"It may seem like any other night at the opera, but I can feel in my bones that this will be a big night for you, Anna," Mama insisted, sounding surprisingly firm through her tears.

Anna glanced over to Papa who laughed quietly and shook his head. Mama always had feelings about things in her bones. After a moment, her words finally sank in for Anna. Her heart did a somersault. She'd been very much looking forward to this night, a night with Mr. Waynford where they could enjoy beautiful, thought-provoking entertainment and share their opinions on it. She always wanted to hear his thoughts and, better yet, he seemed just as interested in hearing hers.

Still, Anna knew she must keep her expectations to a reasonable level. She smiled awkwardly at her parents. "Remember, Mama, do not be disappointed if I do not return from the opera an engaged woman," Anna said firmly but gently, both for her mother's benefit and for her own.

Mama sighed, but it did not sound heavy or disappointed. Instead, it sounded warm and content. She cupped Anna's cheek in her hand, her eyes lovingly tracing the features of her daughter's face, perhaps looking back in time to the child she had once been while a young woman now stood before her.

This surprised Anna once more. Mama did not typically succumb to strong emotion like this. She'd always prided herself on not needing to carry around smelling salts with her like many other ladies did. When she did become overwhelmed, the emotions she experienced usually tended toward frustration and anger with managing her five exceedingly different children.

The older woman took both of Anna's hands in hers. "There is something I love even more than the possibility of you finally finding the happily ever after you deserve, darling. I am so overjoyed to see the change and growth that's happened in you over these past few weeks. You carry yourself with true happiness and confidence—just as you always should."

Tears sprung up in Anna's eyes now. She hugged Mama again, squeezing her even tighter than she'd thought herself capable of. The two women held each other for a silent, heartfelt moment before Anna looked up and found Papa still waiting by the back wall. Anna gestured for Papa to join. He strode forward with a grateful smile, wrapping his wife and daughter in his arms.

"Mr. And Mrs. Parkins have arrived," the butler announced, standing before the door as a footman held it open.

The three Harcourts pulled apart, Anna brushing away any lingering tears while Mama adjusted her daughter's curls. Esther did not seem to notice as she rushed through the door, crying out some nonsensical words when she laid eyes on Anna. The woman hugged Anna tightly, swaying them both from side to side as if they had been separated for many long, painful years.

"You look absolutely stunning!" she squealed as she stepped back, her bright eyes taking Anna in from head to toe. She covered her mouth with her gloved hands, looking nearly ready to burst into tears herself.

Anna laughed, filled with an unfamiliar lightness that only made her crave it more. Mama was right. She had been gaining confidence recently. Instead of feeling nervous about spending an evening with a suitor, Anna found herself excited for a wonderful night spent with wonderful company. She longed to see Mr. Waynford again, to share this experience with him.

In fact, Anna did not feel that she should be nervous around Mr. Waynford any longer. He felt like more than a suitor. He was a friend.

"We really should be going now, dear," Esther reminded them after she regained her composure.

Mama practically pushed them through the front door, leaving Papa to stretch his arm up high so he could wave goodbye to Anna over the commotion. As soon as the Parkins' carriage door closed behind them, the driver sped off through the busy London streets.

"Mr. Waynford is sure to fall in love with you tonight if he hasn't already." Esther smiled gleefully, clapping her hands together as she once again examined every detail of Anna's face, hair, jewelry, and clothing. "As is every other single man in the theater."

Heat scorched Anna's body at that very generous compliment, but she smiled all the same. Clearing her throat, she found just enough courage to look her friend in the eye.

"Esther, there is only one thing I would ask of you tonight."

"Yes, anything!" The woman leaned forward in her seat, her husband putting a calming hand on her shoulder that she hardly noticed.

"Please let me lead the way with Mr. Waynford," Anna said softly. Esther's head fell to the side, her brows furrowed in confusion. "I know you always have the best intentions, Esther," Anna quickly continued. "I certainly appreciate all the training you gave me with how to act and speak and I did my best to put your suggestions to use."

Anna paused, taking a deep breath, summoning a little more strength to finish her request. Esther looked just as confused, turning to Mr. Parkins, asking a silent question with her eyes.

"I've now realized that Mr. Waynford seems to respond better to my true self. Besides, it feels so much better to be myself than I ever imagined…to feel valued as myself, even if I am not one of those charming, glittering ladies I used to admire."

Indeed, Anna did not even feel the need to be like those ladies when she was with Mr. Waynford. She had at first, but over time she'd become more comfortable with him, allowing herself to give up that tiring act every once in a while until it finally dawned on her that she did not need it at all.

"But Anna—"

"Dear, you have done your part for Miss Harcourt. The rest is up to her," Mr. Parkins cut in, taking his wife's hand in his. Anna smiled gratefully at her friend's husband and he returned a knowing nod. They both knew that Esther enjoyed meddling, but that she could get too caught up in it if someone did not gently pull her back.

Esther pouted for a moment, gripping Mr. Parkins' hand tightly before examining Anna closely. A shot of fear raced through Anna. Perhaps she had offended her dear friend by rejecting her help and acting as if she knew the ways of winning a man's heart better.

A cheery smile burst through Esther's momentarily gloomy expression. She reached across the carriage to take Anna's hands. "I am so very proud of you, lovely Anna."

Relief and contentment flooded Anna. She looked out the window as London passed by, her heart humming with excitement, with the feeling of fate unfolding.

Mama had been right about one other thing. Something significant would happen tonight. Anna could feel it in her bones.

∼

AN OVERWHELMING ASSAULT of sights and sounds rushed Anna's senses the moment they stepped out of the Parkins' carriage in front of the Theatre Royal. What looked like hundreds of people had gathered on the street, enjoying jovial conversations and making introductions before pouring into the grand building. Men and women eyed each other, noticing the excellent fashions of their friends and competitors—or perhaps noticing potential matches amongst the crowd. Anna had forgotten how many people flocked to see popular operas like *Artaxerxes*. She prayed that she would somehow be able to find Mr. Waynford in this dense gathering.

"Why don't we wait in the foyer so we can make space for these ladies and gentlemen milling about on the street?" Mr. Parkins suggested, having to raise his voice slightly to be heard over the dozens of separate conversations happening around them.

"Yes, that sounds much better," Anna thankfully agreed, eager to reclaim a little personal space.

Esther, on the other hand, frowned. "I would much rather stay here so I can catch the first glimpses of all the latest evening gowns."

Mr. Parkins smiled patiently as he brushed a finger against his wife's cheek. "There will be plenty to see in the foyer, my darling."

Esther's eyes narrowed in thought for a moment before finally nodding her acceptance of the plan. Mr. Parkins put a hand on Esther's shoulder and Anna took her arm, keeping them all connected as they worked their way up the front steps and through the tall, austere double doors.

Anna smiled as they stepped inside, marveling at the grand beauty of the new Covent Garden theater. She'd been devastated when the original had burned down a few years ago. Though she'd visited several times since its reopening, she still found herself amazed that the architects and builders had done such a remarkable job bringing it up from the ashes again.

She was particularly thankful for the new theater tonight because it would set the stage for Anna to enjoy one of her favorite operas with some of her favorite companions.

Soon, Anna floated away on the magic of her growing hope, the glamor of a night at the opera, and the beauty of the building. She turned around in a slow circle, a wide smile on her face. Her eyes took in all the incredible details around her, from the magnificent foyer that stretched high above her to the happy faces surrounding her.

As she turned to one side, her eyes fell upon a familiar face. She gasped as she came back to the present, recognizing Mr. Waynford standing before her just a few feet away.

"My apologies, Miss Harcourt," the gentleman laughed. "I did not mean to startle you."

Anna's smile grew wider, her heart singing with happiness. "On the contrary, Mr. Waynford. Based on your laughter, you seem to rather enjoy startling me."

He laughed again, the wonderful sound lifting Anna's spirits to a height she'd never thought possible. That smile, that laughter—it was all for Anna. She knew it beyond the shadow of a doubt.

Mr. Waynford took a step closer. "You look radiant

tonight," he whispered. His words made Anna feel as though she'd been set on fire. She felt wonderfully vibrant.

"As do you, Mr. Waynford." Anna returned the compliment with a surprisingly bold smile, yet it did not feel forced or out of place. Everything felt so natural with Mr. Waynford.

"You may thank my valet for that," he chuckled. He still smiled with contentment, but the expression struck a chord of worry in Anna. She had not forgotten the unfortunate news Mr. Milburn had shared.

"Your family…how are they all doing?" she asked tentatively.

"They are very well, thank you. And yours?"

He did not bat a lash at her question, giving no hint at any sadness or pain. Anna's heart sank slightly. He still must not feel ready to share the news with her himself, whatever that news might be. She marveled at how well he hid his worries and prayed that he would soon come to see her as a shoulder to lean on.

Before either of them could say anything else, someone's elbow caught Anna in the back, sending a jolt of pain through her. She stumbled forward, trying desperately not to hunch her shoulders from the ache in the middle of her spine.

Her gentleman caught her easily. He quickly set her back on her feet, but not before Anna's head filled up with the intoxicating feeling of being so close to him—his strong arms wrapping around her protectively, his broad chest pressed against her cheek, a lovely perfume enveloping her in his scent.

"Oh, poor Anna! Are you alright?" Esther's voice barged into Anna's thoughts, sounding impossibly far away. All she could hear was Mr. Waynford asking the same question. She could hear how much he cared for her.

"Yes, I am just fine," Anna assured him. Mr. Waynford's eyes never left her face. Anna could hear the desire in her voice, a self-conscious blush threatening to spread over her face. She hoped that only Mr. Waynford could hear it.

Now that she had her stability back, Anna glanced around. She spotted Esther and Mr. Parkins exchange a meaningful glance. On one hand, she certainly felt embarrassed to have her heart read so easily yet on the other, she did not regret it. She'd seen a flicker of reciprocated desire in Mr. Waynford's eyes.

Seeming to realize his surroundings again, the gentleman cleared his throat, letting go of Anna's arms. "I am glad. You must let me know if you feel any pain from that bump—or in your ankle, as a matter of fact. You only just recently healed, after all. Another tumble could cause further injury to the weakened area."

Anna gave him a warm, appreciative smile, her sense of adoration for him growing by the second.

"It's lovely to see you again, Mr. Waynford," Esther cut in, stepping up next to Anna.

"You as well, Mrs. Parkins, Mr. Parkins. I'll introduce you to my guests, though I suppose you already know—" Mr. Waynford turned with an outstretched arm to the empty space beside him. He peered around the room, an endearing furrow in his brow.

Anna stifled a giggle behind her gloved hand when she spotted Mr. Waynford's friend, Mr. Tilson, whom she'd met at the Serpentine. He stood by the wall, quite wrapped up in a conversation with a pretty young lady. Tapping Mr. Waynford's arm, Anna subtly pointed toward Mr. Tilson and the young lady she hoped would be introduced as Miss Cora Bishop.

Mr. Waynford turned, his eyes softening as they landed upon the pair. "Those two…" he mumbled.

"Why don't we give them a few more moments to themselves? I am sure they already dread having to be parted during the opera," Anna quietly suggested, though the couple in question was far away enough not to hear. Even if they had stood right in front of Anna, she doubted they would have heard anyway.

"Very insightful and kind of you, Miss Harcourt." Mr. Waynford nodded appreciatively.

Without meaning to, Anna let a pensive sigh slip past her lips. They looked so completely in love with each other.

"What might be on your mind?" Mr. Waynford asked, his voice almost a whisper.

Without thinking, Anna responded. "It must be so nice to be true to oneself so publicly, without any worry of impressing others or what everyone else might think of you."

Mr. Waynford remained silent for a moment. As Anna heard her own words replay in her mind, her eyes widened with shock and horror. She'd gotten far too close to her own personal truth. She looked up at him, heart beating against her chest in fear. She must have offended him by speaking so frankly. She'd been too frank as of late. Or perhaps her words had revealed her deceitful act.

The man did not look offended or disgusted or anything of the sort. Instead, he wore a thoughtful expression as he watched Anna that made her heart flutter all the more. He wanted to understand her words. He wanted to understand her. She saw no judgment or mockery in those wonderful eyes.

"I'm sor—" Anna started, her immediate remedy always to apologize.

"Please, Miss Harcourt, there is no need for that." Mr. Waynford interrupted her, holding up a hand in a gesture that told Anna that all was well. "Your words are quite refreshing, in fact. I appreciate when someone can have a truly meaningful conversation, even if it touches on sensitive topics. Have you struggled with such things yourself?"

Anna's stomach did an uncomfortable flip. She knew she should be at least a little annoyed by such a personal question. Other ladies may have blushed fiercely while scolding him for prying with enough playfulness that he would not take offense to her words, even if she'd taken offense to his.

Mr. Waynford gazed at Anna, patiently waiting for a response with no apology on his lips. She soon realized that he did not feel the need to apologize. The question was honest, meant to discover more about her rather than humiliate her. He did not back down from his desire to understand her, even if it brought them to painful truths.

Anna's nerves slowly slipped away. Perhaps she really could confess her earlier tactics, which had not seemed to win her any points with him. Perhaps she could be honest with this man. Anna glanced at the couple again, drawing strength from their confident, loving display. When she looked back at Mr. Waynford, Anna noticed that his eyes had followed hers.

Somehow, Anna appreciated that Mr. Waynford did not politely retract his question. He left her with no way to gracefully abandon the subject. Instead, he gave her an opportunity to express herself, to share this burden she'd been trying to carry, to see if he might carry it with her—or even help her set it aside completely. Again, Anna felt in her bones that if anyone would understand without judgment, it would be Mr. Waynford.

Anna took a deep breath in and slowly let it out, aware of Mr. Waynford's eyes on her the whole time. "I will admit that I have felt a bit plain and outdated in Society lately. I've been trying so hard to emulate the other beautiful, successful ladies I've seen around Town, trying to mold myself after them in the hopes of earning the same admiration that they earn—in the hopes of coming out from behind my wall of invisibility."

Try as she might, Anna could not keep the shakiness out of her voice. Still, she reasoned that a few trembling words were better than a lifetime of silence.

Mr. Waynford nodded, considering Anna's words for a silent moment. "Has that journey been working well for you thus far?"

Anna chuckled almost bitterly, lowering her eyes from his pensive gaze. "I am sure you know the answer to that." She knew she should be burning with shame for essentially admitting to deceiving this man, yet she felt liberated instead.

Though she did not look at him directly, Anna could still see the gentleman's reassuring smile. "I am honored that you would trust me with this insight into your life, Miss Harcourt. I feel that I understand you better, and I am so very glad that I have been able to understand you more every time we meet."

Anna's breath froze in her body once more as awe overcame her. She had not expected judgment from Mr. Waynford, but she had also not expected this level of complete acceptance.

"Are you not terribly upset that my personality seems to have gone through so many different phases in the time we've known each other?"

The sly look in Mr. Waynford's eyes somehow put Anna at ease. "I do have my own confession to make. That did confuse me at first and I really was not sure if I should even try getting to know you better. It seemed an impossible task at first, but I soon came to the conclusion that the Miss Harcourt I am speaking to now has been the real one all along.

"Please, do not be ashamed of trying to find a place in this world just as everyone else is doing. Though I do hope that, from now on, you will be true to yourself without feeling any need to impress others or care what they will think of you for being exactly who you are."

His words stunned Anna; her mouth fell open of its own accord. He really did accept her completely, even after her confession. Her heart soared, elated that Mr. Waynford had seen the real Anna—despite her best efforts to hide herself—and better yet, he'd come to enjoy the real Anna.

"Thank you, Mr. Waynford, for being so kind and understanding and not wanting to flee from me," Anna whispered, afraid that if she raised her voice any higher, her emotions would run away with her.

Mr. Waynford laughed, the sound vibrating through Anna's body. "I assure you that I would never do such a thing. I think, somehow, that I always knew spending more time with you and understanding you better would be worth it. And it certainly has been."

A surge of confidence overtook Anna. She leaned forward, standing slightly on her toes to bring her face just a little closer to his. "You have not been so bad to spend time with yourself, Mr. Waynford."

He threw his head back, his laughter roaring from his body, drawing more than a few confused and irritated glances their way. He seemed not to care and Anna did not either. She thought it well worth the ire of a few members of the *ton* to hear that incredible sound, to know that she'd been the cause of it.

Esther and Mr. Parkins approached, waving goodbye to another couple they'd been chatting with. "We should get inside before we are crushed by these people flocking in all at once," Esther suggested sagely, nodding to herself in appreciation of her own advice.

"Excellent idea." Mr. Waynford stepped away from their

group toward his lovestruck friends. They looked up sheepishly when Mr. Waynford got their attention, as if he'd interrupted them while exchanging embarrassingly romantic sonnets. As they walked back toward Anna and the Parkins, she noticed Mr. Tilson leading the young lady proudly while the young lady's eyes drifted up to his face every few seconds, sparkling with adoration.

"Mr. Parkins, Mrs. Parkins, Miss Harcourt, these are my friends. You already know Mr. Tilson but I am happy to introduce his fiancée, Miss Cora Bishop."

Anna's eyes went round with happy surprise. "Congratulations, Mr. Tilson, Miss Bishop! How excited you must be."

She pressed her hands over her heart, trying to keep it from flying out of her chest with her joy for her acquaintances. They both looked ecstatic to be introduced as an engaged couple. Anna remembered their walk at the Serpentine, where Mr. Tilson had spoken of his desire to impress a young lady by the name of Miss Bishop. Now they stood before Anna, sure to walk down the aisle as soon as they were able.

In the same instant, Anna's heart filled with longing. She prayed that would be her someday soon, looking up at her future husband as if nothing else existed in her world, introduced as his future wife—but not in the general sense that she'd experienced before. Anna quickly realized that her feelings had taken on a sense of purpose.

She glanced up at Mr. Waynford from the corner of her eye only to discover that he was already watching her intently. Had he read her thoughts? Anna found herself almost hoping that he had. While Anna may have felt more confident and bolder recently, she did not yet think she could be so forward as to confess her feelings first.

Mr. Waynford looked at his friends again with genuine happiness, a charming softness in his eyes. He returned his attention to Anna, the softness still there. Perhaps Anna could read his mind as well. A deep certainty stirred within her, a certainty she'd never experienced so strongly in her life. She knew that his thoughts had carried him in the same direction hers had.

Excitement rushed through Anna as Mr. Waynford offered his arm to her. "Shall we find our seats?"

Anna took his arm, reveling in their physical closeness as well as the emotional closeness she felt growing between them. Papa had given Anna permission to use the box the Harcourt family had rented for the Season. She led the way into the theater, rows upon rows of seats and boxes rising up around them. The exhilaration of being on Mr. Waynford's arm had left Anna with just enough sense to look around the incredible room and appreciate its beauty for a moment.

With the help of an usher, they quickly settled into the Harcourts' box, the ladies in the front row and their respective gentlemen in the row behind. Anna so wished that Mr. Waynford could have sat next to her, but she knew that giving the ladies the better seats was the polite and proper thing to do.

Even still, feeling his presence behind her sent a chill through her body. She vowed not to get lost in that sensation. She still needed to take careful mental notes of the opera so she could share them with Mr. Waynford later. After all, as much as Anna loved just being near him, she loved being able to talk with him about their thoughts and experiences even more.

"My goodness, what a lovely box! I doubt we shall have any trouble seeing the stage from here." Esther heaped many praises on the theater, their view, and all the people now filing into the auditorium, pulling Anna out of her world of Mr. Waynford and into Esther's world of glitz and glamor and excitement.

Anna did not know how long she listened to her friend's many remarks about nearly everything her eyes landed upon, but she knew that, in this state, Esther's conversation felt like it took hours even though only a few minutes had passed. As much as Anna enjoyed listening to Esther, she found herself wishing she could return to her own inner world where she had plenty of her own excitement to keep her occupied.

To Anna's guilty relief, Esther eventually turned to Miss Bishop who sat on her other side. To Esther's great credit, she made sure that no one was left out of her conversation for too long. She launched into a series of questions about how she'd met Mr. Tilson, when and where their wedding would be, where they would live, and more.

Anna leaned forward, interested in this part of the conversation. She wanted to learn more about Mr. Tilson and Miss Bishop and hear their love story. Anna had enjoyed hearing love stories since she was a girl. Even her sadness about her own situation could not change that.

A warm breath against Anna's neck stopped her. She turned to her left, her heart leaping into her throat as a rosy red hue spread across her face. Her lips had nearly brushed against Mr. Waynford's cheek. He'd leaned forward in his own seat, his face next to hers. He did not seem uncomfortable about the fact that Anna had almost accidentally kissed him.

In fact, he looked quite eager to talk to her. She noticed Mr. Waynford's eyes drop to her lips for a fraction of a second before returning to her eyes, capturing her in their intelligent intensity and curiosity.

"Remember to take careful notes so you can report back to Mr. Patrick," the gentleman whispered.

A slow, amazed smile bloomed across Anna's face, surprised that he remembered the time she'd talked about her younger brother and his love of theater. It had been a quick moment, so quick that she'd forgotten about it until just now. Mr. Waynford really did see and hear and absorb everything, committing even the smallest details to a secure place in his mind.

Mr. Waynford tilted his head to the side. "Of course I would remember what you said, especially about something or someone important to you."

Anna's blush deepened as she realized she must have voiced her wonder without realizing it. "I-I'm terribly sorry! I did not mean to think out loud."

"No apology needed, Miss Harcourt. I prefer it when you think out loud about anything. If it is important enough to cross your mind, I would consider myself honored to hear it."

A light, warm happiness filled Anna to the brim until she thought she might burst. This man truly was a miracle. Before Anna could say anything else embarrassing, she decided to change the subject back to a safer area.

"When I told my family I would be seeing *Artaxerxes,* Caroline nearly boxed poor Harriet's ears when she asked why anyone would want to see such a boring old opera," she said, smiling fondly at the memory.

Mr. Waynford laughed, his eyes crinkling at the corners. "I am sure Miss Caroline would give anything to attend such a fancy event. But what did Mr. Patrick have to say about Miss Harriet's scathing review?"

Anna laughed, too, completely charmed that Mr. Waynford already seemed to understand the rhythm of the Harcourt family. "Luckily for Harriet, Patrick didn't hear it. His head was buried in a book, reading some play, of course." She gently shook her head as love for her family overcame her—and happiness at sharing that love.

"You are correct in guessing that Caroline was terribly bitter she could not join me. As she comes closer to making her own debut, she becomes more frustrated by missing out, as if all of Society's fun is being dangled in front of her face, just out of reach."

Mr. Waynford nodded with an understanding sigh. "I remember those days very well. My younger sister, Angelica, was so eager to make her debut after watching our elder sister, Emma, have such a grand time."

"Sisters," Anna chuckled.

"We will just have to come back with Miss Caroline next year," Mr. Waynford said absentmindedly.

The comment made Anna's heart leap. She stared at him, unable to regain control of her polite expression. Next year? Mr. Waynford already imagined a future in which they would still be this close next year—or perhaps even closer?

Before Anna could respond, an excited murmur rippled through the crowd. The opera would start at any moment. She only had enough time to nod and turn back toward the stage as Mr. Waynford sat up straight in his seat once more.

Unfortunately, Anna struggled to pay attention despite her best attempts. Her mind swirled with Mr. Waynford's words, rendering her almost deaf to the lines and songs performed on stage. At least Anna had seen *Artaxerxes* before so she could draw on her past viewings to help her later.

She stopped trying to force her mind in any one direction, instead letting it wander to the only place it wanted to go—Mr. Waynford.

CHAPTER 10

*H*aving seen *Artaxerxes* before, Noah knew the intermission would arrive soon. Though he certainly enjoyed the excellent performances of this gripping tale, he could not help being distracted by the back of Miss Harcourt's head.

The lovely, soft dark curls of her hair, the elegant way she held her shoulders back, the moments when she nodded slightly during a particularly moving part as if the words melted into her—it all completely captivated Noah. He desperately wished he could sit next to her so they could whisper to each other about the opera. For now, Noah could only count down the minutes until intermission when they could move about more freely.

Noah looked to his side to see Mr. Parkins next to him and Phineas in the seat over. Both men were more occupied with the women seated in front of them than the entertainment on the stage. To his surprise, Noah felt a certain kinship with those gentlemen. They were all here with the women they admired, adored, loved….

Well, Noah knew from the first moment they met that

Mr. Parkins loved his wife, and there could be no doubt that Phineas loved his bride-to-be. But could Noah claim that word for himself yet?

He looked forward again, his eyes pausing on Miss Harcourt once more. His heart expanded with a warmth he'd never known before, just from being in her presence. Noah became so preoccupied with these new thoughts about Miss Harcourt that he did not notice the intermission starting until she turned around, smiling up at him, her eyes sparkling in the candlelight, sparkling from all her thoughts that he could not wait to hear.

"What do you think so far, Mr. Waynford?" she asked excitedly. Noah noticed something else in her eyes—real, deep, honest interest.

"Would you like to join me for a walk around the foyer to stretch our legs and discuss?"

The young woman nodded happily, turning to the ladies beside her. "Would you like to come with us?" she asked politely. Mrs. Parkins and Miss Bishop both accepted the invitation.

Noah fought off a frown. He'd been very much looking forward to having a quiet conversation with just Miss Harcourt, even though he knew she'd done the proper thing by inviting the rest of their party. Noah had to appreciate that she always kept others in mind, seeking their comfort and entertainment even more than her own.

They joined the sea of theater goers who also wanted to take advantage of the break to mingle or get some much needed movement. Noah held out his arm. Miss Harcourt took it with an endearingly contented smile. That warmth Noah had felt in his heart seeped out, spreading further through his body, knowing that he was the cause of that lovely smile.

Much to Noah's relief, the other two couples took up

stations several feet away from them once they reached the foyer, immediately losing themselves in their own discussions.

Noah let Miss Harcourt's hand slip off his arm as he turned to face her, already missing her touch. He could not help noticing the way her fingers nearly gripped his coat sleeve as she pulled her hand away, as if she did not want to let go either.

She gazed up at him so sweetly, a true, genuine gentleness radiating from her. She seemed to glow with it. A storm of butterflies erupted in Noah's stomach as their eyes locked onto each other. "That aria sung by Arbaces and Mandane in the first act was breathtaking, was it not?" he mumbled, searching for something intelligent to say.

Miss Harcourt nodded, her smile widening. "It was magnificent," she agreed, her eyes bright and eager. "The acting is superb as well. I am always amazed that actors can bring such an incredible, heart-wrenching tale to life."

Without knowing what came over him or having any time to stop himself, Noah stepped closer to Miss Harcourt, completely forgetting about *Artaxerxes* and arias and actors.

"Miss Harcourt, I really must tell you that I am so very glad to be spending more time with you. I am always fascinated by your opinions and I feel relaxed in your presence. You have made an enjoyable evening even more special."

The lady quickly looked down at her hands clasped before her, but Noah could still see her smile. After taking a moment to compose herself, Miss Harcourt looked back up at him, that smile growing into a beautiful sight that Noah wanted to experience again and again.

"And I have been having such a wonderful time this Season, all thanks to you. I hope we will see each other again soon?" A pale pink blush spread across Miss Harcourt's cheeks as her eyes struggled to remain on his.

Noah found her blush and shyness to be so very endearing. He could tell that it had taken a lot of strength to say that. He loved that she'd taken that chance.

A strong, wild urge to grab Miss Harcourt's hands nearly overwhelmed Noah, but all these people gathered in the foyer kept him in check. Acting on that desire would not be appropriate here. The last thing Noah wanted to do was embarrass Miss Harcourt or give her any reason to stop seeing him. He only wanted her to smile and laugh because of him, to long to come closer instead of frown in distress or pull away in shame.

"Mr. Waynford?" she nervously called his name, jolting Noah back to his present situation. He had been staring at her in silent happiness without giving an answer.

"Yes, I certainly would enjoy that." He rushed the words out, already eager to spend another day with Miss Harcourt. "We can plan it all out after the opera is done."

The lady breathed a sigh of relief before covering a laugh with her hand. "I suppose, based on our pattern, it is your turn to choose the next activity."

Noah nodded, though he felt confident that he would still be happy if she chose all their outings. He only needed Miss Harcourt to make his day wonderful.

DESPITE THE INTENSITY of the drama, Noah's heart lifted as *Artaxerxes* came to a close, the two couples on stage happily reunited after their many trials. He watched the back of Miss Harcourt's head again, wondering what she thought as Artaxerxes and Semira as well as Arbaces and Mandane finally reached some semblance of a happy ending.

For the first time in his life, Noah felt that such an ending may not be very far off for him either—or for Miss Harcourt.

He could not quite believe that his thoughts had turned so quickly from suspicion and reluctance at the start of their courtship to genuine affection. Perhaps it should not have been so surprising to him after finally seeing into the real Miss Harcourt.

Truth be told, Noah had always envisioned himself with a woman like her, with a woman he could truly share himself with and receive the same in return.

They again joined the crowd exiting the auditorium, Miss Harcourt's hand back on Noah's arm. He admitted now that he loved the feeling of her fingers gently grasping his coat sleeve, her shoulder occasionally pressing into his side as the room swelled with people all trying to leave at the same time. When they finally made it through the foyer and out onto the street to wait for their carriages, Noah's mind already buzzed with ideas for their next engagement.

As if reading his mind, Miss Harcourt tilted her face up to him without removing herself from his side. "Did you have any chance during that amazing performance to think of what you would like to do next and when?"

Noah smiled knowingly, which caused Miss Harcourt to give a playful frown. Of course Noah had been thinking about it, even while trying to pay attention to the opera. Though he had some ideas, he still wanted to give it proper thought so he could choose something that they would both enjoy. Noah could not waste any chances.

"May I have an extension and write to your home when I have decided on our next adventure? It will be next Thursday, I think, but I shall let you know within three days what I have chosen for us."

Miss Harcourt's mouth pulled to one side, an expression Noah immediately adored. She appeared to be thinking very seriously about his request, though he could still see the teasing glint in her eyes. "I will accept your terms, Mr. Waynford, but I would rather be surprised this time. Whisk me away in a cloud of mystery on Thursday."

Noah's eyebrow rose in surprise. "Are you sure?"

"Positively." Miss Harcourt gave a sharp, confident nod. "I trust you, but more importantly, I know that I'll enjoy myself no matter what we end up doing…because you will be there." Her words grew softer, more self-conscious as she spoke, but she managed to hold Noah's gaze all the same. He grinned, knowing he must look as silly as Phineas did when he started talking to or about Miss Bishop.

They spent another few minutes discussing the end of *Artaxerxes* as their carriages fought their way through the long line of vehicles on the street, all trying to gather before the Theatre Royal. Noah, of course, would prefer if his carriage took a few more minutes or hours or never appeared at all. It would leave him with more time to spend with Miss Harcourt.

"I am always so happy that all those issues eventually led to a good outcome for the two couples. Not a perfect outcome, to be sure, but certainly better than the alternative. I hope they go on to be happy for the rest of their days," the lady sighed happily, lifting her face to the night sky, her eyes reflecting the stars above.

Noah found himself smiling again. He so admired the sweetness in her heart and the way she loved everyone, even these fictional characters, that she would wish them well in their fictional futures.

"I must admit I never really considered their lives after the performance ends. What an interesting idea," Noah pondered quietly.

"You must try it," Miss Harcourt eagerly insisted, patting his arm in her excitement. "There could be even more adventures waiting for the characters—and for yourself—in your imagination."

"I do quite like that idea. I will do my best, but only if you promise not to tease me for my rudimentary attempts at using my imagination in such a creative way. I'm afraid it does not get much practice."

"I am afraid I cannot make such a promise," Miss Harcourt giggled.

Noah huffed playfully. "Then the deal is off."

"No, no! I only said that because I am so sure your imaginings will be marvelous."

Their carriages finally arrived almost at the same time, preventing Noah from arguing any further. Miss Harcourt had won this round, a fact Noah did not mind at all.

The group said their goodbyes and made their assurances of an exceedingly enjoyable night. Phineas helped Miss Bishop into her carriage first before weaving through the crowd toward his own, stationed a few carriages down. Noah watched from the door of his carriage as Mr. Parkins helped his wife into their carriage followed by Miss Harcourt. Their eyes met one more time. They exchanged smiles through the crowd, her eyes reflecting Noah's hope back to him.

Once he saw Miss Harcourt safely into the Parkins' carriage, Noah finally gave his driver the signal to start. He leaned back against his seat, his body feeling loose and heavy at the same time, a blanket of warmth enveloping him. He offered a silent prayer of thanks that he had not shared his carriage with anyone else, leaving him to be a lovestruck fool dazed by an amazing evening with an amazing lady in blissful solitude.

Lovestruck? The word surprised Noah even though he could feel himself running headlong toward it. His mind remained so wrapped up in Miss Harcourt that he arrived home in the blink of an eye.

Noah nearly skipped up the steps, feeling lighter than he had in a long while. As he flew past, a footman informed

Noah that his parents could be found in the library. The footman did not say that Mother and Father wished to see Noah when he returned, but Noah certainly knew that they'd left this message at the door for a reason. Hardly anything could make them stay up this late.

He bounded up the stairs, weightless and energetic. Was this what love made everyone feel like?

Noah threw the door to the library open only to find his parents seated at the small table by the window, moonlight spilling over them while two candles flickered lazily on the table. Mother and Father both snored gently.

Even Noah's elation could not prevent his frown. He made a note to scold them in the morning for staying up late waiting for him. Standing before Mother and Father, Noah gave a quiet cough. He chuckled at their dazed expressions as they pulled themselves out of slumber.

He could feel his joy beaming from his face as he waited for them to register their surroundings. Father came around first, shaking his head before staring up at his son while Mother stifled a yawn.

Father squinted at Noah's expression, as if he suspected his sleepy eyes of playing tricks on him. "How did your evening go then, son?"

Noah took a breath, trying to harness his racing thoughts, all speeding toward Miss Harcourt. Before he could answer, Mother clicked her tongue in a gentle admonition. "It seems obvious from Noah's face how his evening went." Father nodded thoughtfully while Noah chuckled at his mother's assessment.

"You should be off to bed now, dear, and we should do the same," Mother continued, blinking away the tiredness that still clung to her eyes. "I know you will have plenty to say in the morning."

"I will give you all the details at breakfast, I promise."

Noah gave Mother a peck on the check and Father a slap to his shoulder before again floating through the library and the rest of the house, his feet carrying him on invisible wings.

Once in his room, Noah threw himself on the bed, still dressed in his best evening clothes, one leg dangling off the side. He stared up at the ceiling, Miss Harcourt's smile dancing through his memories. That was the only thing his imagination could conjure right now—the only thing it wanted to conjure. At least, despite his earlier warning to Miss Harcourt, his infrequently used imagination could create a compelling likeness of that beautiful face. Of course, Noah would have much preferred to see the real thing, but for now this would suffice.

He had no idea how he would get any sleep tonight with his heart and mind so focused on Miss Harcourt. Noah hoped that when he did finally sleep, perhaps he could dream of her, too.

CHAPTER 11

*A*nna silently sipped her tea in Esther's drawing room while several other ladies, all friends of the very popular Mrs. Parkins, chatted happily on a calm afternoon. Anna liked Esther's other friends well enough, though she did not usually talk much during these occasional gatherings of both married and single women. As usual, Anna was more than happy to listen to their life updates and see the world through their eyes for a while. She'd never felt much of a need to talk about herself in such settings.

Today, Anna found herself even more quiet than usual with one major difference. She did not pay any attention to the other ladies. Her mind remained firmly fixed on Mr. Waynford. It had been a week since they'd seen *Artaxerxes* together and Anna had only seen him once since, for a brief walk around her neighborhood where they confirmed the date and time of their next engagement.

Mr. Waynford had told her, with what Anna interpreted as sincere regret, that he had been so busy with other meetings at his club and with his friends whom he only saw during the Season. Anna could not blame him. Her social calendar had filled up nearly to bursting, mostly with outings with a couple other gentlemen she'd met a few weeks ago, as well as Mr. Milburn, who had greatly increased his efforts to spend time with her.

Even though Anna did enjoy her outings with Mr. Milburn, she could now admit to herself that her mind still drifted back to Mr. Waynford. It was a beautiful feeling. Anna truly understood now why so many people longed for love—though she found herself wondering if she should hope to call her feelings love. What of Mr. Milburn and the two new gentlemen who seemed intent on courting her? Surely they must be given a fair chance, too.

Still, Anna desperately wanted to put all her hopes on Mr. Waynford. Her heart skipped whenever she thought of him and the possibility of love. Despite her hesitation to call her feelings love, conditioned over the last several years to temper her expectations, Anna knew she had finally landed on the right path. Her mind erupted with Mr. Waynford's smile, his knowing but kind eyes, his charming voice, and most of all, his willingness to hear her out on any subject.

She had never experienced such a gathering of warm, happy, hopeful, feelings as she did now, ever since the night at the opera. Esther's drawing room was transformed even though Anna had visited many times before. In fact, Anna herself felt transformed.

Two of the ladies rose from their chairs, momentarily pulling Anna's attention toward them. They looped arms, taking a leisurely walk about the room. The other women remained seated. Anna lost herself in thought once more.

"Anna, I've just had a thought. Would you look at this pianoforte piece I've been learning? You're a better player than me so perhaps you can help me with this section," Esther soon called from her own seat in the middle of her friends. She hopped up, rushing to the instrument on the other side of the room, leaving Anna to smile lovingly at her friend. She had to wonder how Esther managed to have so much energy, but at least she channeled some of that energy into her eagerness to learn.

Anna followed after her friend, passing just behind the two ladies walking by. Her heart froze as she caught a snippet of their conversation. Surely one of them had just said her name.

"You did hear about that Miss Harcourt, didn't you? I'm not sure why Esther holds onto her so, with all these suitors and the bribery—"

"Shh! Let's not talk about this now. When is your new dress arriving?" The other lady quickly pulled her friend along, changing the subject too late. They shot nervous glances over their shoulders to Anna.

Despite the chill racing up and down Anna's body, she did her best to regain her composure, smoothing away her surprised expression into one of serene contentment. As soon as Esther heard Anna approach, she started plunking away at her piece.

Anna tried to listen as her friend played, but she did not hear a single note. She could hear nothing but the words those ladies had spoken in hushed, secret tones.

Normally, she gave no thought to the many rumors that swirled around Society, from the mundane to the shocking to the ones that carried the power to ruin lives. In fact, Anna had heard rumors about herself in the past. Naturally, people wondered why she hadn't made a match yet. She had been embarrassed, but it never amounted to anything too terrible or scandalous. Most had come to the simple conclusion that Anna was just too plain in every way.

As Anna tried and failed and tried again to listen to Esther's piece, one word kept creeping back into Anna's mind, hanging over her like a dark storm cloud—bribery. What on Earth could those women mean by that?

Anna was so caught up in her thoughts, in the uncomfortable churning in her stomach, that she did not notice her friend's hands going still. Anna only found herself back in the drawing room when Esther jabbed her in the arm.

"How did I do? Did you notice any mistakes?"

Anna gave a tight smile, the best she could manage. "You did perfectly fine."

Esther glared suspiciously at Anna. "I know I made many mistakes."

Before Anna could apologize for her lack of attention, Esther's expression softened into concern. She knew that something must be bothering Anna deeply if it rendered her incapable of helping a friend. "What's wrong?" Esther asked in a low voice, glancing around the room to ensure no one could overhear.

"I think I overheard some of the other ladies talking about me. I did not hear much besides my name and something about bribery," Anna confessed, the words cutting her as she forced them out.

Esther bit her lip, no longer able to look Anna in the eyes. This sent Anna's heart pounding. Esther so rarely looked uncomfortable. "Have you heard the same thing those ladies have heard?" she asked, her voice shaking.

The other woman fidgeted with her dress, clearly searching for the right thing to say. Finally, when she met Anna's eyes again, she looked more distressed than Anna had ever seen her, even more so than when Mr. Parkins' family nearly forced him to stop courting her because she'd been too spirited for their taste. What could possibly distress Esther more than that?

"Please put it out of your mind for now. This is not a good time to talk about it, but I promise to tell you what I know after everyone else returns home. Can you stay a while longer than you'd planned?" she whispered, an alarming urgency in her voice.

Anna nodded numbly. She knew she would only grow more anxious the longer she waited, but she knew it must be serious if even Esther did not want to discuss it with company around. There was not much Esther would shy away from discussing, which had gotten her in trouble with Mr. Parkins' family during their courtship; it still did on occasion.

"I will return to my chair and drink more tea. That always helps calm me down." Anna took a step away before turning back to Esther. "And I will help you with that piece later when I have a clearer head." Esther gave her an understanding, worried smile before she turned back to her practice.

Anna had never been more thankful to sit on the outskirts of the group. Esther knew that Anna did not like being too close to the other women for fear that they would pull her into a conversation she was not yet ready to navigate. Instead, Esther had shown her to a seat a few feet away from the other chairs, allowing Anna to listen as much as she pleased and participate when she felt confident enough to do so.

She lifted her teacup, but did not bring it to her lips, her thoughts returning to Mr. Waynford, and even Mr. Milburn, once more. Now, Anna could not help feeling that something wasn't quite right. She prayed that whatever Esther told her would not break her heart.

THE SMALL SITTING room in the Harcourts' townhome sat empty except for Anna. Most of the family forgot about it, which made it the perfect place for Anna to have some privacy and gather her thoughts. She'd gone straight to the small sitting room upon her return from Esther's home. She could not be sure how long she'd sat there, immersed in her thoughts. Eventually, Anna had decided to ring the bell to request two things—tea and Dalton.

The tea arrived first, which was fine with Anna. She took a few calming sips, imagining the warm, delicious liquid smoothing away her worries. Unfortunately, tea alone could not solve this problem. Anna jumped when the door opened again, revealing Dalton's curious expression. She had been so lost in her own world again that she'd forgotten she'd asked for him, too.

Dalton's curiosity quickly gave way to concern as he read Anna's face. He rushed to the seat next to her, sitting on the very edge, the playful light in his eyes darkened with worry.

"What's happened, Anna? Tell me," Dalton insisted when Anna failed to answer at first. She remembered why she'd summoned him in the first place. Anna took a deep breath, her dress suddenly feeling too tight and hot. She could not look Dalton in the eye.

As he often did, Dalton took it upon himself to get to the root of the situation. He leaned forward, taking Anna's hands in his and giving them a gentle shake. Anna looked up at him again. Dalton smiled, trying to bring some light back into the atmosphere.

It was just enough for Anna. "I visited Esther today and several of her other friends were there. I overheard two of them say something…unkind about me. I asked Esther if she knew anything about it and she told me—" Anna broke off, yanking a hand away from Dalton so she could cover her trembling mouth.

"It is alright. Take your time," her brother said gently, clasping Anna's other hand in both of his, his eyes never leaving her face.

"Esther informed me that a rumor has been circulating about me. Some people have noticed that I have more suitors than I did in previous Seasons. That is to say, they've noticed that I have any suitors at all. They say that Papa told some men at White's that he's increased my marriage portion in the hopes of sending me off this Season...and finally getting me off his hands."

She choked on the words as they clawed their way out, her heart breaking at the mere possibility that her beloved father would say or do anything like this—that the relationships she'd developed this Season were all built on lies. She had almost burst into tears in front of Esther. Somehow, she'd managed to keep herself together, allowing the numbing disbelief to protect her until she returned home.

Dalton squeezed Anna's hand, causing her to yelp more from surprise than actual pain. "I'm sorry," he mumbled absentmindedly as he eased his grip. Anna saw an unusual flash in his eyes. He was truly angry. Anna could not remember the last time she'd seen Dalton's anger.

He shook his head, a few locks of light brown hair falling loose. "Ignore that nonsense. That does not sound like anything Papa would ever say and you know it."

Anna nodded. Dalton was right, of course. Papa was not that kind of man. Yet even the idea that someone could think he'd say those things hurt her deeply. Years of self-doubt rushed to the front of her mind, nearly destroying her newfound confidence.

"Why would anyone say such a thing then?" she asked quietly, squeezing her eyes shut against possibilities that ranged from bad to worse.

When she opened them again, she saw Dalton glowering at the corner of the room as if the culprit huddled there, waiting for a proper scolding. "I cannot tell you that. I haven't heard anything of the sort myself, probably since I prefer Boodle's over White's. Now I feel quite justified in that position. I would not like to associate with anyone from that club if they talk like this, and I'm sure Papa would not either if he knew what was being said."

"Please do not bother Papa with this yet, Dalton," Anna begged, realizing that it would be just like her brother to charge ahead to solve this mystery.

"He must be made aware of this." His eyes burned like golden ice, which almost relieved Anna. At least she knew that Dalton would rush to her aid if she ever found herself in need of a champion.

"Not yet, please," she quietly insisted. "I know you must be right, of course. He would not do something like this, especially not without consulting me. I do not wish to trouble him with it. Perhaps I can get to the bottom of it on my own."

In truth, Anna selfishly did not want to confront Papa about this just yet. It was still too raw and painful.

Dalton clenched his jaw. "If you insist."

"There is something else, Dalton," Anna continued, her voice even quieter than before. Dalton leaned forward, straining to hear her. "If other people have heard this gossip, then Mr. Waynford and Mr. Milburn and the others may have heard it as well. What if they are just chasing this supposed fortune? What if they do not actually care for me?"

Dalton softened, the pain in his eyes nearly breaking Anna's heart anew. "There is no way that could be true, dear Anna. I've seen the two of you together and I would bet everything I have, down to the last hair on my head, that he is completely taken with you."

Though he did not say the gentleman's name, Anna knew they had the same one in mind. Dalton's words did bring a little comfort, but not total reassurance.

"But Dalton, you cannot deny that I've generated more

interest this Season than I have in any of my past Seasons combined. How can that be possible if there is a whole new batch of ladies younger and prettier than me to choose from?"

The young man sat up straighter, brows pulled down in a scowl. Anna wondered for a moment if Dalton was going to scold her. Instead of scolding, he sighed and patted Anna's hand. "Even if they did hear this ridiculous rumor and are trying to take advantage of it, they would be fools not to fall for you in the process. Anna, you have so much to offer, not just to potential husbands, but to everyone in your life. You are who you are and that is enough.

"Besides, I know you are really not worried about those other gentlemen. We can speak of Mr. Waynford plainly now. Mention them all you want, but I know he is the only one on your mind."

Anna looked away from Dalton's knowing gaze, suddenly feeling exposed. Her feelings must have been painfully obvious to her brother. After all, he was Anna's closest confidant. His other words settled in a quiet corner of Anna's mind for her to examine later. Though they were kind, she had more pressing issues to deal with at the moment.

"Come now, there is no need to be bashful," Dalton chuckled. "Affection is not something to be ashamed of— especially not around me. You can share anything in your heart with me, sister. You know that. And I will do the same with you."

Anna smiled her agreement, feeling a little lighter. Dalton always knew just what to say and how to say it to improve her mood. Most importantly of all, Anna knew Dalton believed everything he said. If Dalton believed it, maybe Anna could, too. Someday.

"You know I can see the sparkles in your eyes for Mr.

Waynford from a mile off, don't you?" Dalton asked slyly, pinching Anna's cheek.

Anna gasped in mock offense as she slapped Dalton on the shoulder. Their laughter filled the small room, bouncing around them before settling down into a comfortable silence, Anna's chest heaving up and down from the burst of energy.

"Remember, Anna," Dalton continued after catching his breath, "do not give those rumors too much thought. I know in my heart that the man you want feels the same about you —and those feelings cannot be produced by money."

"You really think he is genuine?"

"Yes, I do." Dalton stood and Anna joined him, finding herself pulled into a hug that left her breathless once more.

"Dalton!" Anna wheezed, giving him another, harsher slap on the shoulder.

He released her with a mischievous grin. "Better?"

"Yes, much." Anna bent at the waist, exaggerating her suffering.

She did feel better. Not completely, but better none-theless. She trusted Dalton. He'd always been a good judge of character.

Dalton looked over at the clock on the table next to them. "I think Patrick is probably still reading some play in the library. Shall we go pull a prank on him?"

Anna opened her mouth to argue, but Dalton was up and running toward the door before she could make a sound. With another small laugh, Anna rushed after him, hoping to save Patrick from too much trouble.

CHAPTER 12

The lovely, warm sunlight spilling over Anna brought a smile to her face. Mr. Milburn's voice mingled with the beauty of the birdsong above her, the leaves rustling in the gentle breeze, the relaxed chatter of happy people all around her.

Anna glanced up at Mr. Milburn from beneath her bonnet and saw the gentleman staring straight forward, a confident set to his jaw, steering his horses with expertise. Anna caught a few words about his extremely successful hunting season this past winter.

With Mr. Milburn lost in his tale, Anna took advantage of his distraction to examine his features—certainly handsome, but lacking warmth and curiosity. Transposed over Mr. Milburn, Anna saw another face. She pulled her attention back to the many other people enjoying this fine afternoon in Hyde Park, taking special note of the couples of all ages. She loved to see that so many of them looked completely enamored with each other, lost in their own private conversations.

Anna looked back at Mr. Milburn once more, this time turning her face so she could really see him. Could she really be happy with this man? More importantly, should she try to be happy with him?

At the start of the Season, Anna had felt so hopeless that she would have accepted almost anyone as long as he was pleasant enough. Mr. Milburn fit that description. He may have been more talkative than Anna preferred, a little too haughty and caught up in his material and status, but he was still pleasant. He'd shown Anna on numerous occasions that, for as much as he talked, he also listened closely, and he had a charming sense of humor. That surely would have satisfied Anna a few months ago.

Yet, now that she had come to know Mr. Waynford and grown more confident in herself and her future, Anna did not want to settle for someone simply because they showed interest in her.

Did she not have a right to marry a man who complemented her rather than simply tolerated her? Did she want to spend her life tolerating someone instead of loving him deeply and completely?

Mr. Waynford had transformed Anna's expectations. She did not feel the need to hide herself away, to worry that she would not impress him. He shared himself with Anna as freely as she had learned to do—save for the issue about his father. He wanted to do things Anna enjoyed instead of choosing all their activities himself.

He looked at Anna as though he truly saw her.

Anna had never felt this way about anyone before. She had dreamed of it for so long and now that she had finally experienced it, Anna did not know if she could accept a marriage of anything less.

Mr. Milburn must have felt Anna's gaze. He turned to her,

a pleasantly surprised smile on his face. It was the purest expression she had ever seen from Mr. Milburn. A sharp pain stabbed at Anna's heart as she realized that he must know that he was not her preferred choice. That made his hopeful smile all the more heartbreaking to see.

Again, Anna reminded herself that she must do the right thing for her heart and her future. As much as she dreaded the thought of disappointing anyone, she could no longer live with the possibility that she would carry an irreparable regret for the rest of her life.

"Are you having a pleasant afternoon?" Mr. Milburn asked, his voice unexpectedly soft.

"Certainly," Anna said with a smile.

Mr. Milburn returned his attention to the path ahead once more, holding himself a little taller. "What do you think of this carriage? I thought we would take one you hadn't seen before."

"I admire it very much," Anna insisted. She looked around her at the plush black velvet seats and the gleaming black wood of the body, polished to absolute perfection. Anna sensed that Mr. Milburn still hoped to win her over with his family's impressive wealth. Most people in London could not afford to keep a single carriage let alone multiple carriages, as the Milburn family clearly could.

"We cannot bring them all to London, of course, but we have carriages even handsomer than this one. They are well kept in the country, as are the horses. When we host several families, we often lend them our carriages for rides around our estate. They always love to borrow them for an afternoon."

"That sounds quite lovely." Anna forced the words out, hoping he would not detect the frustration in them. She did not much care for this side of Mr. Milburn. Anna scolded herself for the thought as soon as she had it. He clearly thought the best way to a lady's heart was through his money. Not long ago, Anna had thought the best way to a man's heart was through vapid flirting. She might not love Mr. Milburn, but she did not need to be a cruel hypocrite.

Anna did not have much time to chastise herself before she realized that Mr. Milburn had nearly brought the carriage to a stop. "Is something the matter?" Anna asked nervously, suddenly realizing how rigid the gentleman had gone.

Mr. Milburn coughed, tugging at the bottom of his waistcoat. "I spotted a bench under a large oak just over there. I thought we could sit under the shade for a while."

Anna knew immediately what he intended to do. Her stomach flipped with anxiety. "That's not necessary, Mr. Milburn. I am quite enjoying this ride with you."

"It is no trouble at all," he insisted, already jumping down from the seat. Anna accepted his hand and allowed him to help her down, knowing she could not push back any further without being very rude.

They left the carriage in the care of the groom Anna had brought along. The bench was nestled under a tall oak tree just off the path with many people walking by at regular intervals. Out here, Anna did not worry about Mr. Milburn doing something shocking like trying to kiss her.

Anna and Mr. Milburn sat on the bench, the gentleman leaving little space between them. He coughed again. When Anna forced herself to look at him, she saw that his face had turned still as stone, his back uncomfortably straight. Surely a proposal was a nerve-wracking thing for any man, even one as self-assured as Mr. Milburn.

As Anna waited for him to gather his strength, she wondered at the complete switch she'd done from the beginning of the Season. Here she sat, on the verge of being an engaged woman, yet she prayed for some way out of this situation. All her life, she had dreamed of this moment, but now it felt wrong.

"Miss Harcourt?"

"Yes?"

"May I ask you something?"

Anna's throat had gone dry, but she managed a shaky answer. "Of course."

"Have you enjoyed getting to know me this Season?"

"I have, Mr. Milburn," Anna answered honestly, thankful that it had been a different question than the one she expected. "I hope our friendship has been enjoyable for you as well."

He fell silent once more, leaving Anna to her thoughts, filling with more and more panic. She looked straight ahead, watching the other London residents and visitors walk by, trying to encourage her lungs to take full breaths of air.

Soon Anna realized she had chosen a poor distraction. She noticed a couple send a curious glance her way, at first wondering if they sensed an imminent proposal. When she saw another couple seated on a bench across the path that looked to be having a similar conversation, Anna realized that no one seemed interested in them.

"I certainly have enjoyed spending time with you," Mr. Milburn started again before falling into yet another awkward silence.

Anna's anxiety took on a different tone as she slowly noticed more and more pairs of eyes upon them—no, not them. Her. Their looks ranged from curious to knowing to almost scornful. Anna's breath came in rapid, painful pulses, her eyes darting from face to face. Had everyone in London come to Hyde Park to examine her for some reason, just as they'd done at Richmond Park?

Mr. Milburn adjusted himself to properly face Anna. He

took her hands in his though she hardly noticed. "There is nothing wrong, I promise. In fact, I think you shall soon be the happiest lady in the world, and I will be the happiest man." He gave a nervous chuckle, brushing his thumb against Anna's knuckles, thankfully protected inside her gloves.

"That is not what I am concerned about!" Anna cried, no longer able to keep her frustration and fear at bay.

Mr. Milburn reeled back in surprise. He'd certainly never expected to witness such an outburst from Anna. Anna would have been horrified at her behavior if not for the overwhelming paranoia racing through her.

"Everyone is looking at me and it is making me terribly uncomfortable," Anna whispered harshly.

Mr. Milburn furrowed his brow, tightening his grip on Anna's hands. "Pay them no mind, my dear," he mumbled, clearing his throat. Anna's eyes snapped to the gentleman's face. She knew the truth in an instant.

"You have heard the rumor that my family will offer a large dowry in order to marry me off."

"Y-You make it sound much worse than it is," Mr. Milburn stuttered, baffled by Anna's drastic change.

Pain lanced through Anna's chest at everything Mr. Milburn's words implied. She could feel her throat swelling, her eyes burning with tears that demanded release. Anna forced them back. She would not show her tears to Mr. Milburn or any of these other people.

Anna whipped around to face Mr. Milburn, her fear and anger and pain stripping her of her usual polite demeanor. "Is that why all these people are staring at me?" she demanded, the sharpness in her voice sounding foreign even to her.

Mr. Milburn let go of Anna's hands, his jaw clenching as he tried to find something to say. He squirmed under Anna's intense gaze. She did not relent, even when he took a deep breath, ready to speak. "Word has been spreading, yes."

Anna did not know which she felt first or the strongest—anger, pain, or mortification. "Where did you hear this?" she asked through gritted teeth.

"From my father."

"And where did Viscount Milburn hear it?"

Mr. Milburn paused, a finger tapping on his knee as he thought back. "Well, I believe he heard it from one of Lord Welsted's friends. Or rather, he heard Lord Welsted's friend mention your unexpectedly large marriage portion while chatting with the baron himself."

The words landed on Anna's chest like a stone. Who should she believe now? Who should she trust?

Noticing Anna's distress, Mr. Milburn grasped her hands again. "This must be shocking to hear, but can it really be so bad?" he asked, sounding as if he comforted a child who had lost her favorite toy rather than a woman facing the upheaval of her whole world.

"You are sure to have your pick of gentlemen now. I know this is not the ideal time to say this, but I must confess that my motives may have been inspired by this rumor, as you put it. Please believe me when I say that I truly have come to enjoy your company. Miss Harcourt, I believe we could be happy together, if only you could put all this behind us."

"What of Mr. Waynford? Does he know of his rumor?"

Mr. Milburn's expression soured. "Yes, he does. When I inadvertently mentioned that his father was in a bad way, I meant that he'd made a bad bet and lost quite a bit of money."

"Please take me home." Anna stood from the bench, trying to keep the dreadful feeling in her stomach from bringing her to her knees.

"Miss Harcourt, surely—"

One cold look from Anna silenced Mr. Milburn. He helped her back into the carriage and drove them to the Harcourts' townhouse in silence. Anna mumbled a goodbye to Mr. Milburn as soon as her feet touched the pavement. She'd already made it up the front steps by the time she heard his carriage rumble away. Anna would have flown straight through the foyer if not for the slam in her side that nearly knocked her to the ground.

"Ow!" Harriet stumbled backward, eyes squeezed shut, rubbing her forehead where it had made contact with Anna's shoulder.

"Oh, Harriet! I'm so sorry! I wasn't paying attention." Anna pulled her youngest sibling into her arms, realizing as she did so how desperately she needed to be held. As she let her chin rest on her sister's head—probably one of her last opportunities to do so before the girl outgrew her—Anna offered a silent prayer that Harriet would never have to experience this kind of pain and uncertainty.

"Anna, you're squishing me," Harriet mumbled into Anna's chest.

"I'm sorry, my dear." Anna released Harriet from her grip. "Go on now. Get up to whatever mischief you were about to cause."

She smoothed Harriet's hair, always wild, before pushing her along toward the hallway. The youngest Harcourt smiled with such heartwarming innocence that Anna wondered for a moment if the past hour had been nothing more than a strange dream. As soon as Harriet skipped away, the reality thundered down on Anna once more.

Anna pulled herself up the staircase, her body growing heavier by the second. Perhaps she just needed a nice, long sleep to clear her head. Perhaps she still had time to convince herself that it had all been a dream turned nightmare.

"Look out!" a voice warned, causing Anna to skid to a halt.

Patrick stood before her on his way out of the drawing room, his hands up to stop her from barreling into him.

"I'm sorry, Patrick. My mind is in a fog today," Anna apologized again, shaking her head as if that could rid her of these terrible thoughts.

"I suppose we both have our heads in the clouds today," Patrick laughed, but his smile quickly fell when he saw that his oldest sister was not in a joking mood. "Is something wrong?"

"No, nothing to worry you about. I've just had a long day and could use some rest."

Patrick frowned, his brown eyes round with worry. "I'm afraid your rest will have to wait. You're wanted in the drawing room. We have a guest."

Anna groaned, certainly not in the mood for entertaining. "Who is it?"

"Mr. Waynford," Patrick said with a slight smile.

Anna's heart slowed to a more comfortable pace, knowing that Mr. Waynford sat just on the other side of the wall, but it did not completely eradicate her distress. As much as she always wanted to see Mr. Waynford, the thing she craved most right now was a chance to calm down and gather herself.

"Then why are you leaving if our guest is still here?" Anna asked, using her firm oldest child voice to its full effect. Naturally, it did not have any impact on Patrick.

The boy's eyes narrowed in a sly expression. "I got permission to leave, claiming I needed to get back to my studies, but really I am going to sneak into Dalton's room and see if I can hide something of his."

Anna shook her head. She could not deal with what she'd

heard at the park and this at the same time. "I will pretend I did not hear that."

Surprised, Patrick shrugged and trotted away toward the next staircase. Alone in the hallway now, Anna leaned her back against the wall, forcing herself to take the deepest breaths she could manage. She must get herself under control. She needed to speak to Papa about this at some point, but not in front of the rest of the family or Mr. Waynford. Certainly not today.

After several long moments, Anna found enough courage to signal for the footman to open the door. Happy voices greeted her as soon as she stepped inside. Mama and Papa sat on the sofa in the middle of the room, Dalton and Caroline flanking them in their own chairs.

Then there was Mr. Waynford. He smiled when Anna's eyes found him, looking almost relieved. Anna felt nothing of the sort. Seeing Mr. Waynford did nothing to ease her worries. Instead, he amplified them. Anna could not help wondering now if this man was just a better actor than the rest.

As she watched him for a moment, noticed his fingers twitching toward the empty seat next to him, Anna wondered if she really knew him any better than she knew Mr. Milburn. The other gentleman had been honest about a very uncomfortable subject when she'd pressed it. Anna did not know if she could trust Mr. Waynford to do the same. She would have to find out somehow.

"Come join us, darling." Mama waved for Anna to come closer. Anna wished she could run away, turn around and race to her room. Her feet ignored her, pulling her toward the empty seat next to Caroline, across from Mr. Waynford. Anna could not bear to sit so close to him. She feared what she might see under his charming smile. Mr. Waynford expertly hid his surprise when Anna chose not to sit next to him.

Anna listened to everyone else talk so carefree, as if they were all wonderful friends. Indeed, Mr. Waynford looked like he fit in perfectly with her family. She glanced at Papa, wondering if he'd heard this rumor—if perhaps it was not a rumor after all, but cruel fact. Anna pulled her eyes away, focusing on her fingers twisting the fabric of her walking dress. If she looked at Papa any longer, she may just end up flying from the room in a fit of tears.

The tears threatened to come anyway. How could Anna think such a horrible thing? How could she think her own father would do something like this? Yes, many fathers did this to their daughters. But not Anna's father. Not Papa.

Despite her feeble reassurances, Anna still could not help wondering…where had the rumor come from in the first place? Most rumors had some grain of truth at the center, as the saying went. Anna loathed this seed of distrust that had been planted in her, but she could not shake it no matter how hard she tried.

After all, it made much more sense for all these gentlemen to be attracted to her for a supposed fortune than anything to do with Anna herself. She had known it her whole life. She was nothing remarkable, regardless of what her family and friends told her. They were kind people. They would not tell her that truth.

A gentle pressure settled against Anna's shoulder. She looked over to Caroline, leaning in close while everyone was distracted by one of Mama's humorous tales. Caroline did not usually show much sisterly affection, save to apologize for teasing Anna.

Anna gritted her teeth. She could not bear any of her sister's usual jests right now. Caroline did not make any smart comment about Anna's rigid silence or her inability to look directly at Mr. Waynford. She glanced to Caroline again, even more surprised to see the concern in the younger woman's eyes.

"Are you well?"

Anna looked around the room once more, at her family and Mr. Waynford, willing herself not to lose all faith in them. She gave Caroline a weak smile, the best she could muster.

"I will be."

CHAPTER 13

oah stared out the sitting room window, hands clasped behind his back, staring out at the street below. His mind swirled with the last meeting he'd had with Miss Harcourt. It had not been much of a meeting, in truth. He'd paid a visit to Lord Welsted and Mr. Harcourt in the hopes of also running into Miss Harcourt.

Instead of sweet memories, murky thoughts clouded Noah's mind. Miss Harcourt had arrived home from an engagement with Mr. Milburn while some of the other Harcourts entertained him in their drawing room. Noah had been able to put that fact out of his mind, simply ecstatic at the thought of seeing her again. As soon as his eyes landed on her, a comforting calm settled over his heart, something he'd come to associate with Miss Harcourt.

She had not seemed nearly as pleased to see him. Miss Harcourt had chosen to sit next to her sister on the other side of the room. She had seemed flustered though she'd hidden it under a veneer even more thin than the one she used to wear.

Had she started to fall for Mr. Milburn? Noah glared down at an innocent gentleman walking by on the street. That thought sent a ripple of anger and fear through him—anger because he knew that Mr. Milburn did not care for Miss Harcourt the way he did, and fear because Noah had become so attached to her that any attempts at imagining a future without her twisted his stomach into a knot of pain.

The realization that he cared so deeply for Miss Harcourt still surprised Noah. He had been so unsure of her at first that he felt he'd only just started to understand the real woman beneath her facade. Her behavior the other day in the Harcourts' drawing room reminded Noah of those early days of their courtship, throwing him for a loop once more. Noah stood straighter, lifting his chin up. Staring out the window would not get him anywhere.

"Phineas, how and when did you know you loved Miss Bishop—that you wanted to spend your life with her?" Noah spun around to face his friend with a strange formality.

Phineas's head snapped up from his book. He grinned, patting the empty chair next to him. Noah accepted the silent invitation, trying to suppress the awkward nerves rattling through him. As much as he and Phineas had discussed their determination to wait for love, Noah could not help feeling embarrassed by the topic now that it stared him in the face.

Noah realized for the first time that he would be talking about his own love, a real love, rather than a theoretical one.

"You mean Miss Harcourt, yes?"

"Yes, it is her. I have not really wanted to see any other ladies since I became serious about courting her."

The other man nodded slowly. "I could tell right away during our walk at the Serpentine that Miss Harcourt would end up with your heart."

A small smile tugged at Noah's lips at the thought of Miss

Harcourt having his heart. It sent a shiver of warmth through him. He knew she would care for his heart so gently, and, if Noah had her heart, he would protect it with everything he had.

"Well, based on the lovestruck look on your face, it must be getting quite serious now," Phineas chuckled, setting his book aside on the table next to him before leaning on the arm of his chair toward Noah. "I cannot promise that our experiences will be perfectly analogous, but perhaps you will find some helpful similarities.

"The first few times I met Cora, I certainly found her to be very beautiful, far too beautiful for the likes of me. And I found her to be smart—again, far above my own ability. I did not have much confidence that such a wonderful creature would have any interest in me when so many other men would surely throw themselves at her, and indeed they did. Wealthy gentry, earls, even a duke. The heir to a baronetcy could never hold a candle to that competition.

"As such, I did not allow my heart to open up to the possibility that I had any hope of winning her heart. Yet she always seemed to be there when I called on her brother, so we had opportunities to talk. Eventually, I realized that I could at least ask her to spend a day with me. If she declined, I would be disappointed but not heartbroken. You can imagine my shock when she accepted.

"I know you do not need all these little details, so I will hurry things up," Phineas said, smiling at Noah's impatiently furrowed brows. "Even during those first few outings, I did not believe she could ever be serious about me. Yet the more time we spent together, the more I realized how much we had in common. For all her charm and intelligence, Cora really is as much of a silly fool as I am—and of course I say that in the most loving way possible.

"In any case, it took time to realize that I could love her because she could love me. But when I did realize that, nothing else mattered. It dawned on me slowly, but once I caught a glimpse of the truth, my eyes and heart opened completely to her. I knew I could not live without her smiles, her laughter, her kindness, her marvelous ability to put up with me all while making me feel as though I am the only man in the world. Does any of that sound familiar?"

"On the contrary, it all sounds rather mysterious." Noah frowned, doing his best to absorb his friend's words while doubting their relevance for his situation.

Phineas simply shrugged. "That is love, my friend—the greatest mystery we will spend our lifetimes solving. It will happen for you, too, when the time is right. By my estimation, that time does not seem too far off now."

Noah's frown only deepened as he fell silent, wondering at this mystery he'd landed himself in.

"Has there been a problem?" Phineas asked.

"I am not sure," Noah admitted with a sigh. He explained his afternoon in the drawing room with the Harcourts, how distant she'd been.

Phineas chewed his lip. "Is it Mr. Milburn?"

"It might be. She had just returned from an outing with him that day, but I also know that more gentlemen have been interested in courting her. Still, he seems to be the most determined of her suitors."

"Aside from you, of course." Phineas gave Noah a playful nudge with his elbow.

"What should I do?" Noah asked.

"My situation with Cora is not quite the same, but I think the best course of action would be to go on some outing or visit her again and see how she is. Perhaps she was simply in a sour mood that day. If she still seems bothered by something, ask her to share it with you."

"You make it sound so simple," Noah sighed, running a hand through his hair. It did sound simple, especially for a man who valued honest conversation as much as he did. Yet he could not deny how nervous he felt to receive a particular answer—that she had lost interest in him...or that she had accepted Mr. Milburn or someone else entirely.

Noah leaned back in his chair. He knew Phineas was correct. With some sort of plan in place, Noah thought it time to change their discussion to happier topics.

"Thank you for your help, my friend. Now tell me, how are your wedding preparations coming along?"

As soon as Noah walked into the Harcourts' drawing room behind Mother and Father, he saw the thing he'd been dreading. Quite a few other people already filled the room, pleasantly mingling despite a subtle tension in the air. A quick scan of the room revealed Mr. Milburn and his father, which did not surprise Noah. When his family had received the invitation for a dinner at the Harcourts' home, it had implied a large party of which Noah guessed Mr. Milburn would be a member.

He also saw three other young men with their parents. The Parkins were also in attendance, as well as a couple young ladies and their parents. A large party, indeed. Noah's stomach filled with an uneasy anxiety. How would he ever be able to find a moment with Miss Harcourt with all these people around, many of whom were vying specifically for her attention?

Noah shot a nervous glance to Emma and Angelica, both of whom had noticed the situation as well. Emma looked downright annoyed that her brother would not be given an adequate chance to spend time with his lady, while Angelica's expression mirrored Noah's disappointment.

Pulling his shoulders back and taking advantage of his full height, Noah vowed to make the most of whatever opportunities he could find. Phineas's advice lingered in the back of Noah's mind, urging him to make a decision soon—both for his own sake and for Miss Harcourt's. If Noah truly wanted to take that leap, if Noah truly thought he was falling in love with her, he could not wait much longer to confess his feelings—not with how many other gentlemen were probably thinking the same thing at this very moment.

The Waynford family moved deeper into the drawing room, Mother and Father happily greeting Lord and Lady Welsted. After offering his own greeting, Noah craned his neck to get a better view of the room, trying to find Miss Harcourt.

"I cannot see her. Perhaps she has taken ill," Noah whispered to Emma.

Emma coughed uncomfortably in response. He furrowed his brow, about to ask what bothered her, when he noticed the way her eyes darted to a group on the other side of the room.

Noah followed her gaze. After a moment, he caught a glimpse of Miss Harcourt between the shoulders of two gentlemen as they shifted slightly. From what he could tell, she looked a little overwhelmed. Noah could not blame her. He knew Miss Harcourt did not usually care to be fussed over, so this must have felt quite foreign to her. At least Mrs. Parkins and Mr. Harcourt stood by her on either side, providing a buffer for the reserved lady.

As soon as Mother and Father finished chatting with their hosts, Lady Welsted hurried over to her daughter's group to monitor the situation while Lord Welsted returned to a group of parents. Noah almost did not register that Mr. Milburn avoided Miss Harcourt, standing with Lord Welsted and the older guests instead, immediately resuming their conversation. Noah swallowed nervously, his heart beating faster. He hoped Mr. Milburn did not plan on sharing any special plans with Lord Welsted tonight.

"You should try to work your way in there, Noah." Angelica gently tapped his arm, lifting her chin toward the group surrounding Miss Harcourt.

As much as he wanted to stand next to her, to hear her voice and see her smile, Noah hesitated. He normally did not shy away from group conversations with strangers. There just did not seem to be any room for him over there right now.

"Our little sister is right," Emma heartily agreed, putting a hand between Noah's shoulder blades and pushing him forward. He nearly stumbled, his cheeks flaming. He threw a sharp glare over his shoulder at Emma. His older sister smiled apologetically, as if she did not realize her own strength. Reuben shook his head, leading his wife away while Angelica and Josias followed, leaving Noah with no escape.

When he righted himself, Noah saw a few heads from the group turned in his direction, including Mr. Harcourt. The young man beamed, signaling for Noah to join them. Noah uttered yet another silent prayer of thanks for Mr. Harcourt and his uncanny ability to know just when and how to help him.

With that settled, Noah made his way to Miss Harcourt's party, her brother indicating a spot by his side.

"Good evening, Mr. Waynford. I'm so glad your family could come tonight," Miss Harcourt said with a hollow smile. Just as Noah had feared, she still seemed distressed by something, and not just by the small crowd gathered around her.

That smile was too similar to the one he'd received on his last visit here. Even worse, she used that overly cheery tone that she'd employed when they'd first met, when she'd thought he would like her better if she behaved like a completely different person.

Her attention did not linger on Noah. Instead, she turned back to the rest of the group, listening diligently as the others talked. Though Noah tried to listen as well, he could not help noticing the way her gaze darted away from him whenever their eyes almost met.

Had he done something wrong? Try as he might to figure it out, Noah simply could not determine what he could have said or done to upset her. He would find out tonight and make things right between them again. This, Noah realized, was another important test for him to determine their suitability. Could they overcome this together—whatever this was?

Noah suffered through what felt like an eternity of superficial conversation, all the while noticing the other gentlemen watching Miss Harcourt with interest. Their interest, however, did not convey any sense of affection. He knew they had heard the rumor. It had been spreading even farther and faster lately, it seemed.

Glancing around at their eager faces, Noah suddenly felt as though he'd been dunked in a bucket of ice water. Could he really consider himself that different from any of them?

Yet when his eyes landed on Miss Harcourt again and he saw her lovely features, Noah remembered the many sweet, genuine moments they'd shared, especially after she'd abandoned her facade. He knew that he was different. He may have started out in the same place as these other men, but he had come to care deeply for Miss Harcourt—perhaps even love her, if he let himself.

To Noah's surprise, Miss Harcourt finally met his gaze for

just a moment. He could not quite read her expression, but what he saw sent another shiver through him. She looked as though she wanted to say something to him, but feared his response.

Noah's anxiety nearly spiraled away from him, the conversation now unbearable. He just wanted to speak with Miss Harcourt as soon as possible so he could discover what bothered her and offer his help in whatever she needed. As if answering his prayers, Lady Welsted called for Miss Harcourt.

"Anna, dearest, you should come and listen to this charming story Mrs. Smithly has just told me." The baroness waved for her daughter to join herself and another woman, likely a mother of one of the suitors, by the fireplace.

"Please pardon me for a moment. I shall be back shortly." Miss Harcourt excused herself politely. Noah thought he saw her breathe a sigh of relief when she turned her back to them. Her group dispersed, the other gentlemen frowning in disappointment as they went off in search of other entertainment.

"I am not sure what Mama and Papa were thinking when they invited all these people," Mr. Harcourt said under his breath. Noah lingered by the young man, both for the comfort of having a familiar presence nearby and also for the chance to catch Miss Harcourt when she returned. Noah silently agreed with Mr. Harcourt's assessment.

"I hope you don't mind my asking, but has Miss Harcourt been unwell recently?"

Mr. Harcourt's jaw clenched uncomfortably as he glanced from Noah to his sister. Noah wished he had not asked. Though he did like Mr. Harcourt quite a bit, they had not yet reached the point of familiarity where he could pry into private matters.

Subtly, almost passing Noah's observant gaze, Mr.

Harcourt took a half step nearer to his sister and mother, still chatting with the very animated Mrs. Smithly. "I'm afraid Anna has been feeling a little stressed with all these new... friends she's made recently. I tried to talk Mama and Papa out of inviting so many of them all at once, but they insisted it would be fine."

Noah nodded, his heart heavy with sympathy. He had lost track of the slow progress they'd made toward the three women as he and Mr. Harcourt slipped into more casual conversation. Once more, the gentleman gave Noah quite the helping hand. He'd situated them closely enough to Lady Welsted, Mrs. Smithly, and Miss Harcourt that he could listen for a natural break in the conversation.

"You will not believe this, Anna," he interjected as Mrs. Smithly's story came to an end. "Mr. Waynford has quite an interesting tale of his own that I think will fascinate you. You are quite fond of ducks, are you not?" With a frazzled smile, Miss Harourt pardoned herself from one conversation and joined another.

"Goodness, I should go see what's got Papa looking so perplexed." With a nod to Noah, Mr. Harcourt excused himself, leaving Noah and Miss Harcourt as alone as they could possibly be in this room full of people.

Despite the many sets of eyes Noah felt on him from all corners of the room, he did not waste any time. "Are you well, Miss Harcourt? I'm surprised to see so many people here tonight."

The lady gave another tight smile. "I am very well, thank you. In fact, I insisted that Mama and Papa invite everyone."

Noah's eyes widened for a moment before he regained his composure. He would not have guessed that Miss Harcourt would enjoy such a gathering, let alone request it herself. That would have to wait for now. Noah had more pressing matters to get to and not much time to do it.

"I—"

"Have you heard the rumors swirling around town that my father is offering a large dowry to whoever will marry me by the end of the Season?" she asked, her voice both serious and scared.

The color drained from Noah's face. Like a coward, he wanted nothing more than to run and hide from that ugly truth. He should not have been surprised that this tale had made its way back to her. The London rumor mill was not known for its discretion, after all.

His chest squeezed with pain. Based on her distressed expression, Noah guessed that she had only recently discovered it herself. Surely that could not be a pleasant thing for anyone to hear.

"Yes, I am afraid I have indeed heard something about that," Noah started, feeling the noble strength of truth building up inside him. The flash of pain in Miss Harcourt's eyes nearly brought him to his knees. "But that is not why I began courting you, you see. I truly do enjoy your company and I have developed a strong attachment to you. I only heard those rumors after we'd already met."

Noah had chosen the coward's way out after all. It was not a complete lie, at least, though certainly not how Noah had imagined confessing his feelings to Miss Harcourt. He'd pictured something much more romantic.

Still, he could not bear to see that sorrow in her expression. Noah had never been a liar or a coward, and he could already feel his self-loathing frothing inside him, but tonight he just could not bear it. What harm could there be in a partial lie if all the rest was true?

He knew what the real, ugly truth would do to her—to them. He could not allow that to happen.

Miss Harcourt smiled, still uneasy. "Thank you for being honest with me, Mr. Waynford."

~

NOAH WONDERED if he'd ever sat through a more uncomfortable dinner. Perhaps the one where Reuben's parents had come to visit the Waynford home when he and Emma had still been courting and, through some bizarre misunderstanding, thought that Reuben would be marrying Angelica.

No, Noah decided. This dinner took first prize. He had ended up several seats away from Miss Harcourt. Worse still, Mr. Milburn had a seat right next to her, allowing him to capture her attention as much as he desired.

Noah had no choice but to watch and listen, growing more irritated as the dinner went on. With a sullen frown, he stabbed at his food with his fork, earning him a sharp glare from Mother. Emma snickered into her napkin, earning herself a similar look from Mother.

With a grimace, Noah silently scolded himself. He must get his emotions under control, or get his fork under control at the very least. No matter what he thought of Mr. Milburn or the other gentlemen or his own role in this situation, Noah could do nothing about it now.

His mind was a different challenge entirely. That remained uncharacteristically out of his control. He could not determine which bothered him more—himself or Miss Harcourt.

Currently, Noah despised himself for lying to Miss Harcourt, though he'd done so because he thought it would put her more at ease with him, would bring them closer to where they had been before that strange day in the Harcourts' drawing room. As he spent the entire dinner watching Miss Harcourt undergo a transformation into the woman she'd once tried to be, Noah's frustration with her also grew.

She laughed at Mr. Milburn's jokes and the other men's comments a little too coyly. Noah had thought he'd come to understand Miss Harcourt, but he could not figure out why she would act this way. He tried to convince himself that it must be some sort of defense when she felt overwhelmed and put on the spot. Something told him that was not the case, no matter how much he wished it.

In any case, Noah's jealousy rose to an unprecedented level. He loathed the way Mr. Milburn reveled in Miss Harcourt's attention, as if he were the only man worthy of her smiles.

Noah knew he had no claim on Miss Harcourt since he had taken so long to declare his feelings—and since he'd done so in a less than graceful way. Yet the more he thought about Miss Harcourt accepting someone else, the more it filled him with an empty misery he had never experienced before. He knew in his heart that they had a connection. He'd thought until recently that she'd felt it, too.

Something had changed. Something had pushed Noah out of Miss Harcourt's favor.

He barely tasted the food or heard any of the conversations floating around him. He could only hear Miss Harcourt's voice, fawning over everything the other gentlemen said, as if she had no thoughts or opinions of her own to offer.

Even in his jealousy, Noah knew it was such a shame that none of those men seemed to realize or appreciate just how bright and interesting and thoughtful Miss Harcourt was. Noah had almost made that mistake himself, but he'd given her time to reveal her true identity. It had all been well worth the wait.

The end of the dinner did not bring an end to Noah's suffering. He still had to endure the portion of time set aside after dinner for the men to talk and drink in the dining room while the ladies retired to the drawing room. Noah planned to stay by Father, Reuben, and Josias as much as possible, keeping to himself so he could look back on the night thus far and try to solve this strange puzzle before him.

Noah tipped back his glass, draining the last sip in one gulp. His mind had returned from the exhausting hoops it jumped through only to realize that he stood alone in the center of the room. Father had wandered away to chat with Lord Welsted, Mr. Harcourt, and Mr. Milburn while his brothers-in-law had joined another group of young men.

While Noah could not blame them for seeking lively conversation rather than his gloomy silence, he still did not appreciate feeling so exposed and alone. Noah peered into his empty glass. He supposed a refill would give him something to do besides stand awkwardly in the center of the group. As he made his way to the sideboard, Noah prayed that he would be left alone to his sulking.

"Good evening, Mr. Waynford." Mr. Milburn's voice grated against Noah's ears, sickeningly polite and jovial. He'd joined Noah at the sideboard to refill his own glass.

"Good evening." Noah nodded sharply, keeping his eyes on his drink, afraid that he would unleash an uncontrollable glare if he looked the other gentleman in the face.

"I trust you are well?" Mr. Milburn asked, artfully returning the stopper to the decanter. How did everything about this man annoy Noah so much?

"Very well indeed, thank you. And what of you?" Though Noah wanted nothing more than to turn to the other man and demand answers, demand that he leave Miss Harcourt alone unless he truly loved her, he managed to cling to the last remnants of his quickly fading manners.

Mr. Milburn turned to face Noah, leaning against the sideboard with his glass held casually between his fingers. He looked like he could not care less about spilling a drop of that expensive liquid, while Noah knew that he would not be able to afford such a luxury by this time next year.

The viscount's son took a sip of his drink before answering Noah, a small but content smile on his lips. "I am doing exceptionally well, as a matter of fact."

Of course, Noah knew exactly what he meant; the implication ignited his anger into a burning flame. Was this man really worthy of Miss Harcourt's love? Did he deserve to spend the rest of his life with her?

Noah's stomach squeezed and then expanded with nauseating speed. Who was he to judge Mr. Milburn? Noah had not been too different from the man standing before him all that long ago.

"I'm glad to hear it," Noah muttered, thoroughly put in his place.

"Thank you, good sir. Do enjoy the rest of your evening." Mr. Milburn nodded to Noah before striding off. He looked surprisingly happy, almost innocent.

Noah tilted his glass back once more, willing the liquid to cool him down from the inside out. Before he could take another sip, the door separating the dining room and drawing room swung open, allowing the gentlemen to rejoin the ladies.

He barely had time to locate Miss Harcourt, seated on the sofa in the middle of the room next to Mrs. Parkins, before Mr. Milburn crossed the room in a few confident strides, situating himself across from the two ladies. Noah could only stand, watch, and desperately pray that his eyes deceived him. He knew immediately that this prayer would not be answered. Miss Harcourt paid attention to no one but Mr. Milburn, even as her other suitors approached to join the conversation.

Noah's frustration paralyzed him. He could not bear to force himself into that competition any longer.

The night had not turned out at all how Noah had hoped or imagined. He would simply have to wait until he had a clearer mind and see if he could work the situation out with Miss Harcourt later—if she wanted it to work out.

CHAPTER 14

*A*lone at last, Anna stared glumly at the opposite wall in the small sitting room. She needed to think. She also needed to keep herself from everyone else. The ache in her heart made Anna prone to sudden bursts of emotion—sometimes anger, sometimes sorrow.

With the dinner party from last night still fresh in her mind, Anna's stomach churned with uneasiness and uncertainty. She put a hand to her forehead, letting her elbow rest on the arm of the chair, forgoing proper ladylike poise for now. How could she be proper when she felt her heart crumbling?

She felt betrayed by everything. As much as she had given the benefit of the doubt to Papa, the confirmation she received from Mr. Milburn in the park and the other gentlemen last night had sent her into a downward slope of hurt and confusion. She felt betrayed by herself as well, for thinking she had any chance at real love. Of course, there was Mr. Waynford, too.

Anna had put so much hope in him. She'd even started to think that she could call her feelings for him by that sacred word she'd longed to attach to someone her whole life—love. After the dinner party, he seemed no different than any of her other suitors.

At the core of it all, Anna simply could not tell who in her life was genuine. It tore her apart until she doubted the very things she'd come to believe in. She'd believed in her father's love. She'd believed in herself for a short time. She'd believed in Mr. Waynford. She had never had trouble trusting others, choosing to believe that they all carried some good in their hearts.

Now, with the widespread confirmation of those dreadful rumors making its way through all the single gentlemen in London, Anna did not know who she could trust. After breakfast, she'd spent the morning alone, telling her family that she was tired after such a lively evening. She could not stand to be near any of them right now, but especially not Papa. Her doubt eclipsed the concern she saw in his eyes, concern that seemed genuine but could be just as false as everything else.

The door of the small sitting room opened quietly, interrupting Anna's solitude. "Dalton, please leave me be," Anna snapped without looking over her shoulder toward the door.

"Since you only asked for Dalton to leave, I suppose I must still be welcome." Papa's voice shocked Anna upright.

"My dear Anna." He sat across from his daughter, holding his hand out to her.

Guilt made Anna want to bolt from the room and hide in shame. How could she think that Papa would do something so cruel to her? He'd noticed as soon as he walked into the room that something troubled her. Anna tentatively put her hand in Papa's. Though she still felt far from ready, the time for truth had finally found her.

"You haven't seemed yourself these past few days. How can I help?" he asked, never removing his eyes from Anna's face. She smiled at his choice of words. Papa always wanted to help in his quiet, gentle way.

She took a few deep breaths, gathering her strength. Papa waited patiently, watching Anna. She did not have enough strength to look at her father yet, but she had enough strength to speak. "I am afraid I have come across some rather...unpleasant information."

Papa remained silent as Anna explained the rumor and her reasons for inviting her suitors to the dinner party. He remained silent even after Anna finished. With an uncomfortable mixture of curiosity and anxiety, Anna glanced up at the man seated across from her.

He sat with his elbows propped on the arms of his chair, his fingers meeting in a steeple at his chest. Anna prayed that he would not bring up Mr. Waynford by name. Talking about him would be too difficult right now. It was easier for her to leave him as just one of many in a crowd.

After several long moments, Papa shook his head. Anna's heart plummeted when she saw the shame on his face. Panic raced through Anna's mind. Was Papa about to confirm that he'd orchestrated this whole situation? She held her breath while he figured out what to say next.

The baron dragged a hand over his face, slumping forward in his seat. "I am so very sorry, Anna."

Anna's blood froze and her heart stopped, but the tears still found their way out. "Papa, please tell me this is not true," she whispered, the words fighting to escape her lips. "Please tell me you have not been trying to rid yourself of me."

Papa jerked back up, clasping Anna's hand in both of his. "Dear Lord, never, my sweet girl. That is not what I apologized for. I would never, ever do such a thing." Air flooded Anna's lungs as her father's words sank in. He gripped her chin in his fingers, giving her head a little shake just as he'd done when she was a child. "Nevertheless, I do have something I deeply regret."

"What could you possibly mean?"

Papa sighed heavily, his jaw twitching in frustration. Something had been weighing on his mind for quite some time. Anna could not be sure, but she thought she saw a new line etched in her father's forehead.

"I have known of this rumor for some time," he confessed, his voice no more than a whisper. "I swear I was trying to protect you, Anna," he hurried, seeing the pain in his daughter's eyes. "I've been trying to put an end to it myself, hoping to snuff the gossip out before it reached you. You know how these things go in this cursed town. Words can spread like fire, growing stronger all the while. Clearly, I failed in my mission."

He dropped his chin to his chest, squeezing his eyes shut. Anna leaned forward, putting her other hand over his. "I'm sorry I ever doubted you, Papa. I knew there must have been an explanation, but I was so afraid...so afraid that I had become your shameful daughter that you wanted to send away forever."

"Silly girl," Papa chuckled, his green eyes both soft and pained as he gazed at Anna. "In truth, I would not mind keeping all my children around forever, though your mama may have something to say about that. Besides, you all have your own lives to live. But I would never try to force any of you away."

"Then how did this rumor come about? You know how things go in this cursed town." Anna and her father shared a small smile when she borrowed his words. "There must be some truth in every lie."

"I'm even more ashamed to admit this, but I was there when this whole blasted thing started. My less than tactful friend at White's made a distasteful remark about offering more money to get you married off. I feared others may have heard, since the room is always full of gentlemen walking about. As we now know, someone must have heard it and taken it as fact. Of course, those opportunists who heard that part did not seem to hear me scold my friend and tell him I would never do such a thing to my dear daughter. I've been trying to clean up this mess ever since that day at White's, telling every man who so much as hinted at it to me that it's complete nonsense."

Anna's heart broke for her poor father. "Papa, I hope you will forgive me for ever thinking those awful rumors could be true."

Papa waved a hand through the air. "You have nothing to apologize for, my darling."

A comforting, warm wave of contentment spread through Anna's body. All her doubts melted away. She had known deep down that Papa loved her, would always love her, and only wanted the best for her. She had let her fear cast a shadow over her heart.

"I will forever be sorry that I could not protect you from this cruel turn of events. I cannot imagine how distressing it must be to hear something like this," Papa apologized once more.

"I know you did your very best in a difficult situation, Papa," Anna insisted. "It does hurt, but pain is a part of life. Now having known this kind of pain, I can better appreciate all my blessings in the future."

The baron smiled proudly, patting the back of Anna's hand. "I am so very glad that you have grown up to be such a wise, understanding, positive young lady. You know, Anna, that you do not need to carry on with any of those gentlemen. Neither your mama or I care if you make a match or not this Season. Or ever. We only want you to be happy, and you will always be taken care of."

Anna tried to give an appreciative smile, but she could not quite do it.

"What is the matter, dear?"

"I've always wanted true love like you and Mama have. I did not start the Season with much hope of finding it, but I started to believe it might be possible. I seem to have tricked myself into a false sense of security with all this attention I've been receiving. Perhaps this is not the path my life is meant to take."

Papa took a deep breath, his expression growing serious. "Every parent wants their child to have a life of love and happiness, and, of course, we want the same for you. I urge you not to step off that path just yet, but do keep in mind that more than one type of love and happiness exists."

Anna pursed her lips, confused. "More than one type of love and happiness?"

"Having a marriage like mine and a family of my own certainly is rewarding in its own right, but it is not the only reward in life. You have love for your family and friends, do you not?"

"Of course I do, but I still do not understand what you mean."

"In the same way that you have love for your family and friends, your neighbors and countrymen, you can also have love for yourself. That can bring its own unique happiness. I cannot tell you how many people I've seen in my lifetime who had so much love for others, yet none to spare for themselves. They suffered for it. That is just as important and valuable and rewarding as romantic love. And of course, you will always be loved by us."

Papa's words stunned Anna into silence. What he described sounded so simple, so natural, yet it had never crossed Anna's mind to think of love in those terms. She had always been so concerned with winning or keeping others' love, of pleasing everyone else, that she had left herself out.

"Whatever happens next, Anna, your story is far from over," Papa continued. "You did not trick yourself into a false sense of security. You've just had a glimpse of what enjoying life and finding happiness in yourself looks like. Now, you just need a bigger picture of that view without having to see yourself through the eyes of others."

Anna's heart soared higher than it had in days. Papa was right, of course. This exhilarating confidence she'd felt this Season still belonged to her, even if it started from a place that was not sustainable. Anna's story was not over until she decided it was—and she was not ready to close the book just yet.

She did not know if she wanted to continue any of these courtships given the information she'd discovered last night, and she did not know if she wanted to give up on finding true love completely. For now, Anna knew that she could someday reach a point where she was happy with herself and her life without those expectations. It would not happen overnight, but Papa's words gave her a strong starting point.

Mr. Waynford's face flashed through Anna's mind, sending her heart racing with trepidation.

"Thank you, Papa. You have no idea how much you've helped me." Anna leaned forward, planting a kiss on her father's cheek before rushing away, her hands clutching at her skirt to keep from tripping.

She needed to speak with Mr. Waynford. She needed more answers.

ANNA AND DALTON walked up the front stairs of the Waynfords' home, Anna's nerves urging her to turn around with every step. Dalton put a steadying hand on her shoulder, giving her a gentle squeeze. Anna looked up at him, appreciating his encouraging smile.

"Are you ready?"

Anna gave a single nod. Dalton knocked on the dark wood door. She would have never guessed that she would be standing on a man's doorstep to call on him even though she knew she hadn't broken any of Society's rules. Dalton was with her, but he only acted as a means for her to see Mr. Waynford without being horribly improper.

Once the butler led them into the drawing room, Anna knew she had passed the point of no return. As much as she dreaded this conversation, as distressed and fragile as she felt, she knew she must do this. Time crawled by as they waited, Anna's knee unconsciously bouncing up and down.

"Everything will be fine, Anna. You can do whatever it is you need to do," Dalton said quietly, holding Anna's hand.

She smiled weakly, less and less certain the longer they waited. She supposed they could still go home, claiming she fell ill. She needed to think about this quietly, weighing her options. Could she really be that unhappy accepting one of these gentlemen? They had all been nice. She'd come to appreciate Mr. Milburn and, of course, she could not deny her strong feelings for Mr. Waynford. Could she still accept him, knowing what she knew?

As soon as Mr. Waynford swept into the room, Anna's eyes met his. Her heart yearned for him, cried for her to fly across the room and throw herself into his arms. That was exactly why Anna needed to have this conversation.

Mr. Waynford looked quite surprised to see Anna waiting for him, as did Mr. Tilson, who had followed him into the drawing room. His deep blue eyes never left Anna's.

Dalton gave Anna's hand a squeeze, transferring a little of his bravery to her. Anna cleared her throat, lifting her chin.

"Mr. Tilson, this is my brother, Mr. Dalton Harcourt," Anna mumbled quickly, eager to skip past the pleasantries and get this all over with. "Would you like to join us for a walk?"

"Drat, what poor timing," said Mr. Tilson. "We just returned from a walk."

"Yes, we would love to join you." Mr. Waynford stepped closer, as if he wanted to take Anna's hand right then and there.

"Mr. Tilson, was it?" Dalton asked cheerfully, striding up to Mr. Waynford's friend. "Anna has mentioned you before. She said you are to be married soon. How wonderful! Miss Cora Bishop is your bride-to-be, she said. Tell me, does Miss Bishop have a brother named Isaiah?" He skillfully led Mr. Tilson back out of the drawing room, as if the man had never objected.

Mr. Waynford offered his arm to Anna. After a moment of hesitation, she accepted, feeling everything inside her ignite at his touch. Being so close to him could very well make her unravel and forget everything she'd discovered—about her situation and herself.

Anna clung as tightly as she could to the fragile strength that had been budding inside her. As wonderful as it felt to be on Mr. Waynford's arm, to hear his voice, to see his eyes searching her, Anna knew she could not allow herself to get caught up in all that. She knew, after all, that Mr. Waynford had not been as genuine as he'd seemed.

Once outside, Mr. Waynford took the lead, guiding their small party to a public garden at the end of his street. The walk only took a few minutes of heavy silence, at least between Anna and Mr. Waynford. Dalton and Mr. Tilson maintained a happy stream of conversation behind them. They stepped through the garden's archway, Anna absent-mindedly wishing that she had any energy left to appreciate the pretty space she found herself in. Mr. Waynford walked purposefully toward a bench in the back corner of the garden, while Anna struggled to keep up with his long strides. Dalton and Mr. Tilson lingered by the entrance.

"I'm so very glad to see you, Miss Harcourt." Mr. Waynford broke the silence as soon as they sat down, angling himself to see her better.

The same guilt that had plagued Anna earlier in the day when she'd confronted Papa attacked her once more. Anna chewed her lip, trying to force her mind into forming a simple sentence of greeting, let alone all the complex thoughts and emotions she needed to express.

Mr. Waynford's worried silence told Anna that he had already guessed something bothered her. "Would you like to tell me what's on your mind?"

Anna inhaled the fresh, early summer air, her eyes tracing the blades of grass under her feet. She wished she had the courage to look him in the eye. For now, she would speak to the grass and hope he heard.

"I have been quite distressed after hearing some news recently," she started quietly, her words gaining a little more strength as she went on.

Mr. Waynford stiffened next to her. "I'm so sorry for that nasty situation," he mumbled, an undertone of panic in his voice. That only made Anna's suspicions about Mr. Waynford more concrete.

Her nerves slowly subsided as she pulled her words together. She could not keep imagining a future with this man until she knew the truth—the whole truth.

"A nasty situation indeed. I discovered through the dinner party that every gentleman there had heard this rumor about my father offering a handsome sum of money to the man who married me. That is why I've had so much attention this Season, when before I did not seem to merit a second glance from any man."

"I truly am sorry you had to hear about this in such an unfortunate way." Mr Waynford shook his head, also staring down at the grass, unable to look at her. He looked almost as nervous as she did. She knew he was deflecting.

Anna smiled wryly with a painfully bitter satisfaction. "That rumor is, in fact, false. I've spoken with Papa and he explained everything. A gentleman from his club made a rude comment to him about finally marrying me off; someone passing by heard it, then passed it on, over and over again. Naturally, it became quite the talk of the town since most have already written me off as a spinster."

From her peripheral vision, Anna saw him nod slowly. Her stomach churned as she realized that this information came as a surprise to him, and not an entirely welcome one. Surely, if he truly loved her, that fact would not change anything.

As if reading her thoughts, Mr. Waynford swiveled on the bench to face Anna. He pulled her hands toward his chest, leaving Anna breathless with that same familiar exhilaration as well as dread. "That does not change how I feel about you."

Those words hurt Anna more than she would have thought possible as she remembered what he'd said last night. She so wished she could enjoy this moment with her hands in Mr. Waynford's, sitting side by side in this beautiful garden on what could have been a perfect day.

Anna fought back her tears, still not daring to look into Mr. Waynford's face. "I've known the truth since you said it at the dinner party. You lied to me. You heard the rumor before we started courting. That can only lead me to believe that you initiated our relationship with money rather than love in mind."

"Miss Harcourt, I can expla—"

"I know about your family's financial struggles."

With a small glance, Anna saw his jaw clench and

unclench rapidly, his eyes darting over the ground as if he could find an answer there. Finally, a disappointed grimace passed over his face. He had decided to come forward with the truth, for which Anna felt surprisingly grateful. It had taken nearly all her strength to get this far. She did not know if she would have the strength to reject him if he still denied his motives and insisted he wanted to be with her.

Anna knew she could not allow herself to go down that path, no matter how badly she wanted to. She could not go back to living in ignorance. There was no growth or strength there. Anna needed to do something for herself for once.

"Yes, you are correct," he whispered. Though she had expected those words, they still cut Anna to the bone. Against her wishes, a few tears slipped down her cheeks. Even Mr. Waynford's thumb gently brushing them away did nothing to ease this pain.

"I heard about the rumor before we met. My father encouraged me to get to know you better because, as you already know, we have found ourselves in a rather tight spot," he continued, his low voice cracking with emotion.

Anna's mind reeled back to the early days of their relationship, of seeing that pointed glance between Mr. Waynford and his father during their first dinner together.

"So you really did see me as nothing more than a key to solving your family's problems," Anna scoffed bitterly, surprised at the cold anger in her voice.

The gentleman desperately grasped Anna's hands, leaning forward while trying to pull her closer to him. She stiffened, not allowing herself to be moved. She closed her eyes against the pain thundering through her.

"You must understand that my feelings have changed since then. It may have started out that way, yes, but my situation made it necessary. You see, I never liked the idea of courting someone for shallow reasons like money or status, but learning of my father's debt changed all that. Yes, I thought you could rescue my family, but the more I learned about you—the real you—the more truly I fell in love with you."

Those wonderful, sweet words Anna had longed to hear her whole life, had hoped to hear from this very man, did nothing but shatter her heart. It all felt too wrong now.

"Then why did you lie to me last night?" Anna demanded, ignoring her own shaking voice.

Mr. Waynford sighed, frustrated and disappointed with himself. "I panicked. As cowardly as that sounds, I panicked. I hated seeing you look so hurt. I was not strong enough to tell the truth and I've regretted it every waking moment since. I truly am deeply sorry for causing you the very pain I'd hoped to prevent."

Anna felt her heart trying to pull her back to him, recognizing the regret in his voice. She had expected him to say all this. Thanks to Mr. Milburn's information, Anna had known that Mr. Waynford lied last night. As much as she wanted to believe his sweet words, Anna could not fathom allowing herself to experience an even worse heartbreak in the future —after they were married and it became clear that he hadn't meant anything he'd said on this day in the garden.

"The damage has been done, Mr. Waynford, and I am not sure it can be repaired," Anna whispered, biting down on the inside of her cheek.

"Please reconsider, I beg you," Mr. Waynford continued, his panic growing more intense by the second. "I swear my feelings are genuine now. You can trust me, unlike that Mr. Milburn or any of those other men."

That sealed Anna's decision. He had said the worst thing he could have possibly said, digging his own hole deeper and deeper.

Anna clenched her jaw, her chest heaving with the force

of her breath. "Mr. Waynford, I will not marry someone I cannot trust." Mr. Waynford opened his mouth to protest again, but Anna cut him off, her conviction coursing through her despite the pain. "I would rather live the life of a spinster than marry someone who does not value me enough to speak the truth."

"You must believe me!" the gentleman cried. "I see so much more than that now. I—"

Anger flashed in Anna's eyes as she glared at Mr. Waynford. "At least when I asked him about it, Mr. Milburn had the decency to be honest."

CHAPTER 15

*M*iss Harcourt's words stung as if she'd slapped Noah across the face. In fact, Noah thought he might prefer that to this infinitely horrible, heart-wrenching pain crushing his chest. He stared at her, stunned into silence. She gazed back at him, fierce determination in her eyes.

Noah did not have anything to say to her rebuttal. He really was no better than the likes of Mr. Milburn. How could this have all gone so wrong, just when Noah had started to hope that they could truly be happy together? Miss Harcourt stood, pulling her hands out of Noah's. He leapt to his feet, his mind racing for something he could say to keep her by his side.

"I know Mr. Milburn does not feel the way I feel about you. He is nothing more than a money and status hungry man who sees this all as a game," Noah blurted, panic, fear, and pain fogging his mind. He knew as soon as the words left his lips that they were a mistake.

Miss Harcourt sighed angrily. She looked at him with disappointment in her perfect eyes. Noah knew that her disappointment paled in comparison to his own. Tearing someone else down would not fix the mistake he'd made.

"I know I have not been perfect," Miss Harcourt whispered, her fire never wavering. "I know I tried to deceive you into thinking I was someone else and I deeply regret that. But you see, Mr. Waynford, I still told you the truth. After last night, I am not sure you would have ever told me the truth about why you first pursued me. Your feelings may have changed, but I am not so fragile that I could not bear it, could not understand it if you'd been honest right away."

The coldness in her voice sent daggers through Noah's heart, numbing him to his core. "So you are choosing him," he mumbled, barely registering the fact that he'd just spoken.

Miss Harcourt gazed at him with a passionate bravery he'd never seen before, lifting her up above her pain. "I am not choosing Mr. Milburn. I am choosing myself. I will be returning home to Somerset early so I can gather myself, discover who I really am and how to be happy without a suitor. Goodbye, Mr. Waynford."

"Anna, please!" Noah lurched forward, grabbing her hand. She turned back to him, her surprise overshadowed by pain. He had made such a horrible mess of this situation.

"I cannot change your mind," he muttered, the question transforming into a statement of certainty as he spoke.

Miss Harcourt looked away, forcing her tears back as she slipped her hand out of his once more. She rushed toward the garden entrance, one hand holding her skirts up and the other tapping her brother on the shoulder as she passed. Mr. Harcourt followed his sister, not bothering to look back at the other gentlemen or say a proper goodbye. Nothing was proper about this, after all. It was all so very, very wrong.

"Anna!" Noah called one last time as she disappeared through the archway.

Phineas appeared before Noah, his steps almost silent on

the soft grass. "What's happened?" He looked over his shoulder at the garden entrance, perhaps expecting Anna to return. Noah knew that would not happen. He'd seen the finality in her eyes.

"It is all my fault, Phineas. For all my harping about the value of honesty, I acted like a coward and lied, hoping to spare her pain, but also trying to protect myself and save face." Noah's own voice seemed to reach his ears from very far away. Could he be sure he'd even said anything? Could it really have been Noah who had ruined what could have been the best thing in his life?

"What did you lie about? I'm sure it—"

"When she asked me at the dinner party last night if I'd heard the rumors, I said yes, but only after I'd begun courting her. I tried to explain why, but I just made everything worse. I hurt her so deeply with that lie. I even remember telling myself last night that surely it could not cause too much harm. What a horrible fool I am," he muttered, bitter and full of self-loathing.

Phineas sighed, putting a hand on Noah's shoulder. In a rare turn of events, he was at a loss for words.

"I cannot believe I would lie like that…that I would hurt Anna like that. As much as I pride myself on being observant and reading people, I missed one of the most important things about her. I should have trusted that she could handle and understand the truth. She deserves honesty, even in such a difficult situation. Yet I denied her that basic right. Of course she distrusts me now, Phineas. How can she ever be sure that I am being true?"

Noah fell silent, watching the garden entrance, wishing that he'd been able to catch a better glimpse of her as she'd left, something he could hold on to. All he could take with him now was his pain, betrayal, and those heartbreaking tears in her eyes.

"You never know. She may come back around. Stranger things have happened." Phineas put on a brave smile for Noah's benefit, but it did not reach him.

Noah shook his head, suddenly feeling heavy and lethargic. "We both saw how she looked when she left."

Phineas looked away from Noah. "Why don't we return home?" he suggested quietly, all the naive hope gone from his voice.

Noah nodded numbly, his emotions cycling rapidly from feeling terrible to wondering if this was just an extremely vivid nightmare. He could not grasp onto anything solid. The two men walked back to the Waynford house in melancholy silence, Noah replaying the last few minutes in his head the whole way.

When he'd heard that Anna and her brother waited for him in the drawing room, Noah had certainly had no idea that this would happen. In fact, he'd looked forward to a chance to smooth things over, to reassure her of his feelings, to see if she might reassure him of hers. Instead, he had become his own worst enemy.

Phineas only followed Noah a few feet into the foyer. He knew Noah would want some time alone. Before taking his leave, Phineas paused by the door, opening his mouth to say something, probably some words of encouragement or comfort. When he saw Noah's face, Phineas thought better of it. Noah did not need any pretty words right now. "Please let me know if you need anything," he mumbled instead.

As the door closed behind his friend, a terrible feeling flooded Noah's stomach. He should tell Father about what happened. He'd had as much interest in Noah's courtship as Noah himself had. He quietly groaned, dreading the thought of replaying it all and no doubt greatly disappointing his whole family.

He trudged up the stairs toward the library where he

guessed Father would be. He stopped at the top of the stairs, wondering if he could really make it that far. He needed to rest, preferably for hours—or maybe days. This experience had devastated him, far more than any physical ailment he'd ever suffered.

Noah tried to lift his head, forcing himself to continue. He could not mope around in bed for days over a broken heart. He paused again as that thought crossed his mind.

A broken heart? Had Noah's heart been broken before he'd even fully accepted that he was in love? He balled his hand into a fist, enveloped in anger with himself. He'd let a moment of weakness and cowardice ruin the very thing he'd been trying to protect.

As his anger washed over him in waves of increasing intensity, Noah considered going to his room and telling Father the news later. He shook that desire out of his head. He could not keep avoiding the truth. He'd avoided the truth of his feelings for Anna just as he'd avoided the truth within his lie. He'd been ashamed of himself, of throwing his long-held beliefs through the window.

Noah lifted his head again, a simple movement that took monumental effort. He continued down the hall toward the library. It would be better to get this out of the way now instead of having to reopen the wound later, after he'd had time to process it.

Still, he paused at the library door, taking a deep breath to steady himself. It did not work, but it bought him an extra second before having to disappoint yet another person today. Father answered as soon as Noah knocked. He pushed the door open, another simple movement that seemed to take so much energy.

Father looked up from his newspaper as Noah slipped into the room, his eyes twinkling with anticipation. "I heard Miss Harcourt and Mr. Harcourt paid you a visit."

Noah gritted his teeth as a fresh storm of pain rolled through him. He swallowed the hard lump in his throat, realizing that this would be even more difficult than he'd imagined.

"Have a seat here, son. Tell me all about it." Father patted the arm of the chair next to him, grinning. He clearly had not noticed the turmoil in Noah's face yet.

"That will not be necessary. I won't be staying long." Father furrowed his brows, finally realizing that something was wrong. "Miss Harcourt has chosen to end our courtship," he continued, hesitating as he considered leaving out her reasons. He decided against it after a moment. That would be cowardly, too. "She discovered that I lied to her about my motives for courting her. Understandably, she could not forgive such a transgression."

Father sat in silence for a moment, the newspaper falling limp in his hands. Noah could feel his disappointment from across the room. He longed more than ever to flee to the safety and solitude of his room. Father sat up straighter, a hopeful smile on his face.

"Do not worry, Noah. I'm sure if you keep trying, you can convince her to forgive you. Don't you remember the story of how hard I had to chase your mother in our younger days? You would not even exist if I had given up the first time she sent me away!"

Noah harnessed all his strength, feeble though it was, to keep from lashing out at his father. "She has every right to be angry with me, to cut me out of her life. She is not overreacting. She is protecting herself from a terrible, foolish man," he muttered, his voice still harsher than he'd intended.

The older man stood from his chair, crossing the room to stand before his son. "Noah, you must remember that there is still much at stake here. Think of the money—"

Noah's anger—anger at himself, at Father, at this situation—finally broke free. "It is not about the money anymore, Father!" he yelled, realizing as he did so that he'd never raised his voice like this to anyone in his entire life. Pain and fear made people do and say strange things. "In fact, Miss Harcourt's dowry does not even exist. At least, not the dowry you've heard about."

Father stared at Noah, his eyebrows shooting up in shock. Noah prayed this would put the conversation to rest once and for all. Father clasped his hands together, his eyes racing around the room.

"But you still have time to make a match. Have you not been meeting with the other ladies I introduced you to?"

Noah's jaw clenched. He would soon be unable to contain his anger at all. "It is not about the money. It is about her." Noah's voice was dangerously quiet, but he knew right away that Father heard him perfectly well.

He turned his back to his father, slamming the library door behind him. Noah would have never imagined that he could behave so rudely to Father, but he simply could not stand that man right now. He had tried so hard to bear this situation with strength and grace, yet he had ended up suffering so much more than he'd anticipated. Worse still, he had caused Anna to suffer.

Noah stormed through the house to his room, his fury fueling him. Pain swirled through him in a mad torrent. After everything he'd done to help Father fix the mess he'd created in the first place, he still treated Noah—and by extension, Anna—as a tool.

These false pretenses had cost Noah the real love he had finally found.

When he made it to his room, Noah almost slammed the door shut again. Instead, that impossible weight returned to his body. He closed the door slowly, his energy gone up in smoke. Sinking down onto his bed, Noah propped his elbows on his knees, allowing his face to fall into his hands, the despair pulling him deeper and deeper into a dreadfully cold and dark hole.

Yes, though he had not known it, Noah truly had been doomed from the start.

CHAPTER 16

"*H*ave you made your decision?" Mr. Milburn asked patiently.

Anna sat across from the viscount's son in the Harcourts' drawing room. She nodded, her eyes stuck on his. Unlike the day she'd broken things off with Mr. Waynford, Anna had no issue looking Mr. Milburn in the eyes. Did she have the confidence to do so now because she had already done this once before? Or because she knew neither of them would walk away from this conversation with a broken heart?

As the thought hit her, Anna looked down at her hands in her lap. She faltered now because she realized that she had broken two hearts yesterday.

She still tried to convince herself that it was for the best. Thoughts raced through Anna's mind as she found herself once again second guessing her decision. Mr. Waynford had lied to her about something crucial. He'd clearly regretted it yesterday, but it had still proved to Anna that he was not as trustworthy as she'd first thought.

"I know our time together has come to an end," Mr. Milburn said, bringing Anna back to the present. He said it without anger, only a hint of sadness. Anna looked up and saw understanding in his eyes.

She nodded again. "I am terribly sorry for any disappointment I've caused you." Despite her apology, Anna did not feel very guilty. She knew Mr. Milburn was not the one for her. He knew it, too.

"There is no need for that, Miss Harcourt," he assured her gently. "I really did have quite an interesting and eye-opening Season thanks to you."

Anna's brow furrowed as she set aside her tumultuous feelings for a moment. "How have your eyes been opened?"

Mr. Milburn shrugged, looking slightly embarrassed. "Seeing the genuine connection between you and Mr. Waynford made me reconsider my own feelings toward being leg-shackled. Perhaps finding a love match in the future would not be so bad after all. I've known for quite some time that I could not compete with that gentleman, but my unfortunately stubborn nature kept me from gracefully bowing out." He chuckled ruefully, a light dusting of pink spreading across his cheeks.

Anna gave a small, sad smile. "I'm very glad I was able to bring about a change of heart for you. I'm sure you will find your own love soon."

"That is very generous of you, Miss Harcourt." Mr. Milburn returned the smile.

They settled into a comfortable, friendly silence. Anna truly did wish the best for him, despite his original intentions toward her. She found him easier to forgive because he'd been so frank when she'd first pressed him about the subject, and he'd gone on to explain more of his motives. Perhaps she could forgive Mr. Milburn because her heart had not been so wrapped up in him.

After a few moments of pleasant silence, Mr. Milburn

chuckled, drawing a curious look from Anna. "So, will I be invited to your wedding with Mr. Waynford?"

Anna swallowed the rock that had sprung up in her throat, turning her face away so her tears would not be so obvious.

"Why aren't you marrying him?" Mr. Milburn asked in quiet shock.

Anna cleared her throat, hoping to have enough strength to speak without her voice trembling. She explained her motivation behind the dinner party and the truth she'd learned about Mr. Waynford. Mr. Milburn gave a heavy sigh, sinking back into his chair.

"I am tired of being a sideshow amusement for people to bet on, trying to become the winner of an imaginary prize," she continued, slowly gaining strength. "I am returning home to spend the rest of the Season in the country. My head always seems clearer in Somerset. I will no longer rush myself to find a husband. Before, I thought I could be satisfied with any marriage, but now I know I cannot live in a marriage without a foundation of love. I have my family, my friends, and myself. For now, that shall be enough."

Mr. Milburn gazed at Anna for a moment, contemplating her words. When he did not respond right away, Anna worried that she had offended him with her impassioned speech. His thoughtful expression soon turned to something like pride.

"That sounds like a fine idea to me. Not many would have the courage to face that possibility, and I greatly admire you for it."

"Thank you, Mr. Milburn." Somehow, Anna felt a little lightness return to her. She needed to have more faith in herself and her decisions.

"I think it is about time for me to take my leave," Mr.

Milburn sighed, sounding surprisingly satisfied considering Anna had just broken their courtship.

They walked to the door together, both pausing as the footman held it open for them. Mr. Milburn gazed through the door thoughtfully for a moment before turning to face Anna once more. "I think this period of self-reflection will be very important for you, but do not write love off just yet. I've heard that it has a way of popping up when you least expect it."

Anna nodded appreciatively. "I certainly hope that will be the case for you."

"I hope you do not think me terribly forward for saying so, but I do hope you will forgive Mr. Waynford in time. I cannot speak for him, of course, but I truly do believe he loves you. I have also heard that love sometimes causes people to say foolish things."

"You are very wise in the ways of love for a man who claims he's never been in love," Anna teased as they made their way downstairs.

"I may not have been in love or grown up in a household of love, but I've learned quite a bit from watching it unfold before my very eyes. Goodbye, Miss Harcourt. I wish you all the best."

Anna sighed as the front door closed behind Mr. Milburn, another man she thought she might have married. At least she had ended up with a friend out of it all.

She could not say the same about Mr. Waynford. The thought tore at Anna's heart before she remembered Mr. Milburn's words. Love could still appear in Anna's life at some point in the future. She did not feel much hope for that, given these last few days, but Anna reminded herself that she needed to spend time befriending herself and accept the fact that that might not be part of God's plan for her. If it wasn't,

Anna would still be fine. At least, she hoped she would come to that conclusion soon.

Mr. Milburn's other words left Anna with a strange feeling. As much as she hoped he was right about Mr. Waynford loving her, she just could not revisit that situation yet.

For now, Anna wanted to return to Somerset and make peace with herself. Even as she told herself that, Anna wondered in the back of her mind if perhaps she had been too harsh with Mr. Waynford.

Must she sacrifice a truly loving relationship in order to develop love for herself?

Anna pushed that thought away. She still had plenty of packing left to do, and she certainly needed to write to Esther and invite her over for one last visit before leaving London for good.

ANNA LIFTED her face to catch the sweet rays of sunshine as they filtered through the leaves above, a gentle breeze picking up a few strands of her hair. She truly felt content for the first time since arriving home. She'd spent much of the past month coming to terms with what happened in London, but, on a day like this, Anna decided to let herself enjoy the moment without any worries or regrets.

Caroline laughed beside Anna. She opened her eyes to see Harriet leaning forward, hugging her pony's neck as best she could from her sidesaddle position. Mr. Baldwin, the Harcourts' horse master for many years, tried to correct Harriet's posture to no avail. If Harriet did not want to let go of her pony yet, there was no force on earth that could make her.

The two other Harcourt sisters sat on a soft blanket under a large tree near the small paddock that had been used to train all the Harcourt children to ride. Lush green hills rose in the distance, creating a beautiful landscape that looked almost like a painting.

Neither Anna nor Caroline cared much for riding sidesaddle, preferring the ease and comfort of carriages. However, they certainly enjoyed watching their youngest sibling have the time of her life with the spirited creatures she seemed to take after far more than any member of their human family.

Anna felt Caroline's gaze on her, reading the side of her face. She turned to her sister with a curious smile. They still bickered and Caroline still teased Anna every chance she got, but they had been getting along better than ever since the Harcourt ladies had left London. In fact, Anna had noticed herself loosening up over the past month. She even enjoyed Caroline's jests and sent her own right back at times. She'd had good practice over the last Season in trusting her own wit and humor.

"What's the matter?" Anna asked, smiling slyly. "Is there a giant insect on my face?"

Caroline laughed again. "If there was, I would have long since run away from you." The two sisters' giggles mingled and drifted away on the warm summer wind.

After their laughter died down, Caroline examined Anna once more. "You have been looking very happy recently." She lowered her eyes at the last moment, still self-conscious with this concept that they could share deep, personal thoughts with each other even if those thoughts differed wildly. They had both been making more progress in that regard, growing in their understanding of each other.

Anna looked up at the soft clouds lazily floating by in the bright blue sky, a wistful sigh on her lips. "I am not sure that I am happy yet, but happier. I still have more healing to do after everything that happened, though I have realized since being home that I can be grateful for parts of the experience."

"How can you say such a thing?" Caroline demanded, jerking back in disbelief.

Anna put on her snootiest voice, jutting her chin into the air. "Now, dear Caroline, listen well to a wise lesson from your very smart older sister."

Caroline scoffed in response, not quite able to hide her smile. She leaned forward like an eager pupil.

"The situation was terrible and it devastated me," Anna went on. "In fact, it still hurts when I think back on it sometimes and it probably will for a while yet, but I learned so much from that pain. It's helped me grow into a braver, stronger person who now knows how to appreciate who she is and what she has."

"Truly an insightful lesson," Caroline said in an overly fascinated voice.

"Wait just a moment! I am not finished."

"Oh, carry on then." Caroline crossed her arms with a teasing smile.

"The most important thing I learned actually came in part from Mr. Waynford, and I will always be grateful to him for it. He gave me a window to see myself in a new light, to see myself the way he saw me. I could see myself as an interesting and worthy person in a way I had never been able to before. Now, I have taken up the task of developing confidence in myself, for myself. I do not need to wish I were someone else."

Anna paused, turning her attention toward Harriet again. The girl squealed with delight as her pony trotted along. "Though I still would not mind borrowing a bit of Harriet's wild spirit at times," she added.

"On that we can both agree," Caroline chuckled. She turned serious again, looking at Anna with pride in her eyes.

"I so admire you for enduring all that and not losing the kindness in your heart. I've always loved that about you."

Anna could not help sniffling at her sister's words. "Oh, Caroline!" she cried, throwing her arms around the younger woman.

"Anna, stop that! There is no need for all this drama!" Caroline squirmed in Anna's arms. Her laughter only made Anna squeeze harder. When they pulled apart, Anna saw that Caroline had a few tears in her eyes as well.

"Miss Harcourt, Miss Caroline, our lesson is just about finished," the horse master called for them. The two older sisters giggled at each other as they stood up, straightened out their dresses, and gathered up the blanket.

"Please, Mr. Baldwin, can't I ride for just a few more minutes?" Harriet begged, clinging to the reins of her beloved pony.

"I wonder who Mr. Baldwin preferred—the two of us, who almost never wanted to get on the horse, or Harriet, who never wants to get off?" Caroline whispered into Anna's ear.

"In truth, he probably preferred Patrick out of us all. He's always been the quickest study, so his lessons ended up being the shortest."

Caroline burst into laughter, her head falling back as the sound rippled through her body. Harriet joined in from the paddock, always ready to share in someone else's happiness.

"It's time to go now, Harriet," Anna called from the fence. "Mr. Baldwin is a terribly busy man."

The girl gracefully dismounted before running up to the horse master. "I'm sorry for causing you trouble, Mr. Baldwin. I hope I didn't disrupt your schedule." Harriet looked up at the man with remorseful eyes until he smiled and ruffled her hair, shooing her toward her sisters.

Anna's eyes widened in amazement at Harriet's ability to

feel an emotion like guilt so deeply and then run off into the open field with a grin on her face the very next moment. Anna would not mind borrowing Harriet's ability to let things go, either.

As the Harcourt sisters walked back to Attwood Manor, the grand building rising up high and proud—Anna's forever home—Harriet forgot all about her disappointment at ending the lesson, twirling away in the warm afternoon sunlight. Anna and Caroline walked arm in arm, Anna in deep reflection over her conversation with her sister.

Yes, she was happier now, but not completely happy yet. She prayed she would be soon. She prayed she would not come to regret leaving Mr. Waynford behind. Still, Anna knew she needed this experience, as painful as it was. Just as she'd told Caroline, she had grown and learned so much about herself. The more she learned, the more she enjoyed the person she was.

A cloud of dust from the drive caught Anna's eye, partially obscuring the carriage. The front door of the house flew open and footmen poured out, ready and waiting.

Harriet ran forward, greeting the Harcourt men with excitement. She threw herself into Papa's arms the moment he stepped down from the carriage. The baron picked up his youngest child, swinging her around in a wide circle before setting her back down.

"Hurry on inside and get changed out of your riding clothes," Papa chuckled as Harriet caught her breath.

"But Papa, you said you would watch me ride!"

"Yes, I did, and I expect to see a grand display of your new skills very soon. Mama has written all about your improvements. But first, your old father needs to rest." Papa stretched his arms into the sky, groaning from the weariness of travel. Harriet distributed hugs to her brothers before running into the house, carried on an endless stream of energy.

"How wonderful to see our fine gentlemen!" Caroline gave her own hugs to Papa, Dalton, and Patrick while Anna did the same, quietly welcoming them home.

Papa let out a powerful yawn as he released Anna from a tight hug. "Now I must go find Mama, give her plenty of kisses, and take a nice, long nap," he announced.

Patrick lingered outside with his siblings, his lips pursed. Caroline reached up to mess with his hair, which earned her a disapproving yelp from her younger brother. "Go on inside and get to the library," she chuckled. "We've had a delivery of books from the town and I'm sure there are some new plays in there."

He grinned, giving both Caroline and Anna more hugs before striding up the steps. The remaining Harcourt siblings laughed as they watched their brother prance through the foyer, taking the stairs two at a time.

"Shall we?" Dalton asked, looking from Anna on one side to Caroline on the other, offering his arms to them both. The ladies happily accepted and Dalton led them into Attwood Manor.

Anna had expected them to continue up the stairs, but Dalton paused in the foyer, watching her curiously.

"I am sure you are tired and want to rest before giving a lengthy explanation of the remainder of your Season," Anna said gently though he did not seem remotely phased by the several days of travel.

Dalton smiled, ignoring Anna's words. "How are you doing, my dear sister?"

Of course, Dalton knew better than anyone else what had happened just before Anna and the other Harcourt ladies left London. They had exchanged a few letters in the past month, but Dalton danced around the subject, leaving it to Anna to bring it up if she wanted to. Anna hadn't wanted to—yet.

A small hand landed softly on Anna's back. "She is doing much better," Caroline said proudly.

Love for her sister, for all her family, swelled through Anna's chest. Just as Papa had said, they would always have each other. For that, Anna considered herself blessed beyond measure. She turned to Caroline, taking this opportunity to say what she'd been meaning to say for some time.

"Caroline, I was going to tell you this while we were under the tree, but the timing never felt right so I suppose this will have to do," Anna started. Caroline's brows twitched up, curious. "I am going to tell Mama and Papa to let you make your debut next Season."

Caroline's gasp rang through the large, open foyer. Anna couldn't help giggling as she wondered if everyone upstairs had heard it, too. "Anna, are you really, truly sure about this?"

Anna nodded, intertwining her fingers with her sister's. "I am really, truly sure." She smiled at both her siblings who had become Anna's best friends over the years. "If or when the time for romance comes, I will meet it confidently, showing myself for exactly who I am."

Caroline's bottom lip trembled, about to burst with pride. Dalton, on the other hand, wore a sly smile. Anna turned to her younger brother, brows furrowed. "May I ask what is so amusing?"

Dalton shrugged, his mouth pulling up to the side. "I'm going to my room to nap. Please do not disturb me!" He ran off on his long legs, already halfway up the stairs before anyone could stop him.

Anna and Caroline exchanged perplexed glances. She watched Dalton go, quite energetically for a man who needed a nap. She thought about his strange expression. It somehow made her think of Mr. Waynford for the briefest moment, wondering what her life might be like if she'd let him stay.

CHAPTER 17

The Harcourts' beautiful home, Attwood Manor, rose before Noah. He pictured a younger Anna growing up here, becoming the woman he loved here. Despite his overwhelming nerves, Noah hurried up the front steps, his heart hammering in his chest like it had never done before. A footman still held the door open for him, as Mr. Harcourt had instructed, allowing Noah to sneak in after him.

As soon as he made it through the door, Noah's eyes locked onto the back of Anna's head, devouring her like a man starved almost to madness. She stared up toward the next landing, watching as her brother disappeared down the hall. Only Anna and Miss Caroline remained in the foyer.

Anna turned toward Miss Caroline, perplexed by Mr. Harcourt's sudden departure. She had not turned enough to notice Noah, just a few feet separating them now after this month that had felt like a lifetime. Miss Caroline did catch Noah from the corner of her eye. She did a dramatic double take, her hand flying to her mouth as she whipped around to face him.

"Caroline, what—" Anna started, turning toward the source of her sister's surprise.

Noah had not thought it possible that she could grow more beautiful than she already was, yet somehow she'd managed it. Of course, Noah's imagination could only recreate an inadequate version of her in his mind. His heart soared at the sight of her. He thanked the heavens that he'd made it even this far, that he could stand before her again as the foolish, imperfect, yet completely in love mess he was.

"Anna…" He called her name, breathless and almost dizzy from nerves. It had been the very last thing he'd said to her on that day in the garden. He'd had no idea then that he would have a chance to say her name aloud again.

She stared at him, eyes as wide as the moon, too shocked to reply. He supposed he must seem rather like a mirage, just as she did to him. He'd imagined this moment many times over, yet the reality still felt even stranger than he could have predicted.

Noah cleared his throat, remembering his manners. "Miss Harcourt," he started slowly, reminding himself that he had not truly earned the right to call her by her Christian name yet. "I hoped to have a private word with you." The sound of his heart pounding rang through his voice, but he did not care. He could not waste this chance like he'd wasted so many before. It could be his very last one.

Anna still made no response. Noah's anxiety tripled. Perhaps surprising her like this had been a bad idea after all. Miss Caroline offered some assistance, gently smacking her older sister's arm. "You should go, Anna," she whispered sharply. Noah thanked God for the Harcourt siblings. They always seemed to know just how to step in when Noah could not figure it out himself.

Slowly coming out of her daze, Anna nodded, never removing her eyes from Noah. He threw Miss Caroline a grateful smile which she returned, a joyful gleam in her eyes. Miss Caroline took Anna's arm, pulling her toward the door and nearly shoving her out onto the steps.

"Be sure to stay within view of the house!" she called as she shut the door behind them.

They truly were alone now—save for the dozens of windows behind them, which Noah suspected contained the curious faces of one or more Harcourts.

Anna stood next to Noah, staring out at the beautiful, vast lands that had raised generations of her family. Noah took a moment to appreciate it as well. He'd been too nervous in the carriage he'd shared with the Harcourt men to really notice anything about his surroundings. Now that Anna had at least agreed to talk with him, he allowed himself to relax just a bit. He still had a very long way to go, and he could not predict what would happen, but at least he had made it here.

Taking a deep breath, Noah offered his arm to Anna. She looked from his arm to his face, her expression sending a thrill of hope through Noah's heart. She, too, looked desperate to absorb him. Had she missed him at all? Had she missed him as much as he'd missed her?

Noah smiled reassuringly, waiting to feel her gentle hand on his arm. He reminded himself not to get too far ahead. He had many things he still needed to say before he could even hope to reclaim her heart. Anna slipped her arm through Noah's.

"Lead the way, wherever you wish to go," Noah offered, and he knew his words to be the truest he'd ever spoken. He would follow her wherever she went, if she would allow him to. Anna gave a small, hesitant smile before starting down the steps.

They walked in silence for a several minutes, Anna leading them through the grass on the right side of the house. Noah looked down at her, wondering what she thought of all this. He wondered if he would ever see this view of rolling hills and bright green summer again. That would all depend on Anna. She might still banish him forever, Noah knew, and he would not blame her.

Soon Noah realized that they walked toward a small grove of trees. His heart rose higher in his throat as they closed the distance, longing to pour itself out to Anna. They arrived under the shade of the trees, not venturing too deep. Anna pulled herself away from Noah to stand before him. She no longer gazed at him with shock, but with strength and perhaps even relief. Noah held his breath, wondering if he should start and how.

"Why are you here?" Anna asked, solving the problem for him.

Noah chuckled, also wondering that himself. He still could not quite believe that he'd come to Somerset, that he stood in a beautiful grove of trees with his dear Miss Harcourt.

"It's quite an interesting story, as a matter of fact. I will freely admit that I spent most of the past month confined to my home, not doing much besides wandering around in a melancholy stupor. I only left to visit my sisters and to attend Phineas's wedding."

Anna smiled, her happiness for Phineas evident even through her confusion and suspicion. Her sweet, loving heart had not changed at all, despite the pain she'd suffered.

"My father heard at White's that Lord Welsted would soon be packing up the rest of his family to return home," Noah went on. "I did not think much of it at the time, other than feeling like my final connection to you would disappear forever once your family left London.

"But Father did not leave it at that. He sat me down for a serious talk, apologizing profusely for putting so much pressure on me for a mistake he'd made. He said he knew I loved you, and, if anything good could come out of this situation, it would be that I found the woman I've been praying for."

She blushed at Noah's words, but did not drop her gaze.

"I reminded Father that I'd ruined my chances with you, but he would not accept that. He encouraged me to meet with your family and see if they would be willing to arrange a way for me to get in touch with you. Of course, I did not think any of the other Harcourts would be too interested in seeing me, and our financial troubles still have not been solved. Father would not hear any of that, either. He told me to try again, to let my heart lead me, to let all other concerns fall away. He said we could work everything else out later because, in life, there are so few chances at a love like this."

Noah felt the truth of his father's words reverberating through him as he repeated them to Anna. At that moment, he saw nothing but Anna as she stood before him, a light breeze tugging at her dark hair, the sunlight dotting her face between the leaves above.

Nothing else mattered.

A smile pulled at Anna's lips. "He sounds like a very wise man."

"He has his moments," Noah chuckled.

"I'm guessing that you conspired with my father and brothers to transport you out here so we could talk?"

"You guess correctly."

"Now I would like to know why, if you don't mind."

Noah nodded, accepting the subtle challenge in her words. She would not let him get away with his grand plan without explaining everything first, and Noah knew she deserved nothing less.

He took a deep breath. They had finally arrived at the crux of the matter. He stepped forward, his hands reaching out for Anna's just as they had on that last day. She did not pull away or break eye contact with him, giving Noah courage.

"I know I made a terrible mistake at the dinner party by trying to hide the fact that I was influenced by the rumor. I could see how hurt you already were. It was the most cowardly thing I've ever done, that I chose a lie instead of the truth because I thought it would be easier for you—and, self-ishly, for me as well.

"I hated that I was essentially no better than any of the other men who'd heard the rumor and thought they would take a chance at winning a fortune. I lied because I did not want to hurt you. I did not want you to think me insincere. But, of course, by being dishonest in that moment, I had proved the opposite."

Anna's eyes filled with deep sadness as she remembered those horrible days, no doubt reliving her own struggles and heartache just as Noah did. Now, he knew that he needed to say what he didn't have the courage to say then.

"You have every right to be angry with me. I broke your trust after going on and on about honesty and being true to oneself. I wasn't true to myself or to you. And I am equally ashamed of my behavior in the garden. Like an immature fool, I tried to tear down Mr. Milburn in the hopes of repairing what had happened between us. That was not fair either. After that lie, how could you know that I was different from him? That I had truly come to love you?" Anna's eyes grew wide with shock again as his words registered.

"I truly do love you," Noah continued. "I may have started courting you in the hopes of saving my family, but now I know that you ended up saving me."

Tears welled up in Anna's eyes as she searched Noah's face, searching for the truth that Noah knew she would find. Feeling emboldened, his heart beating with passion, Noah cupped Anna's face in his hands, caressing her cheeks with his thumbs. He'd wanted to do that for so long, longer than he himself realized.

"When we met, you wanted to be someone you weren't. I fell in love with you anyway—the real you. The more glimpses I saw of you, the deeper I fell. When you finally abandoned your mask for good at the opera, I truly fell head over heels in love with you.

"In fact, throughout all the time we spent together, all I thought about was you—how to make you laugh and smile, how to learn more about you, how impossibly wonderful you made me feel. There was nothing else but you.

"I'd always wanted to marry for love, but when the responsibility for saving my family's fortune was thrown on my shoulders, I thought that chance had been stolen from me. As terrible as the situation was in many ways, I hope I will not offend you by saying I'm glad for it all. It led me to you. You appeared in my life in the most unexpected way and you saved me by showing me that true love is worth waiting for, no matter what else happens in life.

"Anna, you are the dream come true I've been waiting for all these years. I know I cannot prove it to you, so I am asking you to have blind faith in me."

She smiled, a tear slipping down her cheek onto Noah's thumb. He brushed it away, taking another deep breath. He still had so much more he wanted to say and apologize for. He could talk for hours about how much he loved Anna, how sorry he was for everything.

"I truly am sor—"

Noah never got to give his last apology. Anna threw her arms around his neck, pressing her lips to his in a deep, miraculous, perfect kiss. Their lips moved together, slowly and sweetly, and Noah felt himself melting into her. He wrapped his arms around her waist, pulling her as close to him as he possibly could. His heart burst with joy, stars erupting in his mind, as he finally held her and kissed her.

He wanted this moment to last forever, but Noah eventually pulled back. He kept one arm around Anna's waist while his other hand moved to her face again.

"Does this mean you forgive me?"

Anna bit her lip as the corner of her mouth twitched up in a sly smile. "I think I can find it in my heart to forgive you." Noah laughed, elated to be able to share playful jests with her again, to bask in her charm and wit.

"Noah, I have something I must say as well," she continued, her voice low and serious.

Despite the fact that she'd just forgiven him, that she'd kissed him, that she'd said his name, Noah still felt a shock of anxiety squeeze his chest.

"I am sorry for not giving you a chance back in the garden. I desperately wanted to believe you, even then, but I needed this time to learn how to find happiness within myself," she mumbled, her words wavering with emotion.

Noah smiled understandingly, his eyes full of nothing but love and devotion. "Do not worry about that, my darling. I hope you have found the peace you needed. You should know that you are the most incredible person I have ever met, and you should hold your head high."

Anna lifted her chin in the air. "I certainly know it."

Noah threw his head back, his sudden outburst of laughter scaring away a few birds from the branches above. Anna's sweet voice joined his, the rustling leaves providing a magnificent backdrop of music for them.

When they finally calmed down, gasping for breath and sides aching, Anna touched her knuckles to Noah's cheek, gently sliding them down to his chin, one finger lingering over his lips.

"I did quite a bit of reflecting over the past month, and I

am glad for the growth I experienced during that time and during our courtship. My good friend Mr. Milburn told me just before I left London that love can happen when you least expect it."

Noah smiled, a serene sense of happiness bubbling up in his chest. Not even the mention of Mr. Milburn could knock him off this cloud he'd landed on, the beautiful cloud of happiness he now shared with Anna. In fact, he was glad that she'd left on good terms with Mr. Milburn. Despite his jealous display in the garden, Noah bore no ill will for his former rival. He had played an important part in their story, after all, the story that had brought him back to Anna in the end.

"I thought at the time that I needed to choose between a loving husband and love for myself." She paused, a beautiful grin dawning over her face. "Now I know that I can choose both if I want to."

"And do you want to?" Noah asked with a raised eyebrow.

Anna giggled, the sound filling Noah's heart with an elation that he'd thought impossible for any one man to experience. How had he come to be that lucky man? "Yes, of course. I love you, too, Noah. I am so glad you talked my family into bringing you back with them."

"I shall thank them profusely in a moment," he laughed, leaning down to kiss her again. "But first, may I ask you one more question?"

Anna gazed up at him, her eyes soft and golden in the afternoon sunlight. "Of course, my love."

"Can we promise to keep rescuing each other?"

She nuzzled her head into his chest, pulling him into a tender, loving embrace. "I want nothing more than to keep pulling you out of the mud if you will keep picking me up when I twist my ankle."

Noah kissed the top of her head, whispering into her hair, "Do you think we're being watched?"

Anna stood on the tips of her toes to peer over his shoulder at Attwood Manor. "Most certainly," she chuckled. "But I do not care at all. All I see right now is you."

"And all I see is you."

CHAPTER 18

*T*he full-length mirror showed Anna an incredible sight, something she'd once thought she would never see. She stood before the mirror in her beautiful cream wedding dress. Tears sprang up in her eyes as joy and amazement overwhelmed her.

"Save some tears for the ceremony, Anna," Caroline laughed.

"I assure you, I will have plenty left," Anna huffed playfully.

Harriet sighed from her spot on Anna's bed. "You look just like a princess." Her green eyes traveled up and down Anna's body, absorbing the finely embroidered gold roses that flowed up her skirt and through her bodice.

Anna smiled at her reflection in the mirror. She did look rather like a princess today, and she certainly felt like one, but not just because today was her wedding day. Noah adored her with every fiber of his being, reminding her that she was special on the days she needed a little extra help believing in herself. Now, for the most part, Anna could see herself as the strong, smart, capable woman she had always been.

She knew Noah loved her for exactly who she was, on the days when she beamed with confidence and on the days when she doubted herself. Anna knew without a doubt that she would never again have to pretend to be someone else.

Caroline handed her a small bouquet of flowers, picked just that morning from their garden. Anna's heart sang as she took the bunch, knowing that she would soon be Noah's wife —Mrs. Waynford.

This was better than anything she could have ever dreamed. She had been blessed beyond anything she deserved.

Mama came into view in the mirror, standing behind Anna as she adjusted a few curls. Her eyes brimmed with tears as well. She kissed her oldest daughter on the cheek, Anna giggling as some of Mama's tears landed on her skin.

"I am very thrilled for you, my dear Anna. I know you and Noah have a lifetime of happiness ahead of you," she mumbled, unsuccessfully choking back her emotions.

Anna pulled Mama into a tight hug, her tears freely flowing now. "Caroline, Harriet, come here," she called, waving for her sisters to join. Harriet hopped up from the bed immediately, throwing her arms around Anna and Mama.

"Truly, Anna, do you want to walk down the aisle in a wrinkled gown?" Caroline moaned.

Anna's laughter filled the room as she gestured for Caroline to hurry. "I could not care less about a few wrinkles in my dress. Now come here! I must share this moment with the most important women in my life."

"Oh, my sweet daughter!" Mama wailed through stuttering sobs. They all laughed, even as Caroline teasingly scolded Mama for getting her tears all over her.

A soft knock reached the ladies through their laughter. "Come in!" Anna called, raising her voice over the cheerful noise.

"No, Anna!" Harriet shrieked. "It might be Noah! He's not supposed to see the bride before the wedding!"

"Hush now, Harriet." Mama brushed her youngest child's hair back over her shoulders, playing with the golden locks for a moment. "Noah is waiting patiently—or perhaps not so patiently—for his beautiful bride at the church."

The door creaked open tentatively, giving Mama a chance to usher Caroline and Harriet back, leaving Anna to stand in the middle of the room in her wedding dress holding a bouquet of flowers as Papa came in.

Having already seen Mama's emotional display, Anna could not believe her eyes when Papa went above and beyond, bursting into tears the moment he saw his daughter, one hand gripping the doorknob while the other covered his mouth.

Anna rushed forward, offering soothing words the whole way. She pulled Papa into a hug, locking her arms around his neck, which forced her to stand on the tips of her toes. She did not mind. She felt almost like she had when she was a child, engulfed in her father's embrace. He wrapped his arms around her, his body trembling with sobs.

She still did not care about her dress getting wrinkled or her hair falling out of place or her flowers losing petals. All she cared about was sharing this incredible, dreamlike moment with her family.

After all, Anna knew how much this moment meant to Papa, too. She knew how much he'd suffered in London as well, trying to make things right and protect his child. Now, despite all that, Anna would get her happy ending.

"I am just so happy that my beloved daughter is marrying such a wonderful man," he sputtered, needing several tries to get all the words out. "But make no mistake, Noah is a very lucky man to have you as his wife," he added sternly.

Anna laughed, patting Papa's cheek. "I will remind him of that fact often, I promise."

"Goodness, we need to get the boys and head over to the church. We'll be almost late at this rate!" Mama cried, grabbing her younger daughters' hands and nearly dragging them from the room.

Papa chuckled as he watched his wife fly by. "Almost late is as good as late to your mother. But do not worry, I doubt they would start without you."

Anna reached up, wiping her father's tears away. "I love you, Papa."

"I love you, too, my dear girl."

"Anna, hurry!" Caroline's sharp voice called from the hall, Caroline herself appearing in the doorway a fraction of a second later. She wrapped her hand around Anna's wrist, pulling her older sister forward while Papa brought up the rear.

Harriet ran ahead of everyone else while Mama called after her to slow down or else she would trip on her dress and scratch up her knees.

"A scratched knee is nothing to worry about, Mama!" Harriet cried over her shoulder.

"Dear me," Mama groaned, rubbing at her temple.

"It will be fine, Mama!" Anna put a comforting hand on her mother's shoulder, feeling oddly calm on what should have been the most exhilarating day of her life.

Of course, an excited buzz vibrated deep in Anna's chest. She could not wait to stand before the altar, before Noah and all their friends and family, and marry the love of her life. Yet through it all, she felt a comforting sense of peace. Even if everything went wrong today, nothing could really be wrong as long as Noah became her husband.

At Mama's urging, they thundered down the stairs, the noise causing Dalton and Patrick to turn and look up. Their eyes fell on Anna, Patrick's mouth dangling open while Dalton's eyes glistened.

"You look beautiful," Patrick whispered as he gave Anna a hug. She buried her face in her youngest brother's shoulder for a moment, idly wondering when he'd gotten so much taller than her. It seemed just a couple years ago that Anna could still see over his head.

"Dear Anna," Dalton said quietly, his voice cracking ever so slightly as he held his arms open for her. In his typical fashion, he squeezed Anna nearly breathless. "I am so very, very happy for you. And I am so very glad that our scheme to bring Noah back with us worked so perfectly."

Anna pulled back, looking up into her brother's face, her heart overflowing with appreciation for him. "Thank you for always being there for me and encouraging me to never give up. Without you prodding me almost a year ago now, I would have stayed at Attwood Manor and missed out on Noah."

Dalton grinned mischievously, pinching Anna's cheek. "Yes, as a matter of fact, you are quite indebted to me."

Anna shook her head, slapping him on the shoulder. "You mustn't pinch my cheek anymore, Dalton. I am a grown, married woman now after all. You should have some respect for your elders, don't you think?" she teased.

"Oh, you will always be my silly sister." For good measure, Dalton pinched Anna's other cheek.

"Hurry now, hurry now! The carriages are waiting!" Mama called, shooing her family toward the door.

In record time, they piled into the two carriages, one for the ladies and one for the men. The trip to the village church took almost no time at all as Anna's excitement picked up speed, pulsing through every vein in her body.

She stared at the church through the window as they approached, knowing that Noah and the rest of her life waited for her just beyond those doors.

~

ANNA'S FACE ALREADY ACHED, but she could not stop smiling at Noah. "Have you had a good day so far, my husband?" she asked.

Noah gazed down at her with such warmth and love in his eyes that it sent a burst of flutters through Anna's chest. "The best, my wife."

They spun around the empty ballroom of the home Anna had grown up in. Now, she danced with her dear husband, just the two of them, with no music and a few candles spread throughout the room to see by. Despite the fact that it was their wedding day, this was the first moment they'd had just to themselves.

Anna thought back on the whirlwind of the day, from the beautiful ceremony surrounded by their loved ones where she and Noah promised themselves to each other for the rest of their lives, to the lovely lunch they'd had on the grounds of Attwood Manor.

She'd loved every moment of it, but she sighed happily as she relished the feeling of Noah's arms around her, their feet effortlessly carrying them through the dance steps.

Noah kissed the top of Anna's head. "I've just realized something."

Anna looked up at him with a teasing smile. "Did you realize that you must call me Mrs. Waynford now?"

"You say that as if it is a bad thing, but it is the best thing I've heard all day—aside from you saying 'I will' at the church," Noah laughed. "It is my greatest honor to call you

Mrs. Waynford. But I've just realized that this is the first dance we've ever had."

Anna's eyes widened. She had not even thought about that. Their one and only opportunity at a dance had been interrupted by her sprained ankle. She smiled lovingly, brushing a lock of Noah's hair out of his eyes. "It was well worth the wait."

"It certainly was. And I am sure we will have many more dances together in the future."

They came to a natural stop, falling into a warm embrace for a few blissful moments. Anna pulled back just enough to tilt her head up. Reading her mind, Noah caught her chin in his hand and brought their lips together.

"We will have many more kisses in the future, too," Anna said. Noah laughed, his thumb gently brushing against her chin.

The smile slipped from his face, his expression growing serious and thoughtful. "What are you thinking about, husband?"

"I have something to tell you. I spoke with your father during lunch."

Anna chuckled sheepishly. "I hope he did not badger you too much about taking care of me."

"No, it was nothing like that," Noah assured her. "In fact, he seemed very confident that I will do everything I can for you and he is, of course, completely right about that."

"Then what did you discuss?"

"Your father has agreed to help my family with our financial troubles. He will work it all out with my father later, but he knows we have been thinking of ways to recover the money we've lost. Father has been in talks with the county to sell a portion of our land so they can cut a new canal through to provide an additional water source for the nearby towns. Lord Welsted has offered to give us enough to cover what remains of the debt after that transaction."

Anna's mouth now fell open. She'd had no idea this day could get any better. The issue of money had weighed on them during their engagement. Noah's father had been thinking long and hard about ways to make more money from their land. Anna and Noah had been thrilled when he came to them with the canal idea. Offering part of one's land to the county usually came with a generous reward. This gift from Papa would help the Waynford family recover the rest of their losses.

"How wonderful, Noah!" Anna cried, wrapping her arms around his waist. "I am so glad it all worked out in the end, just like you'd said it would. As long as we are together, everything else falls into place."

"I will forever, forever, forever be grateful to your family, my darling. I will make them proud by caring for you and giving them many grandchildren and nieces and nephews," Noah whispered in her ear, the heat from his breath sending a shiver down her spine.

"I cannot wait to have a little Noah and a little Anna—and who knows who else—running around our home," she sighed, a warm contentment flooding her from head to toe. She propped her chin on his chest, gazing up at him. "Have you told your father yet?"

"Goodness, no. I thought the joy of finally seeing his son married would be enough for one day. Adding this news would just send him into a true stupor. Besides," he added, lowering his voice, "I selfishly wanted to keep this day about our love for each other, the journey we took to get here, and the start of our new chapter."

"That makes perfect sense to me." Anna buried her face in Noah's shoulder, breathing in his scent, feeling his heartbeat matching hers.

"Thank you, dear wife."

"For what?" She looked up, surprised. She'd had nothing to do with Papa's generous decision.

"For being my wife. I love you, Anna." Noah smiled, his perfect, ocean blue eyes bright with joy.

"I love you, too, dear husband." Anna lifted herself on her toes, pulling Noah down for a long, warm kiss.

Suddenly, Noah let go of Anna completely, taking a few steps back. Before she could ask why, he bowed low with his hand outstretched.

"May I have another dance, beautiful lady?"

Anna smiled, her hand slipping into his effortlessly, perfectly.

EPILOGUE

"*I*t must be true now. It must," Anna whispered to herself, tiny beads of sweat breaking out along her hairline. She clapped a hand over her mouth, fighting another wave of nausea.

She should find Noah and tell him. That thought rang through loud and clear in Anna's mind even as her stomach flipped again. He'd been fretting over her so much recently, noticing how tired she seemed and how often she had to excuse herself because she felt faint. He had not said it in so many words, but Anna could see the concern in his eyes every time he looked at her. Wouldn't he be so very relieved to finally learn the cause of Anna's strange behavior and discomfort?

After a few moments, the uneasiness in her stomach settled back down to a manageable level. Her exhaustion, however, remained. Now that she knew for sure, Anna supposed it made sense. Surely growing a child had been taking up most of her energy these past three months.

Anna slowly sat up straighter, beyond grateful that she occupied the drawing room of Shambrook Lodge alone, while everyone else went about their days after breakfast. She would have been mortified to be sick in her new family's drawing room, let alone have one of them witness it. Even that small effort seemed to knock the wind out of her. Anna remained seated for several more moments, trying to catch her breath, her morning dress already feeling too tight though she'd not yet begun to show evidence of her condition.

When she finally managed to push herself up from the chair, she slowly crossed the room to ring the service bell. Anna paced along the wall as she waited, surprised that she felt better with a little movement. Somehow, this new knowledge still felt far away to her, as if it happened to someone else. Anna had often imagined this moment throughout her life—discovering that she carried a child. Just the dream of it had sent her heart racing with excitement and her eyes watering with joy.

Yet now that Anna experienced it, it still did not feel quite real. Would they really be holding a baby in their arms in just six months? Anna had no idea what to do next or how to prepare. Well, she did know what to do next. She must find Noah. He would help her prepare.

A small smile spread across Anna's lips. She wondered how he would react to the news. Would he shout and jump for joy? Would he burst into tears? Would he stare in shock and amazement? Imagining her husband's reaction to the news that he would soon be a father sent a jolt of excitement through Anna. It had finally started to sink in, to feel real. This was not a dream anymore. She felt it in her bones—and certainly in her still queasy stomach.

"Good morning, madam." The footman greeted Anna warmly when he found her in the drawing room.

"Good morning, David. Do you happen to know where I might find my husband?"

The footman thought for a moment with a slight frown. "I'm afraid I do not, but I can find out for you."

Anna nodded, looking out the window at the lands that had become her new home. The landscape in Essex looked so different than what Anna had grown up with, yet she'd immediately felt a sense of belonging here. She belonged wherever Noah was.

A small figure walking across the lawn toward a line of trees caught Anna's eye. "Thank you, but there is no need now. I've found him."

She made her way through Shambrook Lodge as quickly as she could, given her lack of energy and her still sensitive stomach. Her growing excitement propelled her, though, as she made it down one flight of stairs, to the ground floor, and out to the back veranda. Though she'd only lived here for a few months now, Anna knew the layout of the house perfectly, as if she'd always been meant to live here.

By the time Anna made it outside, wrapping her shawl tighter around her in the crisp autumn air, she'd long since lost sight of Noah. She did not need to see him to know where he'd gone.

Since their wedding day, Anna had discovered a wonderful thing about marriage. Even though they spent most of each day together, even though they had courted for months in London, Anna still learned new things about her husband. Some of them surprised her, like his tendency to pull his cravat loose when he felt comfortable. Some of them made perfect sense, like the shaggy mess of his hair in the morning, which proved difficult for his valet to tame, resulting in that occasional loose strand that Anna found so endearing.

Anna had also discovered what she thought to be the best part of marriage—that she could love someone more the next day than she had the last. As Anna made her way across the lawn, the cool breeze and warm morning sunshine refreshing her, she wondered how such a thing could be possible. Yet she found herself growing more and more amazed by Noah, even when he frustrated her or they disagreed on one thing or another. She'd also grown more and more amazed by herself, by how much freer she felt with each passing day.

With a new gust of energy, Anna found herself at the tree line much faster than she would have guessed. Of course, thinking about Noah and the wonderful life they shared—and the new life they'd created—helped pass the time. It still took Anna a few seconds to locate the barely visible path between the trees, the path Noah's grandfather had first established as a secret escape when one needed a little wilderness.

Noah had only briefly described Shambrook Lodge for Anna when they courted in London because he had feared that his family would lose it. Anna had been happy to discover within her first week of living with her husband at Shambrook Lodge that he still returned to a beloved child-hood spot. It was one of the first new things she'd learned about Noah during their next chapter.

She slipped between the trees, keeping her eyes on the path that seemed more like a suggestion. Noah had warned her that tree roots snaked beneath the earth, sometimes pressing up into the path. Keeping one hand on the trees next to her, Anna carefully picked her way through the grove. She'd forgotten how chilly it would be under the shade of the trees. She wished she'd brought an additional shawl or had put on her coat. Surely the baby would not feel the cold, bundled as it was inside her.

The baby—their baby. That thought enveloped Anna in an impossibly warm bubble of happiness, her heart swelling with so much love for this person she had not yet met, could not yet feel or see. This was another wonderful part of marriage—creating a family, growing their love for each other through their children.

The sound of the stream trickling nearby alerted Anna to the fact that she had almost reached her destination. She picked up her pace, eager to find Noah. When she finally passed through the copse of trees onto the bank, she saw her husband standing with his back to her, watching the stream roll by. Her heart leapt when she saw him, as it still did every day since they'd met, instinctively pulling her toward him.

This was his favorite place on their estate, Anna had discovered. He came here when he needed to think or simply wanted to be alone. She watched him for a moment, his broad shoulders filling out his coat, his back straight and confident, wondering what had inspired him to come out here today.

In her haste, Anna did not notice a protruding root, disguised by a tuft of grass. She yelped as she felt her toes make contact with the hard root. She squeezed her eyes shut, waiting for the impact of cool, wet mud.

"Are you alright, my dear?" Noah asked, his strong hands gripping her arms, holding her steady.

Anna shouldn't have been surprised that Noah had caught her before she fell. He'd promised to rescue her whenever she needed it. He somehow always knew just when she needed him most.

"Yes, darling, thank you," Anna whispered, still trying to catch her breath. She could not tell what affected her more—the near fall or the fact that she was just moments away from revealing her secret to Noah.

"You look a little pale," he mumbled, his eyes searching her face for pain or discomfort of any kind. "Come, sit here with me."

Noah led Anna to a natural bench made from a large

PENNY FAIRBANKS

stone a safe distance from the edge of the stream. Anna sat first while Noah watched every movement with his sharp, observant eyes.

"Are you going to sit with me?" Anna asked with a chuckle, patting the smooth surface of the stone beside her.

"Are you sure you are not hurt? Wasn't that the same ankle you twisted on that fateful evening?" he asked, finally joining Anna.

"No," Anna assured him, resting her head on his shoulder. "It was the other one."

"Are you cold?"

"A little, yes."

Noah stood again, unbuttoning his coat and draping it around Anna's shoulders.

"Well, I don't want you to be cold," Anna protested even as she pulled the coat tighter around her.

"I am not cold at all, I assure you." Noah wrapped his arms around himself, blushing slightly when Anna raised an eyebrow. When he returned to his spot next to Anna, she shrugged off one side of the coat, throwing it across Noah's back.

"Thank you, my darling, thoughtful wife." He kissed the top of Anna's head as he'd made a habit of doing. "What brings you out here today?"

"I was going to ask the same of you." Anna burrowed herself into her husband's side, absorbing his warmth and charming scent.

Noah stared straight ahead at the stream, the water dancing by, both elegant and playful. "I've just had some worries on my mind," he admitted, the babbling stream nearly drowning out his words. "I was not sure if I should share them with you."

Anna pulled back, peering up at Noah's profile, his brow furrowed and his mouth fighting a frown. "Of course you can, my wonderful, troublesome husband. Has the canal project hit a snag?"

Noah's frown turned into a bemused smile. He turned to Anna, his eyes softening. "No, as a matter of fact, the canal is coming along very nicely. You see, the thing that has been worrying me is, well…you."

Though she did not like to see such anxiety in her husband's face, Anna could not suppress the glee that rose up inside her, threatening to spill out at any moment. She knew why he worried for her, and soon he would have an explanation. Anna did not want to simply blurt out the news, so she bit down on the inside of her cheek, willing herself to wait for the right moment.

"I know I have not been feeling well, but I'm sure whatever it is will pass soon," Anna assured him, rubbing her hand up and down his arm both to comfort him and restore a little warmth.

"Are you sure?" Noah snatched Anna's hand, placing it over his heart. She could feel it beating, strong and steady. "It seems that you have not been quite right for weeks now. I have never seen you so tired, even though you sleep through the night and rest during the day. And at least once a day you complain about feeling faint and run off to lay down somewhere until it passes."

Anna removed her hand from Noah's chest, cupping his cheek with it instead. Her thumb brushed over his skin, covered in fresh stubble since he had not yet shaved. She knew she must ease his concerns soon. The poor man looked hardly able to bear another moment of this mystery.

Anna returned her gaze to the stream ahead of them, imagining Noah's past spent on this bank, imagining a new future unfolding. "Noah, have you ever fished in this stream?"

Noah eyed his wife quizzically. "Yes, I have, though not

much recently. When I was a boy, though, Father and I would come here a few times a week to fish or look for birds or otherwise laze about. Why do you bring that up now?"

She could hide her smile no longer. As her eyes swept over the landscape—the stream before them, the trees on the other side of the bank, the bright blue autumn sky above—Anna could see their children sharing this special space with their own father.

"Will you bring our son here to fish?" she asked, breathless again.

"Certainly, someday." Noah continued to watch her, utterly puzzled by this abrupt change in conversation.

"And what about our daughter?"

Noah's bottom lip poked out for a moment as he pondered this. "Well, it might be unusual for a girl to fish, but I suppose if she wanted to learn, I would teach her."

Anna dropped her head against Noah's shoulder once more. "What a wonderful father you will be."

Noah propped his chin up on the top of Anna's head. "And you will be a magnificent mother. I cannot wait for that day."

"We have many preparations to make," Anna hinted, wondering when Noah would grasp it.

"I suppose, though we should wait until—" He cut himself off, sitting up straight, his half of the coat slipping away. He stared at Anna, his chest rising and falling rapidly.

"We shouldn't wait too much longer, my love," Anna said through her tears. "These next few months will pass quickly, I am sure. Our baby will be here before we know it."

"Anna!" Noah leapt up, standing before his wife with his hands in his hair. "Are you sure?"

"Very, very sure," she chuckled, putting a hand over her stomach. "That is why I have not been feeling very well recently. I just wanted to wait until I had no doubt."

"Good Lord! We're going to have a child!" Noah cried, his face trapped in an amusing mixture of shock and elation, fingers entwined in his hair.

"See? You do not need to worry about me after all." A tear slid down Anna's cheek as she watched her husband process the happy news.

"On the contrary, darling Anna, I shall worry about you even more now." Noah fell to his knees before her, grasping her face in his hands. Tears filled his eyes as he gazed at his wife. "I love you so very much."

"I love you, too, Noah." Anna leaned forward, placing a gentle kiss on his forehead. "But you should really stand up now. Your trousers are going to be covered in mud."

"You know I do not care about a little mud," Noah laughed before jumping up again, holding his hand out to Anna. "We should get started on our preparations, don't you think? We must tell Mother and Father, and send letters to my sisters and your family. We should invite everyone to stay so we can celebrate properly."

Anna's giggle filled the air around them, mingling with the sweet music of the stream. "I did not think we needed to get started right at this very moment."

Noah nodded thoughtfully. "You are right. Of course, you are right. We should enjoy this moment for now."

"Yes, we should." Anna took Noah's hand, rising to stand before him—the man she loved, the man she shared her life with, the man she would raise a family with.

She wrapped her arms around his waist, resting her ear against his chest, just over his heart. A new heart grew inside of her, one that contained both of them as well as its own uniqueness.

They stood together for several minutes, or perhaps hours, holding each other in peaceful silence. Anna's once impossible dreams had become reality in the most incredible way.

She wished she could go back in time and tell her younger self that everything would fall into place—that she would be happier with herself and with her life than she'd ever thought possible. But, Anna realized, despite the pain and the many twists and turns she'd taken to get here, she would not have changed a thing.

It had all been worth the wait.

THANK you for reading Anna's and Noah's story! You can join the Harcourt family again in Dalton's journey here. Want to catch a glimpse into Anna and Noah as parents? You can meet them again in their daughter's romance tale here. If you want to stay updated on my new releases, you can sign up to my newsletter and receive my stand-alone novella, *A Lifetime Of Love,* or you can hang out with me in my private Facebook Group.

If you would like to read my complete Regency Romance series, Resolved In Love, you can find find them here.

ABOUT THE AUTHOR

Penny Fairbanks has been a voracious reader since she could hold a book and immediately fell in love with Jane Austen and her world. Now Penny has branched out into writing her own romantic tales.

Penny lives in the Midwest with her charming husband and their aptly named cat, Prince. When she's not writing or reading she enjoys drinking a lot of coffee and rewatching The Office.

Want to read more of Penny's works? Sign up for her newsletter and receive A *Lifetime of Love*, a stand-alone novella, only available to newsletter subscribers! You'll also be the first to know about upcoming releases!

Made in the USA
Middletown, DE
04 December 2023

44339555R00172